MUSLIM
WRITERS

PUBLISHING

THE GIFT

Zaipah Ibrahim

Muslim Writers Publishing
Tempe, Arizona

The Gift

Muslim Writers Publishing
P.O. Box 27362
Tempe, Arizona 85285
USA

www.MuslimWritersPublishing.com

ISBN: 978-0-9793577-7-0

Illustration by Shirley A.Gavin
Book design by Leila Joiner
Edited by Debora McNichol

Printed in the United States of America

FOREWORD

Bismillah Ar-Rahman, Ar-Raheem
In the Name of Allah, Most Gracious, Most Merciful

All praise be to Allah, the Most Gracious and the Most Merciful, for helping me to complete this Islamic novel. When I began toying with the idea of a fiction alternative for young Muslim adults, I realized the task would not be easy. For one, an Islamic romance novel written in English would not be well accepted in my region in Malaysia. The majority of readers prefer books written in Malay. Moreover, most of the local young adult fiction is usually inspired or influenced by Western non-Muslim literature. Despite this, I maintain my belief that Islamic fiction should be a practical alternative to the other literature available to our teenagers and young adults these days.

The best home is the heart of your loved one
For how could one not remember
The person who lives in his or her heart...

ACKNOWLEDGMENTS

Special Thanks and love to my family, my father, brothers and sisters.

Special Thanks to Dr. Ungku Maimunah Mohd Tahir for her literary critiques on the story and characters.

Special Thanks to Nurshidah Abdul Wahab for reading and commenting on 'The Gift'.

Special Thanks to Johari Abdul Aziz for his honest critiques in shaping up the Islamic characters in 'The Gift'.

Special Thanks to my friends, Zuraida Zakaria and her husband, Amir Abdullah for editing the language and style.

Special Thanks to my friend Sumayyah.

A Very Special Thanks to my dear friend and author, Linda Delgado.

THE GIFT

CHAPTER 1

Saleha smiled at the young nurse who accompanied her out of the doctor's office. She felt calm. She was glad that she still had six months. Both doctors had said that sometimes miracles happened and a patient lived longer. "Humans plan, but *Allah Ta'ala* is the best Planner of all," she whispered to herself. Allah willing, she could have more time. "That's what Ani always says." She was so grateful to Allah *(Subhanna wa Ta'ala)* for granting her a friend like Ani.

When Saleha and her family moved to JB, or Johor Bahru, twenty-five years ago, Ani and her husband Zaid were their first neighbors. Ani was a full-time housewife, and her husband was a religious teacher at Maktab Sultan Abu Bakar, which used to be known as English College. They had no children. Ani always said that Saleha's children were also her own.

About eight years ago, Ani started taking orders to make *Muslimah* clothing from the neighborhood women. Later, with her husband's encouragement, she opened Ani's Boutique, a successful upscale shop in JB. For two years, she had also been a dealer for her friend's boutique in KL, or Kuala Lumpur.

Her husband was a freelance religious speaker since his retirement a few years ago. Zaid had been a good friend to Kamal, Saleha's late husband. About three years before his death, Kamal bought a house in another neighborhood in JB. Though no longer close neighbors, the friendship between the two families persevered.

Saleha's family treasured the bond they shared with Ani and Zaid. They especially held dear Zaid's ability to impart religious knowledge to the family. Zaid, in return, viewed this as a gift and an opportunity to gain rewards from Allah.

Ani and Zaid had always been there for her family since Kamal's death. Only Ani knew about Saleha's cancer; Saleha wanted the illness to remain a secret for a while longer. Since Ani always reminded Saleha of the way to Allah (swt), she became stronger in facing even bad news, and the news she just received was certainly not good.

At fifty-four, Saleha, with her graceful figure and head covered with a white *hijab*, looked peaceful. Her sharp features and light-colored skin made her look younger than her age. She was content and grateful for what Allah (swt) gave her. After getting into her car, she took Kamal's leather wallet from her handbag. She took out the small photos of her children and smiled. Those faces always lifted her spirits and gave her strength to face the world.

"*Alhamdulillah,*" she whispered, before leaving the hospital parking lot. Instead of going home, she headed for Lido Beach, not far away. After parking near a tree, Saleha opened the door to let in the mid-morning breeze. She sat in the car and looked beyond the shore.

The water moved gently under the steady morning sunshine. Saleha was entertained by the delightful glitter on the surface of the graceful moving water. She took a deep breath. "*Subhanallah,* so beautiful. Alhamdulillah, I'm still here to appreciate this."

The beach ran along the banks of the Johor River and faced Singapore. It had been a locals' favorite before tourists discovered the river's scenic beach. Now, though not as pristine as it used to be, the beach continued to be a popular destination.

Saleha gazed across the straits at the skyline in front of her as she listened to the soothing sound of small waves hitting the sand. The rhythmic sound was a familiar greeting to her. Those days with Kamal and the children were the best times. Soon, she would be with him again, insha Allah. But she would have to leave her children and that memorable beach.

She remembered her children playing, laughing and talking during their regular picnics on the beach. But Imran was thirty-four now, and had been the CEO of KS Holdings for five years. He was like his father in character, but more serious-looking. Looks are easily deceiving, though, because Imran was quite agreeable to those close to him.

Imran was as tall as a typical Malay man, but he looked impressive with his short, dark, backcombed curly hair that matched his heavy eyebrows perfectly. His deep dimples— Kamal's dimples, Saleha thought—had always been his most attractive features. They cheered his brooding face every time he smiled or laughed.

He avoided talking about marriage, saying that he preferred to take care of his mother and siblings first.

Saleha remembered how composed Imran had been during his father's funeral. He was shocked but never cried a tear: not when they received the police officer's call on the night of the accident, and not at the funeral. He shed no tears, at least not in front of anyone. *Death only meant losing the presence of someone,* he reminded his family. *They did not lose their father because they never owned him, for he only belonged to Allah (swt). He only returned to his Owner.*

Those were Imran's constant words of encouragement to the family. Saleha knew his son had learned about loss before

Kamal's death. Saleha was always thankful and amazed that Imran was always there for the family and stayed strong during those painful times. Imran said the family had to stick together now that their father was gone. He made a promise to look after all of them and he really had kept his promise.

Imran's younger brother was hard-working as well but was much more cheerful. Iskandar, three years younger than Imran, loved to make others laugh. He was taller and thinner than Imran, and wore glasses. He resembled Saleha and, like her, looked young for his age. In fact, he looked the youngest of her three sons. He was the accountant at KS Holdings. He and Imran were very close and worked side by side since Kamal's death. A few years ago, Iskandar married Marina and the twins came soon after. Kamal would have been proud of Iskandar, Saleha thought.

Hanim, a younger version of Saleha but with Kamal's dimples, was twenty-one when her father died. His death affected her terribly. Imran was there by her side through those hard times, and as a result, Hanim and Imran were closer than ever. Hanim was a computer programmer at UiTM in Melaka and was engaged to Sufian. Saleha smiled, remembering the first time Hanim told the family about Sufian and how Imran, taking over their father's role, had a long talk with his sister about it.

Then there was Hidayat, Saleha's youngest. At nineteen, he was a cheerful, active, and ambitious young man who looked a lot like Iskandar, except his hair was curly. He was the most athletic among the three brothers. He was studying journalism at a college in KL, where Saleha would visit him when she was out that way. When Hidayat enrolled in the college, it was Imran and Saleha who accompanied him. Thinking back on these memories, she felt so blessed and grateful to Allah (swt). She was so proud of her children, especially Imran. She could not have managed the family alone if Allah (swt) had not made him stand by her.

The sound of Ani's car interrupted her train of thought. Saleha had asked Ani to meet her there. Ani had, from time to time, accompanied Saleha to Hospital University in KL. For Saleha's family, a business trip with Ani had always been the reason for her going to the hectic city. They did not know about her appointments or her illness. Her local doctor and Dr. Norman at Hospital University had been in contact with each other for about a year now.

Holding each other's hands, Saleha and Ani walked to the bench. Then Saleha looked into her best friend's eyes and broke the news.

"Thank you, Ani." Saleha paused and smiled at her dear friend. "Alhamdulillah. Thank you for all that you've done for me and my children, for always being there for me especially, praying for me to find the courage and strength to face this ordeal."

Ani watched Saleha and felt her serenity even after devastating news. Saleha seemed always to be at peace. "Sal, you're my best friend, my sister. We are family. And like always, your children are mine." Ani returned Saleha's smile.

Saleha nodded. "Alhamdulillah. That is why I need your help." She looked at Ani, searching for agreement.

"Of course, I will do anything I can, insha Allah. Is this about the children? Have you told them?"

"No, and I don't intend to. Well… at least not yet." Saleha turned to face the water. The small waves moved in rhythm with her calm, but a strong determination overcame her.

"But Sal, don't you think it's time for them to know? You're their mother and they love you. At least it could prepare them…"

Ani looked concerned. She knew the family was very close. It had become even tighter since Kamal's death. She had always admired and respected the strong bonds within Saleha's family and her children's loyalty.

Saleha faced Ani. "I can't tell them yet, especially not Imran." In a deep, strong voice, Saleha continued, "He has done so much for the family since Kamal's death. He always wants to be strong for us. That night is still fresh in my mind…he was trying so hard to keep himself together. First Kaira, then Kamal. It was so hard for him!"

"And since then, he has thrown himself into work and more work. He has taken care of us for so long. I know I can count on him when that day comes. No doubt he will be there—always— for Iskandar, Hanim and Hidayat. Just as he was for me when Kamal died. Insha Allah, he will."

Saleha paused to watch the water. The waves moved peacefully toward the beach. At the perfect timing set by their Creator, they left the beach so obediently after hitting the sand. It was the law of nature governed by the Lord of the Universe, the One that dominates the timing for everything, including human lives. Not even a second late will His creation be when the time comes to return to Him.

Saleha and Ani doubtlessly accepted Saleha's fate as Allah's (swt) decision. However, as the reality sank deeper, one thing remained unsettled. Saleha had to tell the children at some point. But would revealing the illness change Saleha's condition? Saleha didn't want to drag the family into an abyss of uncertainty and gloom. And she knew Imran well enough not to tell him yet.

Ani had seen Imran grow into a fine man. She knew almost all chapters of his life. He was nine years old when Ani first met him. He was a quiet, easy-going little boy. Unlike most boys his age, he had a strong sense of loyalty. While the other boys would play with their friends, abandoning their siblings, Imran would not leave his alone. He was very protective.

"I see Kamal in him, Sal—strong in facing life and in believing in himself. And his family is so important to him." Ani also knew how much the young man respected her and her husband. After his own parents, they were the ones Imran would turn to for advice, especially since he returned from the United Kingdom ten years ago. Since then, Ani and Zaid had been Imran's guides and confidants. His father's death caused Imran to grow even closer to Zaid.

Turning to Ani again, Saleha said, "That is why I want to do something for him before I return to Allah Ta'ala, insha Allah, and I need your help to do it."

Ani quickly nodded in response. "What about Iskandar and Hanim?"

"I don't want to worry Iskandar. He has Marina and the kids to take care of. And Hanim...I don't want her driving back and forth checking on me. You know her when she's worried. As for Hidayat, this would be too much for him and would affect his studies."

Ani agreed. "So...?"

"Well, I know this may sound wishful, but I'm his mother. It's every mother's wish..."

"You want to see him married," Ani interrupted, reading her friend's thoughts.

Saleha nodded. "Only then will I tell him and the others about the cancer." Saleha smiled and at that moment Ani noticed she looked different—serious and yet very determined, and well, happy. She did not at all look like someone who was dying.

"My dear friend, insha Allah I will help you." Ani smiled.

Saleha got up and looked down at Ani. Almost whispering, she told her friend, "I knew I could count on you, Sis. Thank you. Alhamdulillah!" Saleha returned the smile.

As the women walked toward Saleha's car, Ani related that she was going back to her hometown for her niece's wedding and invited Saleha to go with her.

"It would do you good to get some fresh air in the country," Ani suggested with a smile.

"Oh, Ani...I don't know. It's a family thing. I don't think..."

Ani stopped walking and interrupted her. "Sal, you are my family. Sarah would love having you for the wedding. Come on...just three days. We can stay longer if you like. Hey, maybe we could talk about this plan of yours while we're there, insha Allah."

Saleha said she would call Ani later. As Saleha was getting into her car, Ani stopped her.

"Sal, who knows, maybe your wish will come true this weekend," Ani joked with a twinkle in her eye. Saleha laughed. "I could be right, you know. I mean, not that I have anyone particular in mind..."

Before Ani could finish her sentence, Saleha cut in. "Don't tell me we are going to pick one of the girls for Imran at this wedding?" Saleha continued laughing.

"Well, the thought did cross my mind. But you know what I mean."

"Thanks for the thought, Ani. I'll give you a call, insha Allah. When exactly is the wedding?"

"A week from today, but we can leave a few days earlier." With that, they left Lido Beach.

While driving home, Saleha smiled to herself as she recalled what Ani had said. She thought the whole idea was funny. But Ani could be right. In fact, that was how she met her late husband. It was at her neighbor's wedding and Kamal was the groom's best friend. With that enjoyable memory lingering, she said to herself, "Well, Ani, I think I'm going with you, insha Allah!"

~

"Well, Mr. Imran Hakim, I guess we have a deal here."

"Yes, indeed." Imran shook hands with Mr. Chow, the representative from KS Holding's newest customer. "I'll make sure the paperwork is done by this week. We'll give you a call when we can seal the deal, Mr. Chow."

Mr. Chow and his assistant asked to leave, and Imran walked them to the door. Later he picked up the phone.

"*Assalamu'alaikum*, Iskandar. Hey, it's finally done. We got the contract, alhamdulillah."

"Alhamdulillah…good! Congratulations, big brother!"

"We both did a great job, as usual," he said in all mock-seriousness. They both laughed. "Hey, let me buy you lunch!"

"Oops, I can't. I promised Marina. We have a lunch date to-day. Her mother is looking after the kids. But I'll take a rain check, bro."

"Well…okay. Say *salam* to Marina." He hung up. Imran looked at his watch. It was almost noon. He had promised to call his mother about her doctor's appointment. Just about then, the telephone rang.

"Assalamu'alaikum, pal. Want to grab some lunch?" Umar asked at the other end of the line.

"Great! I was afraid I'd have to eat alone. See you at the usual place, say, in about half an hour, insha Allah. I need to make a quick call first."

"See you then, insha Allah. Assalamu'alaikum."

Imran called home and Saleha picked up the phone. She knew her son would be calling at this time.

"So how was the appointment?"

"Oh, alhamdulillah. Everything went fine. And I'm feeling great."

"I'm glad, Mom. Alhamdulillah. Oh, I'm coming home early today. I was thinking perhaps I could take you out to dinner tonight...a date?"

Saleha chuckled and teased her eldest son, "Hmm...a dinner date, Son? What's the occasion?"

"I need an occasion to take my own mother out to dinner?"

"Well, dear, for three months now you've been staying late at the office. I forgot the last time we went out together with the family."

"Actually, the company landed a new contract today, alhamdulillah. I've been working for months to get it. Now that it's ours, I'm taking a break. So what do you say?"

Saleha laughed and agreed, "Great! But one day you have to find a real date, you know."

"Okay, Mom. I'll talk to you later, insha Allah," Imran said abruptly with a small laugh. They hung up, both knowing that they had just touched the topic that the son avoided most.

~

Umar glanced at his watch. Imran was five minutes late. He decided to order for both of them. Just then in walked Imran, who approached the table with a salam and sat.

"Sorry, Umar...the traffic. You've ordered?"

"Yeah, the usual. Hope you don't mind."

"Nope. I just don't feel like eating by myself today."

"How come? Isn't that part of your routine when you don't have a business lunch?" Umar asked playfully.

"Yeah, but today I just feel like celebrating. Remember the contract Iskandar and I have been working on for the last two months? Alhamdulillah, we got it!"

"Alhamdulillah! Congratulations, pal! So I guess lunch is on you then?"

"Insha Allah!"

As they ate and talked, Imran noticed a young woman entering the restaurant. Her bright red and white *baju kurung*, which perfectly matched the red scarf on her head, stood out in the restaurant. She seemed familiar but he thought no more of this and continued his conversation with Umar. However, the woman saw Imran and approached the table.

"Assalamu'alaikum. Excuse me...Mr. Imran Hakim, right?" The woman greeted.

"Yes, *wa'alaikumussalam.*" Imran politely smiled and got up.

"I'm Melissa. Melissa Annuar," she introduced herself.

"Oh, yes...Dato' Annuar's daughter, right? We met at your father's office, I think?"

"That's right. Nice meeting you again, Mr. Imran."

Umar got up and smiled at her.

"Nice to meet you, too. This is my friend Umar Shukry."

"I'm sorry to interrupt. I just wanted to say hi," Melissa apologized.

"Care to join us?" Umar invited her.

"Thank you, Mr. Umar, but I'm meeting a friend."

"Perhaps next time, insha Allah. Say salam to your father."

"I will, Mr. Imran, insha Allah. Enjoy your lunch, both of you. Bye." Melissa left.

Umar smiled at his friend. "Did you mean that?" he asked with a grin.

"Mean what?" Imran asked.

"About the 'next time.' She seems nice."

"Don't even start, Umar. You know I was being polite. Her father is a very influential businessman."

"Right, right. It's business as always. Imran, I'm sorry to say this, but when are you going to enjoy life a bit, huh?" Umar asked with a concerned voice.

"Isn't that what I'm doing now?" Imran raised his thick eyebrows. Then he smiled at Umar, flashing his dimples.

"Well, besides business. A little bit more on the personal side, maybe?"

"Where are you going with this, Umar?" Imran said, uncomfortable.

"C'mon, Imran. I've known you for like, what— fourteen, fifteen years? You've been ignoring your personal life for too long now."

"I'm not up for it, Umar. After all, what's the rush?"

"I know, but look at you. You've been blessed with so much, alhamdulillah! You have almost everything you want in your life—a family who cares a lot for you, a satisfying career. There's just one thing missing. A person who would love and care for you."

"My Mom's the one, then!"

"Imran…"

"You know something? It's weird that you mentioned this. My mother said something like this too today. Am I missing something here?"

"Well, I don't know what your mother said, but I think it's about time that someone bugged you about it."

"Umar, this is getting way too serious now. Can we continue this some other time? I'm trying to enjoy my lunch, you know. And you'd better not spoil it or lunch will be on you." Imran laughed.

Umar knew his friend was good at avoiding this subject. He shook his head and smiled. Then, with a sigh he told his friend, "Whatever, Imran. But know this: things will never change unless you let yourself change first. May Allah Ta'ala open your heart, pal!"

~

Imran was driving home when he remembered what his mother and Umar said that day. He had heard that many times before. Even his father used to tease him when Imran mentioned in passing any woman that he met through business. But this was the first time this year. He looked at his watch. It was almost six o'clock.

Imran drove to Lido Beach, where he had so many happy family memories. He left his car and headed for the embankment. It was peaceful here. He recalled how unspoiled this still-beautiful beach used to be. And he remembered the other beach where he and Kaira were happy so long ago. She would have loved Lido Beach. He closed his eyes, picturing her lovely face and charming smile. The wind gently swept around him, as if consoling him. He contentedly recalled their time together until he remembered the accident. Alhamdulillah, the years had lessened the pain. But after ten years, he still missed her.

He felt he could imagine how *Rasulullah* felt long after the death of his beloved wife, Khadijah (*radiallahu*). It was far from his mind to compare Kaira to Khadijah (ra), but she was the best

Muslim woman he had ever loved. A sad smile touched Imran's face. He whispered, "Will I ever meet someone like her again?"

Across the sky, the last flock of birds was flying home for the night. He remembered his mother saying: *"To Allah we belong and to Him is our return"* (Qur'an 2:156).

CHAPTER 2

A black Suzuki pulled into the parking lot of the Language Center at Pine College. A young woman wearing a dark blue dress with a light gray hijab exited the car. Five-foot-four and slender, her fair complexion contrasted pleasantly with the color of her dress. Her straight nose and full lips complemented almond-shaped eyes. Her serious demeanor belied her age.

Taking her books and a briefcase from the back seat, she headed toward the Language Center. On her way, she met a couple of students who greeted her with a salam. As she climbed the stairs to her office, she bumped into Yasmin.

"Assalamu'alaikum, Syira."

"Min...wa'alaikumussalam," Syakirah returned the salam with a tired voice.

"Hey! What's with you? You look exhausted and it's only Tuesday."

"Yeah, I'm wiped out. I stayed up late last night finishing those tests."

"I thought you were almost done with them."

Syakirah groaned. "Yeah, the neighbor kid had an accident last night and I took him and his mother to the hospital. Twelve stitches on the back of the poor little boy's head. I waited in the ER and then brought them home."

Yasmin was not surprised to hear this. She knew her friend well. Syakirah was someone to rely on in time of need. And she loved children.

"I see. Well, classes don't start until nine, so why don't we go and get some caffeine?" Yasmin asked with a smile. Syakirah agreed.

On their way to the main office, they stopped at the notice board. A flyer from the Language Center was posted about the upcoming Language Camp.

"I heard we're opening it to more students," Syakirah said.

"The last one was so successful. Mr. Johan was really impressed." Mr. Johan was the Head of the Students Affairs Department.

"Alhamdulillah. Last time students were disappointed because they couldn't participate. When do we find out for sure?" Syakirah asked.

"Hopefully today in our meeting with Mr. Azmi. And then maybe we could fix a meeting with the committee members for Friday."

"That would be helpful because last year we had such a short notice... But alhamdulillah the whole thing turned out great!"

～

It was about twelve-thirty when Yasmin and Syakirah left Mr. Azmi's office. He confirmed that the Language Center had in fact increased the number of camp participants. The two friends stopped by the lounge of the Language Center before going back to their offices.

"Alhamdulillah. Hopefully the students who missed the last camping trip will have a chance to go this time," Syakirah said. "Camping always reminds me of the good old days. Did I tell you Manaf and I used to go camping when we were in college?"

"Really? I know that you love camping, but Manaf too?"

"Yeah, our last trip was a one-day jungle-trekking and treasure-hunting at Gunung Jerai in Kedah. It was so exciting. I could just close my eyes and remember the smell of nature and the fresh air. We were on the same team. The mission was to find all the clues leading us to the treasure." Syakirah paused dramatically, "which turned out to be an old pair of slippers." Syakirah and Yasmin laughed.

"It was fun." Syakirah sighed and stared at the newspapers on the lounge table in front of her as the memory ran through her head. Yasmin looked at her. She knew those fun memories triggered painful ones. It had been a long time since Syakirah talked about Manaf.

Yasmin remembered the first time she met Syakirah. She was amiable, but quiet. As their friendship developed, Syakirah opened up to Yasmin about her past and Manaf. A handsome co-ed, he and Syakirah met during a Student Association meeting and became close friends.

When Manaf left for Australia to pursue his degree, the friendship continued through letters and they came to realize they had fallen for each other. But during Syakirah's final undergraduate year, she was accepted for an American post-graduate program. Manaf, in the meantime, gave up his studies and returned home. Syakirah was grateful to see him, but worried about the upcoming separation. Manaf insisted, though, that she pursue her studies. Soon after she left, the two broke up. Losing Manaf made Syakirah turn completely to Allah (swt) for peace and spiritual strength. Syakirah once told Yasmin, "Allah Ta'ala guided me through the hard time. I'm a better and a stronger woman now. Alhamdulillah."

Yasmin believed that the Syakirah she knew now was not the same as the one who was involved with Manaf. Yet the older and wiser Syakirah inevitably caught a case of melancholy now and again.

"Syira…"

Syakirah came out of her reverie. "Hmm?" She turned to face Yasmin. "Yes?"

"Nothing. Sorry to interrupt, but I know what you were thinking. And before you get too carried away, let me pull you back to the real world."

"And where would I be if not in the real world, Mrs. Yasmin?"

Yasmin's raised eyebrows answered the question without a word.

"I guess all this camping kind of triggered the good old days… What has happened is for the best and Allah Ta'ala has decided that." Syakirah recalled the verse fully well:

"And put thy trust in Allah (swt) and enough is Allah as a Disposer of affairs" (Qur'an 33:3).

"Well, okay, if you say so. I just don't like to see you torturing yourself." Yasmin believed that Syakirah was over Manaf, but needed a reminder occasionally.

Syakirah was a strong person, in faith and emotionally. *That* Yasmin found out after Syakirah had lost her mother a few years back. Syakirah held on during that difficult time, somehow effectively coping with work and family obligations. Yasmin became her best friend during that time. Yasmin was the first to hear the good news that her father remarried.

"Min, it was a long time ago. I'm past all that now. Promise."

Syakirah smiled to reassure her best friend. The memories used to hurt but she'd rather think of the good times. She truly believed that the break-up was best for both of them. "See, I'm all smiling here, Mrs. Yasmin!"

As they were talking, Sudin, the office assistant, told Syakirah she had a phone call. It was her stepmother. Her grandmother—her late mother's mother—was sick.

"Mom, can it wait till this weekend?" Syakirah and her stepmother had grown to love and respect each other since the elder woman became a member of the family.

"She really wants to see you, Syira," her stepmother pleaded.

Syakirah felt guilty for taking this lightly. "Okay. I'll take a couple days off, insha Allah."

"I'll tell her you'll be coming home very soon, dear." The elder woman sounded relieved.

"I'll see you then, insha Allah. Assalamu'alaikum."

CHAPTER 3

The telephone rang and Ani picked it up. "Hello, Ani's Boutique."

"Assalamu'alaikum. It's me."

"Oh, Sal. Wa'alaikumussalam. How are you?"

"Alhamdulillah, I've never felt better," Saleha replied in a cheerful voice.

"You're really in a good mood today, alhamdulillah," Ani commented.

Saleha got straight to the point. "I want to know what your niece told you."

They both laughed. Saleha was especially cheerful since they came back from Sarah's.

"Ani, I don't want to talk about this over the phone. Do you think you can come over today? I need to discuss a few other things too."

"About...?"

"Just come over when you're free, okay?"

"Insha Allah, I'm closing the shop in an hour. Good?"

"Great, insha Allah. I'll be waiting. See you then. Assalamu'alaikum."

"Wa'alaikumussalam." Ani put down the phone and smiled. She had not heard her friend this excited for a long time. She

thanked Allah for His blessing and for making Saleha happy
again. Ani looked at the clock and continued to work until
closing time.

~

The light blue living room was decorated with a tasteful
feminine touch. A set of antique wooden sofas anchored the
room. White and sage curtains over the windows and French
doors protected the room from the bright Malaysian sunlight.
Small, black, round tables guarded the curtained doors at each
end. Atop each were well-arranged flowers set in beautiful
porcelain vases. Framed pictures of Prophet Muhammad's
(*salallahu Allahi wa salaam*) mosque, Masjidil Nabawi, and the
exquisite Ka'bah graced opposite walls.

Saleha sat on the sofa thinking of how to break the news to
Imran, eventually deciding that she really needed Ani to bounce
ideas back and forth.

She had a feeling that her son would like this girl. From what
she knew of her, Saleha liked her already.

And they had yet to meet.

It all began the weekend of the wedding. They were talking
about their children. Ani and her sister decided to tease Saleha
a little.

"Sarah, do you think maybe Sal could find a wife for Imran?"
Ani began, her eyes twinkling.

"Ani..." Saleha interrupted, embarrassed.

"Well, I'm just trying to help. Don't worry, Sal, this is just
between the three of us. Right, Sarah?"

"I don't know, Ani," Sarah paused, looked at Saleha and
continued slyly, "You know... Maria has a friend..." Sarah

paused melodramatically and continued in a rush, "Her name is Syakirah Sulaiman. She called an hour ago to congratulate Maria. They've been close friends since primary school. She's teaching English in KL...very nice girl. Pretty. Smart. Good Muslimah. She can't come to the wedding, but her grandmother might be here."

The ladies listened, Sarah's narrative sparking their imaginations.

"Every now and then she comes to visit when she's back home...a little quiet but very friendly once you get to know her."

That was how it started. Saleha wondered why she wasn't married. Sarah didn't know, but explained that after her father remarried, she chose to concentrate on her career. This girl seemed to be a lot like Imran. Saleha wanted more information, but Syakirah turned out to be a private person, a quality Saleha liked in a daughter-in-law, and decided to wait until Ani and Sarah had a proper opportunity to grill Maria. That would have to wait until after her wedding.

The next day during the ceremony, Saleha met Syakirah's grandmother and sister. They were friendly and seemed very nice, and Saleha was sure Syakirah was the same. Several times she checked her hopes from getting too high. But she could not stop thinking about the girl. She wanted to meet her soon.

*   *   *

As Saleha sat mulling over her thoughts, she heard a car pulling up to the house. For some reason, Imran decided to come home early, and he brought Umar with him. Her conversation with Ani would have to wait. She opened the door to welcome the boys in.

"How are you, Aunt Saleha?"

"Alhamdulillah, Umar. How's your family, the children?"

"They are great, alhamdulillah."

"Imran, you're early today!"

"We have a tennis game. I left my car at the office. We're here to get some stuff and change."

Saleha was relieved. "Perhaps we all can have some tea before you leave. Umar…?"

"Thanks, Aunt Saleha, I can't say no to you! I need to use the restroom first and do the *Asr* prayer."

"Insha Allah. While you two do your prayer, I'll ask Mak Jah to prepare tea."

Umar dutifully followed Imran to his room.

As Saleha waited for the tea, she heard Ani's car and ran out to meet her.

"Ani, Imran's home but he's leaving soon," Saleha blurted in a not-so-hushed tone. "I don't want to say anything yet to him. He's with Umar."

Ani laughed as she got out of the car. "You sound like a kid who's been caught with her hand in the cookie jar."

Realizing Ani was right, Saleha giggled.

As they came into the living room, Imran and Umar joined them.

"Assalamu'alaikum, Aunt Ani. When did you get here?"

"Wa'alaikumussalam. I just got here and I came to visit your mother. She says you're not staying long."

"We have a tennis game today."

"Good. You spend too much time at the office."

Umar glanced at his friend. "You're right, Aunt Ani. I've been trying to get him out of that office for some time. The last time we played was two months ago."

"I've been busy," Imran joked, feigning a self-righteous tone.

"Imran, working hard is good, but spending the whole day at work? Do take time to relax as well. Rasulullah (saws) divided his day into three portions, remember?" Ani said with a caring smile.

"And he was much busier than you, dear," Saleha added. They all laughed and enjoyed their tea time.

Shortly after the men left, Saleha and Ani went to sit in the garden.

"So what did you find out about Syakirah?"

Ani told Saleha what she learned. When she mentioned where Syakirah worked, Saleha sat up.

"Did you say Pine College?"

"Uh-huh."

"Subhanallah… that's where Hidayat is studying."

"Oh… *that's* why it sounded familiar when Maria mentioned it."

"Do you think maybe I could meet her? Ani, my appointment with Dr. Norman is coming soon."

"That can be arranged when we're ready. But will Imran be receptive?"

The question took the smile from Saleha's face. She didn't know. But she knew that she had to try. "Ani, I would wait if I had the time."

Ani understood, a little sad, knowing how much she would miss her friend. "I know, Sal. I pray to Allah Ta'ala that he's ready, too." Ani smiled to reassure her friend.

CHAPTER 4

"Hey, Syira, assalamu'alaikum! You look like you're in a hurry. Class at eight?"

"Wa'alaikumussalam Min! Yeah, double period, and I need to get to the office to collect some stuff. You too?"

"Yup, eight to nine, but we still have fifteen minutes. So how's your grandmother?"

"Fine." Syakirah's tone changed. So the visit hadn't gone too well.

"Oops...that doesn't sound fine. I hope your grandmother's okay... "

They reached the Language Center office. Before opening the door, Syakirah stopped and turned to Yasmin with a funny look on her face. "Min, I need to talk to you about something after class," she said in a low voice.

Curious, Yasmin asked, "Sure. What's up?"

Syakirah kept silent and opened the door. After picking up her exercises, they walked on to class. On their way, they met Mei Lin.

"Syira, when did you get back? How are things at home? How is your grandmother?"

"I got back last night. She's doing fine, and I saw my friend who just got married."

"Great! The whole visit was good then. Hey, remember the student I told you both about on Monday?"

"The high scorer on the writing test?" Yasmin asked.

"Uh-huh. Hidayat's his name. He's been chosen to be a regular writer for the *Daily Pine*. And guess what? He's been assigned to write a series of articles about the Language Camp. So he will be seeing both of you about the camp activities and their progress."

"We're having our first meeting with the committee members this afternoon at three. I guess you can tell him to attend the meeting," Yasmin suggested.

Syakirah said, "Sounds good to me."

Mei Lin agreed. "I think it's fine to let him sit in on the meetings… Okay, you two. Mine's on the first floor. Boy! I'm glad today's Friday. Talk to you later!" Mei Lin headed for the first classroom of the building.

Yasmin and Syakirah climbed the stairs to the second floor. "Don't forget, Min, see you at the cafe after ten, insha Allah," Syakirah reminded her friend as she entered her classroom.

～

The cafeteria at Pine College was always busy in the late morning. The lecturers and other staff members all used the cafeteria for breaks and conversation. Yasmin was sitting alone when Syakirah walked in. She greeted her friend with a salam.

"Let's not sit here, Min. We can sit over there," Syakirah spoke in a low voice, motioning her friend to a table in the corner. Unquestioning, Yasmin followed her. This must be something really personal.

Leaving her books on the table, they walked to the counter to get lunch. Yasmin glanced at Syakirah, who apparently didn't want to talk until they returned to their table. When they finally sat, Yasmin could wait no longer and asked her friend, "So what is this about? I've never seen you like this before."

"Well, you won't believe what happened to me yesterday at my grandmother's."

"You said she was sick. Is she okay?"

"Alhamdulillah, she's fine... which reminds me that I have classes to make up. You see, she... hmm..." Syakirah chuckled. "She was sick when she called, but was miraculously cured by the time I got there."

"What do you mean?"

"You remember what I told you last month? That she asked me, as she always does, when I'm going to settle down. Well, she did that again yesterday. Only this time, she had the answer, too."

"I don't get it."

"They told me about this man from JB."

"Wait, wait...they? Your parents are in on this too?"

"Of course." Syakirah stopped to sip her tea.

"So your grandmother wasn't really sick?" Yasmin laughed.

"Yes and no, just a mild fever. I guess she thought the timing was right. She wasn't feeling too well and this Imran Hakim would be the man for me..."

"And he is...?"

"A businessman whose mother is apparently trying to find him a wife."

Yasmin took the information in. "Kind of a deathbed wish on your grandmother's part then. You aren't mad at her, are you?" Yasmin was smiling now. Syakirah's family had been pushing her to get married since her younger sister got married last year.

"I'd be lying if I said no. I was happy to see her but I also had to miss classes for two days, remember?" Syakirah replied, looking a bit annoyed.

"Hey, your classes aren't going anywhere, Sis! This is good news, right? Insha Allah, you're about to meet your Mr. Right," Yasmin said with a chuckle.

"Yeah, right. My Mr. Right," Syakirah responded. "Come on Min, don't tell me you're on their side too. You're supposed to help me out of this mess."

Syakirah did not like the smile on Yasmin's face. She knew her friend well. Yasmin had always told her to find someone and settle down. "Of course I want to meet my Mr. Right, whoever he is. If he exists. But not this way. I feel…" Syakirah stopped.

"What? Hey, this isn't a problem that needs a solution. I think it's great. Matchmaking in modern days. He could be the right man for you. Otherwise, your grandmother and parents wouldn't let him anywhere near you. Congratulations, my friend! I'm happy for you. It's finally going to happen, Syira, insha Allah!"

"Oh, Min, please…you are the last person I thought would agree with them."

"Who else agrees then? Does Nadhirah know yet?"

"Yeah. She reacted just like you did," Syakirah replied, staring at her drink. "And Ashraff too. He wants to get married, but he doesn't want to hurt my feelings by getting married first, dear brother."

Yasmin paused. As usual with Syakirah, there was more than met the eye. "Come on, Syira. Don't tell me you're against this because of Manaf again? You told me you've closed that book for good. It's been what? Five, six years? Oh, Syira…you've got to move on." Yasmin's voice was soft now.

"No, Min. It's not Manaf at all. He's not in my life anymore. I'm way over him. I regret letting myself be absorbed in a romance with him. *Astaghfirullah.*"

"No, Syira. Allah Ta'ala made the two of you meet and love each other, but you two were just not meant to be together."

"But now it's different. I don't know what…" Syakirah stopped and sipped her tea.

"I know what," Yasmin said abruptly. "It's been so long since Manaf. It's like starting all over again. You're afraid of getting hurt, of investing yourself in someone. But, Syira, how long are you going to wait? You have to pick things up somewhere, sometime. This guy is …what? The fourth proposal since Manaf? This is Allah Ta'ala's work. He knows best. So don't dismiss this Imran before you take the opportunity to see for yourself."

With a sigh and a forced smile, Syakirah responded, "Funny, Min. I'd rather invest my time in loving Allah Ta'ala…very rewarding, as you know, my dear friend. And you talk as if I'm engaged to this guy, and I've never even met him."

"You think he knows anything about you?"

"I don't think so. What I know is Grandma met his mother during Maria's wedding last Friday. She said his mother was very nice. Maria's aunt invited her."

"So how did your name come up?"

"Well, that was the first time they met and Grandma didn't know that this lady was looking for someone for her son. Two days after the wedding, Maria's mom called Grandma to talk about me."

Yasmin spoke. "I think it's a good start…very different from Manaf. Maybe the old saying will be true for you. Love will bloom after marriage. Who knows? Remember your mother's wish? It's been five years. I'm sure she'd be happy to see you get married now, insha Allah!"

Syakirah gazed at the flowery tablecloth in silence. Then Yasmin touched her hand. "You're my friend, Syira. I love you.

Just give it a thought, okay? Don't say no just yet. Seek guidance from Allah Ta'ala. Do *Istikharah* prayer. I have a feeling this is good for you. I don't know why."

"This is so funny. For all I know, this might lead nowhere. It'll just go away on its own. Grandma just likes to make a fuss over me. It's not like anything is confirmed."

"Do you want it to be?"

"Min, I still don't like the idea. Can we just drop this, please?"

"If you say so."

"I do. I'm happy with the way things are. I have peace. Allah Ta'ala has granted that to me. Alhamdulillah!"

Yasmin let go a sigh, and then smiled. "Alhamdulillah."

"Oh! By the way, are we still going to visit the campsite this weekend to check on the layout for the treasure hunt?" Syakirah asked.

"You're changing the topic, Syira, but yes. Nik and the kids are coming too, insha Allah. We can have a small picnic there."

"Cool!" They smiled at each other.

∼

Imran was on the phone when there was a knock on the door. He was pleasantly surprised to see his sister and he motioned her in.

"I'll get in touch with you very soon. Bye." He hung up and greeted Hanim. He held out his hands for a salam. Hanim accepted and kissed them. They hugged and sat on the couch in his office.

"To what do I owe the pleasure of this visit?" he asked lovingly.

"Are you in the middle of something important? I can…"

"No, no. Nothing as important as my little sister," Imran interrupted. "So what brought you here? Have you seen Mom yet?"

"Not yet. I came straight to your office. But she's the reason why I'm here first. I was worried about her."

"Oh…her doctor's appointment, you mean?"

"Yes."

"You could have just called me."

"*Abang* Imran, I don't know what, but I feel like she's not telling us something. The last time I was home, she looked like she had something on her mind. I tried to ask, but she said it was nothing to worry about. You know Mom—she's good at not making us worry even when there is something upsetting her."

Imran reassured his sister. "I talked to her after her last appointment and she said everything was fine. She looked much better, too. Last week she went to KL with Aunt Ani. I guess the trip did her good because she's looked great ever since, alhamdulillah!"

Hanim was relieved to hear what her brother had said. "Alhamdulillah. Now I can breathe easier."

Imran got up and went to his desk. He looked at his watch. "You worry too much, Sis. Look. It's almost noon. I promised Mom I'd have lunch with her at home today after Friday prayer. She'd be so happy to see you."

"Okay, sounds good. Oh, Suffian sends his salam. He offered to drive me here, but I took a bus instead." She smiled when her brother nodded, approving her decision. It would not be Islamically proper for her to share a ride with Suffian because they were not yet married.

"Wa'alaikumussalam. How is he?"

"Good, alhamdulillah. Oh, I forgot. I promised to call him as soon as I got here safely. Can I use your phone?"

"Go ahead." Imran smiled at his sister as she talked to her fiancé on the phone. She knew how protective he was of her. Hanim remembered a few months ago, before her engagement to Suffian, Imran had badgered her about her choice of husband. He wanted her to be sure of what she wanted and gave Suffian the third degree. After she hung up, Imran asked, "How long will you be here?"

"Not long. I have a meeting on Monday morning, so I have to be back by Sunday."

"I'm going to KL on Sunday. I can drop you off on my way, insha Allah."

"Alhamdulillah, thanks!" Hanim said cheerfully. Imran smiled at her.

"We should get going now, Sis!"

"Insha Allah, I'm right behind you, big brother!" They laughed and headed for home.

CHAPTER 5

There was a knock on the door of Syakirah's office. She looked up from her reading. "Yes?"

The door opened and a student entered.

"Assalamu'alaikum, Miss Syakirah. Can I see you for a second? It's about the article on the Language Camp. I just need a few finishing touches before I can hand it in for printing."

"Wa'alaikumussalam, Hidayat. Please come in and have a seat. I'll call Mrs. Yasmin."

"Actually, Miss Syakirah, I went to her office already but she was out."

"Okay then. What can I help you with?"

"I need confirmation on the lecturers in charge of all the activities."

"Oh that. Well, as of now I only have this." Syakirah showed the short list to Hidayat. "I'm still waiting for the complete list. I'm sure we'll get it by this afternoon, insha Allah. You can come and check later, insha Allah."

"Okay, thank you. And another thing…I was wondering if outsiders will be allowed to visit. I mean, like parents or the students' relatives."

"I don't know, but I'll find out. I'm meeting with the Head of the Language Center in an hour. I'll ask him, insha Allah."

"I'll come by later to check then."

"If I'm not around, just go to Mrs. Yasmin."

"Thank you very much for your time. Assalamu'alaikum." Hidayat smiled politely and left. Syakirah continued with her reading until Yasmin entered her office.

"Assalamu'alaikum. What's up? I thought you said we're going to have a meeting with the Head today?"

"Wa'alaikumussalam. Yes, in fifteen minutes. Oh, Hidayat will drop by this afternoon for some info on the camp. Will you be around then? I have to go to the administration office at two, so I might not be around when he gets here."

"Fine, I'll be in my office, insha Allah. So let's head to the Language Center now. We don't want to be late." They both left Syakirah's office.

"Any news about Mr. Imran, Syira?"

"Good that you asked. I received a call last night from Maria. She told me that her aunt, who is a friend of Mr. Imran's mother, called her."

"So what did Maria say?"

"She was asking Maria about where I work and some other stuff about my educational background. Maria suggested they meet me myself."

"When?" Yasmin asked excitedly.

"When what? I'm not meeting her. I feel like I'm being spied on or something."

"Maria meant well, I'm sure."

"I know that. I just don't like being investigated."

"What about your grandmother?"

"Well, I haven't heard from her since the last time I visited her. I thought the whole thing had been dropped until Maria called me. Now I think there's something cooking between my parents and Grandma."

"Like what?"

"Well, I called home after talking to Maria. They said Grandma came over and asked about me. They said she was just concerned."

"Maybe Mr. Imran's mother called your grandmother?"

"I don't think so. I think she was just curious because nothing much happened since Maria's wedding. She was afraid that those people have changed their mind about me." Syakirah laughed.

"You think this is funny?"

"I'm not happy about the spying part, but the whole thing is kind of funny, Min. I'll let you know what happens next in this soap opera, insha Allah."

CHAPTER 6

Imran didn't usually go home this early, but today Saleha had asked him to. His mother didn't say much on the phone, and Imran could not guess the reason.

As he pulled up to the house, he noticed Ani's car. He felt the hood, which was still warm. As he opened the front door, he could hear the women's voices in the living room. Saleha saw him walk in.

"Assalamu'alaikum."

"Wa'alaikumussalam," The women returned his salam.

Imran sensed that Ani must be in on what was going on. "Something special brings my two favorite ladies together?"

"Do I need a special reason to visit you and your mother?" Ani joked.

After he and the friends exchanged greetings, Imran went to his room to change.

"Ani, he knows something's up," Saleha whispered.

"There's nothing to worry about, Sal," Ani responded, calming her anxious friend.

"I just don't want him to get upset. You know this is not his favorite topic." Saleha looked worried.

"He loves and respects you. You're his mother, Sal. How upset could he possibly be?" Ani tried to put the matter into perspective.

"It's just that…it's been a long time since I spoke to him about marriage. Am I being selfish, Ani?" The question left a sad look on Saleha's face.

"No, you're not. And even if you are, it's for his own good. We're not forcing him to do anything, Sal. We're just giving him a little push. If he's okay with it, we'll go and meet Syakirah, insha Allah."

"Are you sure Maria won't mind?" Saleha looked a little hopeful.

"Well, Maria said she's willing if Syakirah is." Ani smiled.

"How will we know Syakirah is willing too?"

"Just leave that to me, insha Allah. We need to hear what Imran thinks first."

Imran went to the living room and joined the women. He decided not to say anything until they began first.

"Tea, dear?"

"Yes, thanks, Mom." Imran smiled at his mother and sat on the couch. They all talked for a while about work. Then Ani changed the subject. "Imran, can I ask something personal?"

"How personal, Aunt Ani?"

"Well, I've known you since you were small. I watched you grow from a little boy to a successful businessman. You're a good, young Muslim man, alhamdulillah. But there's something incomplete about you… something that I'd like to see…"

"Let me guess. See me get married, am I right?" Imran smiled at his mother and Ani.

"Imran, your Aunt Ani is not the only one who wants to see you get married."

"Mom, I know but I think I want to see Hanim get married and Hidayat graduate first."

"There's nothing wrong if you get married first."

"I'm not sure I'm ready," Imran smiled.

Ani saw a disappointed look on Saleha's face. She knew that Saleha was trying her very best not to upset him. She also knew that Saleha would not ask for anything from Imran for herself.

"Imran, what if I said I found someone nice for you?" Ani told him with a smile.

"Ah...playing a matchmaker, huh, Aunt Ani?" Imran laughed. "And who could this unfortunate girl be, insha Allah?"

"The girl would be fortunate enough to have you. Or maybe it would be unfortunate that you wouldn't be having her, insha Allah." Ani said casually but with a hope in her heart.

"Oh, I see. So this must be some girl then. Anyone I know, Mom?" Imran smiled to his mother.

Ani cut in, "The question is, would you like to meet her?"

"As much as I don't like the idea, I guess I'll play along as long as no one is going to force me into anything," Imran answered and cracked a smile.

"So is that a yes, Imran?" Saleha looked anxiously between her son and her best friend.

"For my mother and you too, Aunt Ani, I'd do anything, insha Allah, but don't make me promise anything."

"Alhamdulillah. Fair enough," Ani responded and they all laughed. Saleha was relieved. She felt a little bit awkward for asking Ani to do most of the talking. But she thought this would make Imran see how much this meant to her. "I'll set the date and we'll see, insha Allah."

"Okay, Aunt Matchmaker, whatever makes my mother happy, insha Allah. You still haven't told me who she is."

"Her name is Syakirah Sulaiman. That's all I'm telling you for now."

After talking for a while about work and Hanim's upcoming wedding, Ani left. Imran was about to leave for the study when

Saleha stopped him and sat next to him. "Imran, are you sure you want to do this?"

Imran looked at his mother lovingly and smiled. "Mom, like I said, if it makes you happy, I'm okay with it. But I can't promise anything. I know how much this means to you. If not, you wouldn't have let Aunt Ani do the talking. And she was good, wasn't she?" Imran added jokingly.

Saleha chuckled. "I'm doing what is best for you. You've done so much for the family since your father passed away. And now as your mother, I want to do something for you, and I hope it will bring you happiness, insha Allah." Saleha felt tears in her eyes.

Imran grasped his mother's right hand. "Having you as a mother is the best thing. Alhamdulillah, I feel blessed. We're a family and nothing makes me happier than seeing this family happy. I'll do anything for that. That was the promise I made and I intend to keep it forever, insha Allah."

Saleha was touched by what Imran said. She knew it was true, and she worried because he never seemed to care much about his own future as much as he did the rest of the family. He had always been open to Saleha about his personal life until his father died, and since had mostly kept to himself.

"Imran, may I ask a question?"

"Mom, since when do you need permission to ask me about anything?"

Saleha nodded. "I knew you would say that, but it seems you have all but shut me out of your life."

"I'm sorry, Mom, I never meant to do that. You always taught us how important it is to be open about our feelings. It's just that with Dad gone, I know how important it is to protect the family. My needs are secondary to my mother's and my family is my top priority… always, insha Allah."

"Masha Allah, I have such a good son! You are so much like your father, alhamdulillah. But you do yourself and your family a disservice by living your life for us and not including yourself in your plans for us.

"Is it Kaira?" Saleha paused. "My son, you have to move on. Remember, Allah Ta'ala determines everything for us. We both know that everything in this life belongs to only Him. He is the ultimate Owner of each one of us, and of all things and people that come into our lives. All are loaned to us. There are some things in life that He wants us to be with only temporarily. But not having them in our lives doesn't mean we should deprive ourselves of other things He has reserved for us."

Imran listened to Saleha. Zaid said the same thing to him when he came back from the U.K. ten years ago. He still missed his late wife sometimes, but he told himself regularly that he didn't.

What they had together was one of a kind. He had yet to meet anyone who could replace her. He prayed to Allah (swt) often, seeking His guidance in starting all over again.

"After your father died, there were times I thought I lost everything. But your Uncle Zaid and Aunt Ani made me realize how I could not lose someone I never owned. Allah chose him for me to share our lives together. But Allah Ta'ala gave him to me as a trust, and that trust was lifted when Allah took him back. He just returned to his true Owner—Allah Ta'ala.

"Then I remembered Allah Ta'ala has entrusted me with you children. Even though I don't have your father with me, and Allah Ta'ala only knows how I miss him, there is a part of him in all of you. I have something beautiful and meaningful to live for. And that is a blessing from the Almighty Allah."

"I'm not holding on to Kaira, Mom. I learned to move on years ago, alhamdulillah. Allah Ta'ala made me see that it was wrong to hang onto the past like that. I did the right thing when I finally let her go. But when Dad died, his accident triggered flashbacks of my accident, and I miss her sometimes."

Saleha watched her son with much concern.

"So I pray to Allah Ta'ala for the strength to concentrate on my work and my responsibilities. I even pray one day, insha Allah, to have a life like I had with Kaira… with someone I could love as much as I loved her." Imran ended with a smile.

Saleha listened compassionately to her son. How strong and confident he was on the surface, and so vulnerable underneath. His sincerity increased Saleha's hopes that Syakirah, with Allah's (swt) guidance, would help end his suffering soon. It occurred to her how strange it was to have this feeling about someone she had never met.

"Imran, I'm your mother, and I love you. I wish I could make your pain go away, but I can't. I just want you to keep an open mind and heart. Give yourself a chance?"

Saleha waited for an answer with teary eyes. Imran smiled and nodded. She patted his shoulder and left him sitting on the couch.

Imran remembered Kaira.

It was Friday. The wedding ceremony was in the morning, with a small reception after the Friday prayer, and a trip to the beach later that afternoon. They were supposed to leave for a short honeymoon that night, and afterward, return to Malaysia.

They went to the beach in two cars. Imran and Kaira shared a car with Tamrin and Farah. Izwan and Ita were with another married couple and their son in another car. The nine of them occasionally had picnics at the beach.

"Will you miss this?" Imran had asked Kaira as they walked toward the beach.

"Yeah, very much," Kaira said in a whisper.

"Same here." Imran stopped. "Thank you."

"For what?" Kaira asked, curious.

"For spending your life with me. You are mine for life now, insha Allah."

"I love you, Imran Hakim. There is nothing I want more than to be your good, *solehah* wife, insha Allah."

"I can't wait to get home and start our life together. I made a promise before Allah Ta'ala this morning to do my very best, with His help and guidance, to take care of you. Insha Allah, I intend to honor it as long as I live." Imran smiled lovingly at his new wife.

He had proposed to her there during one of their regular picnics. Kaira joked that it was a Western proposal. It wouldn't have been that way if they were at home. Both sets of parents gave their consent for the marriage in the U.K., and they planned a big wedding when the couple arrived home.

"Insha Allah, I was meant to be in your life, Imran, since the day we first met. Allah created Adam for Hawa, and you for me. But we must always remember that we truly belong to only Him, Allah Ta'ala, forever."

They both smiled. She looked so happy that day.

How young I was, Imran thought to himself. The phone rang, interrupting his thoughts. It was Hidayat.

"Wa'alaikumussalam, Hidayat. What's up? I was about to do *Maghrib* prayer."

"I'm calling to tell you and Mom that I'm leaving for home on Thursday night."

"Are you cutting classes on Friday?" Imran asked sounding curious.

"Hey, of course not! My Friday class was cancelled," Hidayat sounded almost offended that his brother would suggest such a thing.

"Just kidding. Anything you want me to tell Mom? Or do you want to tell her yourself? I'm sure she's done praying."

"No, it's okay. Just tell her I called."

They talked for a while before they hung up. He was heading to his room when Saleha came down the stairs. He told her about the call. Saleha was happy to hear the news.

After dinner Imran went to the study, where he was always reminded of his father. He closed the door and stood near the big chair facing the window. That had been his father's favorite spot. Imran spent most of his time in this room when his father died. He would sit in the chair, contemplating for hours. His thoughts again returned to Kaira.

Imran had met her during the *Eid* celebration. Both had been at the university for three years but had never met. The Eid began their one-year friendship before they married. He went home over the summer and Saleha noticed a change in him. He told his mother about Kaira and was happy when she approved of their friendship.

Imran picked an album from the study's bookshelves. He looked at a picture of his parents and smiled. His father teased him about marrying his friends' daughters. This was their private joke.

His father stopped teasing after learning about Kaira. He respected Imran's decision and was looking forward to meeting his daughter-in-law. Imran remembered telling his father about Kaira and Kamal's reaction. "She must be very special, Son. May Allah bless your marriage."

Imran sat down with the album. "You were indeed special, Kaira." After Kamal's death, Imran sometimes wondered if his father really had wanted to arrange Imran's marriage. A few years after Kaira's passing Kamal revisited the topic of marriage occasionally, but they both knew that Imran was nowhere near ready.

Imran sat down at the desk. He pulled the top left drawer and reached for a blue diary and a picture of Kaira on graduation day. She was wearing a blue long dress and a white hijab. It was the first picture of her wearing a proper hijab. She had always worn a scarf, which covered only her hair. She decided to wear the hijab a month before graduating. Imran was not surprised when she told him of her decision. Kaira's family was not religious but while in the U.K. she found and befriended a treasure trove of practicing Muslimahs from around the world. Her interest in Islam renewed through these connections, she strove to perfect her religion.

Imran's interest in improving himself coincided with Kaira's, and among other things, Kaira's interest in Islam attracted him to her. Consequently, his parents were happy with his choice.

"I have a surprise for you tomorrow." She called him the night before graduation.

"Give me a clue," Imran pleaded.

"Okay. It has to do with our future." He later learned that she planned on wearing it since their unofficial engagement. He remembered her reciting the verse from An-Nur:

And say to the believing women that they should lower their gaze and guard their modesty; that they should not display their beauty and ornaments except what (must ordinarily) appear thereof; that they should draw their veils over their bosoms and not display their beauty except to their husbands... (Qur'an 24:30)

Imran put the picture inside the album. He recalled what Zaid told him.

"Dwelling too much on the hardships and future fears will wound your heart and cause you problems. Use your intelligence to know Allah Ta'ala and seek Him. Then all things will be there for you, or else all things will be against you. Don't be saddened by a misfortune in life; rather, put your trust in Allah Ta'ala. With *Iman* and *Taqwa*, insha Allah, you will successfully manage your pain and sadness."

"What should I do?"

The elder man caringly told him, "Let her go, Imran, let her go. Accept her death as His decree...*redha*. Tell yourself that whatever Allah Ta'ala does is good. To Him belongs everything, and everything returns to Him. He does whatever He wishes, for He knows what's good or bad for His creatures."

It had taken Imran a while to realize that letting Kaira go was the best thing to do. The good moments with his late wife made him feel happy, and he would like to remember her that way—remember her and her faith in Allah (*swt*).

CHAPTER 7

Yasmin and Syakirah had just finished their last classes and planned to have lunch together. On their way back to the office, they met Hidayat and his friends. Some students were gathered around the benches in front of the Language Center.

"Assalamu'alaikum, Mrs. Yasmin, Miss Syakirah." Hidayat greeted the two women, followed by his two friends.

"Wa'alaikumussalam, Hidayat. That was a nice piece you wrote in the *Daily Pine*. Miss Syakirah and I were impressed," Yasmin commented on Hidayat's article.

"Alhamdulillah, thank you. I couldn't have done it without your input."

Syakirah stated, "You're quite welcome, Hidayat."

Hidayat asked, "Could I get help with the next as well?"

"Sure, we'd be glad to help, insha Allah." Syakirah told him.

~

After lunch, Yasmin was on the phone when Syakirah dropped by her office. She sat facing Yasmin while she flipped through the *Daily Pine*.

"Okay, honey. Mommy has to go now. Assalamu'alaikum." Yasmin hung up the phone. She smiled, thinking of her four-year-old son. She planned on taking him swimming after work but cancelled since he had been sick the night before.

"Must be Ridhwan," Syakirah said smiling. Yasmin caught Syakirah up on Ridhwan's illness then changed the subject.

"Do you have plans for the break, Syira? If no, you could come with us to Sunway Lagoon. We're taking the kids there on Sunday."

"Umm, no thanks. I'm staying here a couple of days. Then I'm going home to visit the family."

"Staying here…as in working? Syira, take a break!"

"Don't worry, I don't plan on working myself to death," Syakirah laughed. "I'd like to get a head start on some teaching materials for after the break, insha Allah."

"Well, if you change your mind, let me know."

"Thanks." Syakirah's phone rang, so she left to answer it. A few minutes later, she came back to Yasmin's office.

"That was Maria. She's coming to KL for a holiday and guess what? Her auntie is meeting her here, insha Allah."

"And they want to see you, right? Is Mr. Imran's mother coming, too?"

"Yeah… I missed Maria's wedding, so when she said they're coming, I thought I'd treat her and her husband to a special dinner. But she mentioned this other thing and I suddenly have a feeling I'm not going to enjoy this visit."

"Well, I don't know what to say except I hope it turns out for the best insha Allah."

"What best? For me or them?"

"For everyone," Yasmin teased.

CHAPTER 8

Saleha woke up early in the morning. After Fajr prayer she and her housekeeper, Mak Jah, got busy preparing Hidayat's favorite dishes. Imran came down for breakfast and saw all the food on the table.

"Masha Allah...all these for Hidayat! What about me?" Imran said jokingly. His mother laughed.

"Well, I wasn't sure what to cook. He said he misses home breakfast so much. I figured I'd cook some of his favorites."

"You don't think Hidayat can finish all these, do you? There's enough here to feed the entire neighborhood!" Imran sat for breakfast and enjoyed the fruits of his mother's benevolence.

Saleha and Imran had almost finished eating when Hidayat rang the doorbell. Mak Jah let him in and he headed straight for the kitchen.

"Assalamu'alaikum!" Hidayat greeted his mother and brother.

"Wa'alaikumussalam! We knew you'd be late, so we started without you. We left you some food, hope you don't mind," Imram joked.

Hidayat said "no" as he kissed his mother's hands and gave her a hug. He did the same with Imran before sitting next to Saleha.

"Mom! You cooked all my favorites!" Hidayat sounded like a little boy as he eyed the spread his mother prepared for him. "Life is good, alhamdulillah!"

"Hey, don't you want to clean up first, after sleeping the entire night on the bus?" Imran teased his brother. "You might spoil the smell of the food."

"Nope! I cleaned myself at the bus station. I want to eat first. After all, these are all for me. A bath...I can do that later, right Mom?"

Saleha laughed and poured a cup of coffee for Hidayat.

"Wash your hands first," Saleha said, which Hidayat quickly did and returned to the table.

"Well...*bismillah*! Eat your heart out. I have to get going now. I'll talk to you later, bro. Mom, I'll be home early today, insha Allah. We can all go out for dinner."

Saleha nodded. "Insha Allah." Imran always took them out to dinner on the first day Hidayat came home from college.

After Imran left, Saleha sat down to eat with her youngest.

"So how's school, honey?"

"School's fine. In fact, everything's great, Mom. Alhamdulillah! I really enjoyed it this semester."

"Go on," Saleha encouraged. She wondered what made her youngest son more excited than usual, vaguely hoping that two weddings would be in the works soon.

"Remember I told you about my writing? Well, I've been assigned to write a series of articles about the Language Camp we're going to have soon. One was published last week. I'll show it to you later. The next one will be after this break, insha Allah."

"Alhamdulillah. I'm proud of you, Son. But is there anything else you'd like to talk to me about?" Saleha smiled, knowing for sure that there was something else.

"Like what? And what makes you think I'm leaving something out?" Hidayat asked mischievously.

"Honey, I'm your mother. You're not that hard to read. Does this have to do with someone at the college, someone special maybe?" Saleha teased him.

With a sigh, Hidayat answered, "Mom, you're hard to keep a secret from. Well, not that it's a secret or anything."

"What is it then?" Saleha looked at her son. Hidayat had never kept anything from her. His openness reminded Saleha of Imran when he was Hidayat's age.

"It's not what you think, okay? She's..." Hidayat began as Saleha smiled.

"Oh...what do I think, dear?" Saleha teased her son, continuing, "Did I hear 'she'?"

"I know what you're thinking, but it's not even the least bit close to that. She's helped me a lot with my writing."

Saleha interrupted, "Aha...so she's one of your lecturers, I guess?" She suddenly remembered Syakirah. Ani told her that Syakirah taught English at Pine College.

"That's a good guess, Mom. Her name is Miss Syakirah Sulaiman, but I don't have a crush on her, okay."

Saleha stopped short but tried not to look surprised. Hidayat didn't notice. "So what is she like? She must be really nice for you to be going on about her. But then again, as a student you respect all your lecturers, right?"

"Of course. But for some reason, I feel particularly close to her. She's like *Kak* Hanim." Saleha smiled. Hidayat was comparing Syakirah to his own sister.

"Hmm. That's great. Now it won't be hard for you to get help with your writing then." Hidayat agreed with his mother.

"Right! And you know what, Mom? I think she'd make a great wife for Imran."

"Oh really, now?" his mother said, surprised both at Hidayat's confirming her expectations, and the effort he expended in considering his brother's needs. *From the mouth of babes*, she thought, immediately scolding herself because Hidayat was no longer a child.

"Yes, Mom, but don't tell him anything, because I'm afraid it'll scare him off."

Perhaps Imran was an open book after all.

~

It was almost five when Imran got home. Saleha was alone, setting up tea at the dining table. Hidayat was visiting his friends down the street. Placing his briefcase on the small chest across the dining table, Imran joined his mother for tea.

"He must really be full of energy. He didn't take a nap after that long trip last night?" Imran asked. "He usually would be sleeping by now. What's up?"

Saleha answered, "Well, he sounded excited on the phone with Raju. He was talking about his newspaper article... All he could talk about this entire morning was his new post at the college."

"Yeah, I've been wanting to talk to him about that, too. I happened to meet an old friend a couple of days ago. He's in the publishing business, and I told him about Hidayat. He told me about a university in the U.K. that has a good journalism school..."

Before Imran could finish, Saleha interrupted, "Imran, are you saying you want to send Hidayat abroad?"

"Well, it's a good school. And Hidayat has such talent. It shouldn't be wasted, I think."

"I know but...Imran, he seems very happy at Pine College. Why change that?"

Saleha was unexpectedly annoyed. She wanted Hidayat to get to know Syakirah better. Hidayat and Syakirah being brought together was not coincidental. Allah (swt) meant for it to happen. Insha Allah, Saleha was on her way to have her wish come true—her wish for herself and for Imran. On top of that, she did not want her baby to be on the other side of the globe when her own days were numbered.

"I know, Mom. But don't we want what's best for him?"

"We do, Imran, but I think we should let Hidayat decide this for himself. He's been at the college for almost a year and a half now, and he's doing very well. And I like knowing that he is not oceans away from home." Saleha looked at Imran and then at her tea.

Imran noticed his mother was upset. Hidayat and his mother were very close and the prospect of his living abroad couldn't be an attractive one for her. Even after Hidayat decided to study at Pine College, she continued to hope that he would study at one of the colleges in JB.

"Of course you're right, Mom. Maybe we can talk to him about it tonight." Imran smiled at her lovingly. He was instantly rewarded with her visible relief. "Now that reminds me that I have to call Iskandar. I was supposed to have dinner tonight with Dato' Annuar, but Iskandar is going instead."

"But Imran, you shouldn't miss it. Dato' Annuar is your father's friend. And what about Marina and the twins?"

"Marina and the kids went to visit her parents; they left this morning. And Iskandar will probably join them tomorrow, insha Allah."

"Imran, we can have this dinner tomorrow night."

"No, no. Iskandar and I have agreed to do this, and I'm looking forward to my dinner with my beautiful mother and favorite baby brother. Nothing to worry about, okay?"

Saleha nodded and Imran smiled at her. The last thing he wanted was his mother feeling guilty about dinner.

~

"So where are we eating tonight? Same old place?" Hidayat asked Imran.

"Unless you have somewhere else in mind. It's your pick."

"Well, Raju told me about this new place at Jalan Skudai. They have all sorts of seafood there. So Mom, how does seafood sound? Okay?"

"Sounds good, dear."

"Seafood, then!" Hidayat cheered.

"Yeah! Seafood, here we come!" Imran added and they all walked out the door laughing.

The seafood restaurant was indeed new. Everything looked shiny and clean. There were not many people yet when they arrived. The night was beautiful. The twinkling stars in the clear sky welcomed them there. The air too smelled fresh. They chose a patio table facing the beach. They were enjoying deep-fried shrimp when Imran asked Hidayat about his studies.

"Well, I'm having a wonderful time this semester, and I really love this writing job. I get to put into use what I've learned and I'm practicing what I want to do when I finish college. And the people at the college…wow! They are so wonderful too… I can talk on and on about this forever, you know."

"Obviously," Imran teased. He had never seen his brother look so excited. Maybe his mother was right. Hidayat should stay at Pine and complete his studies. But he wanted the best for Hidayat and that British school sounded great.

"You have my full support, dear."

"Thanks, Mom. But I already knew that." Hidayat smiled at his mother. "Anything you want to add, Mr. CEO?"

Imran smiled at his brother. "Well, I think you've got something great going on, but that doesn't surprise me. Ever since your first article was published, I knew you'd go places." Imran remembered Hidayat's first published work in the *Students' Voice*. He was only in fourth grade, but he was already showing his journalism skills.

Saleha watched her sons talk about Hidayat's writing. She hoped Imran would not bring up the British school at all. She remembered what she went through with Imran, and didn't want to go through that again.

Hidayat saw that Saleha was deep in thought and brought her back to the present.

"Mom...hello..."

"Sorry, dear. I was just thinking about something. Imran, you should've seen the article Hidayat wrote. It was good, very nicely written. Alhamdulillah!"

"Alhamdulillah! I guess I should have. It must've been good if it gets high praise from Mom," Imran teased. He changed his tone, "Well, Hidayat, that brings me to something that I've been saving to tell you tonight. There is a university in the U.K. It has one of the best journalism schools in the country. I thought perhaps..."

Hidayat interrupted Imran, "That I might be interested in going? Well, yes and no." Saleha listened to her son, praying hard that Hidayat would decline the offer.

Hidayat continued. "Yes, I was interested. I've heard how good that school is, and I did give it a thought. But no, I don't want to study there. I think I can do pretty well at Pine College. They have a good journalism school, and the longer I'm there, the more I like it.

"I don't know how it compares with other schools in the world, but I like Pine College. I like studying there and I want to start my future from there, insha Allah... Well, if there is a future for me in journalism."

Imran listened to what Hidayat was saying. He knew that his brother had a point. He had the talent. He could make it anywhere if given a chance. "I've no doubt about that, insha Allah. If you keep up the good work, I don't see why you wouldn't. Are you really sure? I mean, don't you want to give studying abroad a second chance?"

"I am sure." Hidayat was resolute.

"Your brother's right, dear. Insha Allah, if you work hard, you can become a good journalist no matter where you study." Saleha smiled at her youngest son.

"Thanks, Mom. And Abang Imran, thanks again for the offer. I know you want the best for me, and I respect and love you for that always. But I want to stay where I am and to continue what I'm doing right now. I might want to go to the U.K. one day to pursue my M.A. or something, insha Allah. You never know, right?" Hidayat looked at his brother and smiled.

Imran nodded. He respected his brother's decision. Relieved, Saleha silently thanked Allah (swt).

"Okay. Now that's done, right? Can we move on? We're scaring these delicious shrimps. See, they're cold now." They laughed at Hidayat's remark.

It was almost nine when they finished eating. They were about to leave when Imran asked his mother about her trip with Ani.

"You're going to KL, Mom? How come you didn't mention it this morning?"

"It must have slipped my mind. It's just one of those business trips your Aunt Ani has from time to time."

"So when are you leaving tomorrow and for how long?"

"Well, your Aunt Ani booked the early flight, and we don't plan on staying long. We'll probably be back Monday morning, insha Allah. Since you're home, honey, I don't want to spend too much time away from you," Saleha patted Hidayat's hand.

CHAPTER 9

"Yes. Go ahead with that. I'll be in by eleven, insha Allah."
Imran hung up the phone. He would take his mother and Ani to the airport before he went to his meeting.

"Imran, we can take a cab." Saleha knew that he had to attend that meeting.

"It's fine, Mom. The meeting is at ten-thirty, and I won't miss much. Iskandar will be there."

Saleha nodded.

"So where's Hidayat?" Saleha asked. On cue, her youngest showed up with newspapers in his hands, joined by Ani, who greeted Saleha and Imran with a salam.

"Ani, I didn't hear your car."

"No, I took a cab. I sent the car for a service checkup. And Zaid had to leave early this morning. So are we ready?"

"All set, right Mom?"

"You sound cheerful, Hidayat. I thought you were going to miss your mother."

"Of course I will, Aunt Ani. But I'm not a little boy any more. I'll be okay without her." Hidayat responded, imitating a little boy's tone. The women laughed at him.

Imran interrupted him, "Well, last night you said you were going to catch up on sleep, right?"

Ani and Saleha laughed more.

"That and…well, something else," Hidayat replied, looking mischievous.

"Now that sounds like a scheme, Hidayat," Ani pitched in.

"Do I want to know what that something else is?" Saleha asked, curious.

"You'll see when you come back, insha Allah." He grinned at his mother.

"We'd better not spoil his plan, Mom. Let's get going. It's eight o'clock now." Imran said as he picked up Saleha's overnight bag. Hidayat picked up Ani's. As the brothers walked out, Ani stepped closer to Saleha.

"So are you ready to meet Syakirah? Anyone suspicious?"

Saleha smiled at the second question and shook her head as she said, "Not a one, alhamdulillah!"

～

It was a quarter to ten when Saleha and Ani walked out of the airport. Saleha's appointment at the University Hospital was at eleven. They promised to meet Maria at three. Since they didn't want her to know anything about the doctor's appointment, they decided against checking in at the hotel where Maria and her husband were staying.

They took a cab to the hospital after choosing another hotel. There they had a drink at the canteen while waiting for Saleha's appointment. Ani looked at her friend, who seemed so calm despite the fact that she was seeing Dr. Norman again.

"You're not nervous, Sal?"

"A little perhaps, but I have you with me," Saleha answered calmly and smiled at her friend.

Ani did not want to see Saleha in distress, and was so grateful that the thought of meeting Syakirah kept her distracted.

It was almost noon when Saleha finished her appointment.

"Thank you for everything, Dr. Norman."

"Just take good care of yourself, Mrs. Saleha."

"I will, insha Allah."

Saleha had been seeing Dr. Norman since her doctor recommended him ten months ago. He was a kind man. His full gray beard and square glasses gave him that professional look, and his tall, lanky figure commanded attention.

"Have you decided to tell your children?"

"Insha Allah, soon, Doctor. Right now I have something important that I have to see to first."

"I respect your decision of course, but it will be easier for you if you have your children's support now."

"Thank you for your concern. I will when the time comes. For now, I want to keep it a secret." With that Dr. Norman nodded and smiled politely.

"So you're going back to JB today?"

"Oh, I'm staying here a while to meet my future daughter-in-law, insha Allah." Saleha smiled and noticed mild shock from Ani.

"Have a nice time then, insha Allah."

"Insha Allah. Thank you again, Doctor."

As they left the office, Saleha was smiling but Ani scowled.

"Future daughter-in-law, Sal? Don't you think it's too soon for such high hopes?"

"I just feel good about my wish." Saleha smiled happily.

"I don't want to see you hurt if it doesn't work out."

"I believe it will, insha Allah," Saleha stated confidently. Ani hoped and prayed that she was right.

~

Syakirah was looking at her watch when she heard a knock on the door. She opened it and there was her old friend, standing with a big smile.

"Assalamu'alaikum, gorgeous!"

"Wa'alaikumussalam!" Syakirah said with joy. They hugged as Maria's husband watched them. "Aidil, come in. You guys make yourselves at home, okay?" They walked to the living room.

"I've missed you so much, Syira. When you didn't come for my wedding, I was heart-broken, you know. But it's okay now that we're here."

"I'm so sorry I couldn't make it. Congratulations to both of you. But you know what? Since I missed the wedding, I promise to make it up by taking you out to dinner tonight... That is, if you two haven't planned anything romantic yet," Syakirah said, teasing the couple.

"Alhamdulillah! What a nice treat, Syira. You invited us for lunch—and dinner too?"

"Be grateful to Allah Ta'ala. That's what you get for having a friend like me!"

The couple laughed, and she continued, "And my roommate made our lunch before she left for vacation this morning, so you're not stuck with my cooking, either," Syakirah giggled.

Later after *Dhuhur* prayer, Syakirah drove them back to their hotel. The ladies dropped Aidil off before heading out to Saleha and Ani. When they reached the hotel where Saleha and Ani were staying, Syakirah turned to Maria before getting out of the car.

"Maria, I have to say that I don't like this. You know that I'm doing it because of you and your aunt."

"I know. I would feel the same if I were you. But you know what? After this meeting you won't have anything to wonder about."

"Wonder? Why would I?" Syakirah feigned.

"Well, once this is over you don't have to think about what could've or would've happened. For all we know, this might be the first and the last meeting ever."

Syakirah frowned. "What makes you think I'd ever wonder about this if I didn't come today?"

"Syira, give me some credit. I've known you for what? Two, three days?" They laughed.

"You're right, you're right. That's my nature. But still..." With that they got out of the car and entered the hotel.

Saleha and Ani were talking when Syakirah and Maria approached them with a salam. Ani hugged her niece as Saleha shook hands with Syakirah. After ordering drinks, Maria began the conversation.

"Aunt Saleha, thank you again for coming to my wedding."

"The wedding was beautiful. It was a pleasure to be there, Maria. So where's Aidil?"

"He's at the hotel. This is a woman thing, he said." Maria grinned.

"Syakirah, you're not going home this break?" Ani asked.

Syakirah was mildly surprised that Ani knew the college was on break. "In a couple of days, insha Allah."

Maria interrupted with a laugh. "Aunt Ani, Syakirah is a hardworking person. She's been like that since we were in school. No wonder she's a college lecturer and I'm just a primary school teacher."

Syakirah blushed and in a teasing voice, added, "Well, it wasn't work all the time, Maria. We did have fun too, remember?"

"Yeah, we did, didn't we? Although I think I had more fun than you did, since you were always worried about studies."

"Now, let's not get into that. You're making me sound like a nerd!"

The four women laughed as the two younger ladies waxed upon their adolescence. The subject changed to Saleha and Ani's visit to KL, then to Syakirah's job.

"I like teaching at Pine College. It's a good college."

"Yes, I've heard," Saleha told her.

"Oh, you have?" She wondered how much Saleha had learned about her.

"Well, my youngest son is studying there."

Syakirah was mildly surprised. Maria too, by the look on her face. "Oh, really? What is he studying?"

"Journalism. His name is Hidayat."

"Hidayat? Hidayat is your son?" Syakirah almost kicked herself for not making the connection between Hidayat and Imran.

"So you've taught him?" Ani took a turn asking.

"Yes. He's a great student. He's writing for our weekly magazine. But then, I'm sure you already know."

Ani nodded. "Saleha told me."

"He is so excited about it. It was all he talked about yesterday," Saleha added.

"He's very talented." Syakirah told Saleha about her son's task in the coming Language Camp.

"He showed me the article." Saleha smiled and they continued talking. Saleha liked Syakirah, who seemed comfortable talking to the elder women. There was so much more about Syakirah that she wanted to know, but she thought this was enough for now. She could proceed with the next step of her plan.

"Well, it's almost four-thirty. I'm sure you girls have other plans. And I promised your uncle to call him at five," Ani told Maria.

"Yes, we should go. I need to get freshened up before dinner tonight. Syakirah is taking us out to dinner."

Syakirah wished she could stay a bit longer to talk to Saleha. Somehow Saleha reminded her so much of her late mother, agreeable and gentle.

"I'll call you tonight, Maria, insha Allah...about tomorrow."

"Okay, insha Allah. But make sure to call after nine-thirty." They said goodbye and parted.

When they reached the car, Syakirah let go a sigh of relief. "Alhamdulillah! Am I glad it's over or what? That was worse than a job interview."

Maria laughed and teased her friend, "Syira, you are so full of it! You like Mrs. Saleha and Aunt Ani and you know it! And I think they like you, too—and might want to meet you again, insha Allah."

"Oh, Maria...once is enough, though I think Mrs. Saleha seems like a sweet lady, don't you think?"

"Yeah, she is. Well, if Mrs. Saleha is nice and her son Hidayat is nice too—that's according to you, okay—I guess her other son must be nice too, Syira." Maria grinned mischievously. Syakirah didn't like what she was hearing. Maria sounded just like Yasmin.

"Whatever, Maria. As far as I'm concerned, I'm finished."

"Uh-huh." Maria continued teasing her friend.

They drove back to Maria's suite, and Syakirah promised to pick them up later for dinner.

"I like her, Ani. I think Imran will too, insha Allah. What do you think?" Saleha asked as they entered the hotel room.

Ani studied her friend. She was amazed at how this woman could be so happy knowing she did not have that much time left. She seemed to forget the fact that only that morning they had gone to the hospital. Thinking about it made Ani too choked up inside to reply to her question.

"Well, I like her too." Ani felt tears in her eyes. She really hoped it would work out. "Imran will like her, insha Allah."

"He has to, Ani. He has to. Ya Allah, I'm so glad I met her today. I feel like today was the beginning of a wonderful ending. I just hope I'll be there when the ending happens." Saleha smiled. "I'm so excited and grateful to Allah Ta'ala, alhamdulillah!" Ani just managed to return her smile and nodded in agreement.

"So where are we going tomorrow, Ani?"

"Shopping? Or maybe we can go to Bukit Cerakah? I've promised to have lunch with Maria and Aidil. You can join us."

"Okay, insha Allah. That sounds great."

CHAPTER 10

As they waited for Imran to pick them up, Saleha reminded Ani of the next step in her plan. "Don't forget to call Maria tomorrow night, insha Allah." Ani nodded, reassuring her friend as Imran pulled up to the curb.

On the way to Ani's house, the women told Imran about their trip, omitting the doctor's visit and their meeting with Syakirah and Maria. Imran told them about Hidayat, who had been working on his secret since that morning. As Imran and his mother left Ani's place, Saleha brought up the subject of Syakirah.

"Imran, there's something I want to tell you. Well, when your Aunt Ani and I were in KL, we met Syakirah."

With a small laugh, Imran asked teasingly, "Oh, you did, did you? Did you plan this with Aunt Ani?"

Imran's response made Saleha a little nervous. "Well... umm...yes."

Imran chuckled.

"Ani's niece, the one who just got married, was in KL. Since she's a close friend of Syakirah, we asked to arrange a meeting with her."

"Hmm...and Syakirah agreed?" Imran was grinning now. He wondered why this person would agree to meet his mother.

"I could tell she did not like the idea at first. She seemed uncomfortable, but then, so was I at first. Anyway she's a nice person. Insha Allah, you're going to like her, Imran."

"Mom, how do you know?" Imran asked as he glanced at Saleha. He pretended to be nonchalant.

"I don't, but I have a feeling you two have a lot in common… a mother's intuition, insha Allah," Saleha responded with assurance.

"Now let's not go jumping the gun. I didn't promise to commit myself to anything, Mom." Imran reminded his mother politely.

"Of course. Well…she's working at Pine College."

"Hidayat's college? Really?" Imran asked.

"Yes. You're surprised, huh?" Saleha had her confidence back as she remembered what she had told Ani. It was not just mere coincidence that Hidayat and Syakirah were both at Pine College. She believed it was a sign from Allah (swt).

"I guess I am."

"Well, I was too but then it dawned on me that this could be destined by Allah Ta'ala. I mean, who would have thought I would meet a nice girl for you and she's known Hidayat all this time?" Imran was smiling and shaking his head as he listened to his mother. Saleha made Imran agree not to mention this to Hidayat yet.

When they reached home, Hidayat was waiting for them on the porch. As soon as Saleha got out, he approached his mother.

"Assalamu'alaikum. So how was KL, Mom?" Hidayat asked as they entered the house.

"Someone who studies in KL should know what KL is like, Hidayat," Saleha smiled, after replying to his salam.

"It went well, I presume?" He smiled at his mother.

"Well, not as exciting as what you've been up to, I think." Saleha responded, trying to get a hint of Hidayat's project. Hidayat grinned.

Imran looked at his watch and decided to have lunch at home before returning to the office. As they all sat in the living room, Imran asked Hidayat about his secret again, but Hidayat refused to reveal his secret.

"It'll be ready in half an hour. So why don't you and Mom go freshen up a bit?" Hidayat smiled and walked to the kitchen. Saleha looked at Imran, who then raised his eyebrows and shrugged his shoulders.

Half an hour later, Hidayat was flipping through a magazine when both Imran and Saleha came down to the living room.

"So?" Imran asked his brother.

"This way, please..." Hidayat motioned his brother and mother to the dining table. Mak Jah, who was pouring the drinks, smiled at them.

"Voila! This is the secret project I've been working on," Hidayat squealed with excitement. "Fish curry, fried chicken, stir-fried vegetables...cream pudding and washed fresh fruit." He pointed to each of the dishes on the dining table. Imran and Saleha were speechless.

"You did all this, Hidayat?" Saleha finally asked. Imran was about to ask the same question.

"Umm...well, not exactly. Mak Jah here helped me, right Mak Jah?" Hidayat explained, looking at the woman who had been like his second mother. The helper laughed at him and explained how Hidayat had been planning the whole affair since the morning Saleha left for KL.

"Hmm...a college journalist turned chef. You're a fast learner, Hidayat. But are these as good as they look?" Imran teased him.

"Let's find out!" They laughed as they sat around the dining table and enjoyed the feast. As they ate, Hidayat told them of the many minor disasters narrowly averted but for Mak Jah's skill and experience. Saleha in turn told him about her trip but did not mention Syakirah. Imran listened, but was silent.

~

Imran looked at his watch. It was past five-thirty. He was driving home but decided to stop at Lido beach for a while. After parking his car, he took off his shoes, coat and tie. Rolling up his shirt-sleeves, he surveyed the area. There were not many people today, he thought. He headed for his favorite spot.

Walking along the embankment, he thought about what his mother had told him in the car. He stopped and stared in the distance across the straits at Singapore's skyline. He sat on the embankment and took in the stunning view, which worked to distract him from himself for a few moments.

"Subhanallah!" he whispered, then reminded himself of his mother's scheme.

Ya Allah, has the time finally come? Am I about to start it all over again? Imran recalled his talk with Ani and Zaid. It was months after he returned from the U.K. He was still coping with Kaira's death then, and these two people were the ones from whom he sought advice.

"Did you love Kaira?" Zaid had asked Imran.

"Yes, with all my heart. That's why it's so hard... to let her go, Uncle Zaid."

"I know it's hard, but that's what a Muslim does when the one he loves dies... he lets her go and is pleased with the Almighty Allah's decree—that's redha! Then he seeks His help with patience and prayer...hoping for reward from Him."

Imran thought before responding. "I once told her she was mine for life. But she was never mine to begin with. What was given to me was her presence in my life. A presence does not last. It can always be replaced with an absence when Allah Ta'ala sees fit."

"Yes. And only a misguided man regards death as an absolute loss. In Surat Ar-Rum:

Glory be to God, when you enter evening and when you enter morning. All praise is to Him in the heavens and on earth and at nightfall and when you enter noon. He brings forth the living from the dead and brings forth the dead from the living, and revives the earth after its death, and so you will be brought forth.

Zaid continued, "Then in verse fifty:

Look upon the signs and imprints of God's mercy, how He revives the earth after its death. Surely He it is Who will revive the dead (in the same way). He is powerful over all things."

"It's just that what happened on that day keeps flashing back. It wouldn't have happened if..."

Ani interrupted. "Imran, a strong believer is better and more loved by Allah than a weak believer even if they both have goodness. Do not show weakness in your struggle. When something bad happens, never say, 'If I had not done so and so, then such and such would not have happened.' Instead, say, 'It was ordained by Allah for me and He allowed what He wished.' Always remember that the word 'if' would open the door for Satan to manipulate you."

"I know, Aunt Ani. Kaira was such a good person. I guess that's why Allah Ta'ala took her back so soon. By doing that

He wanted to teach me to be a better and stronger person. As I struggled to live without her, Allah Ta'ala was guiding me to His path. But I will miss being with her...someone who was blessed by the Most Loving Allah Ta'ala."

"You are still young, Imran...twenty-four, right?" Zaid asked and Imran nodded his head. "The time will come when you will meet someone as good as Kaira again, or perhaps a much better person, insha Allah. One of Rasulullah's wives was a widow known as Ummu Salamah. When her husband was martyred, Rasulullah prayed that she would remarry a much better husband. Indeed, Allah Ta'ala rewarded her with the best husband."

Imran glanced at his watch. It was six-thirty. Before heading for home, he whispered, "I guess I won't know until I meet this Syakirah Sulaiman." He wondered how, in this modern day, a person could agree to a matchmaking. With that thought, he shook his head lightly and a smile lit his face.

CHAPTER 11

Syakirah was in her room packing when the telephone rang. It was Maria. She told Syakirah that her Aunt Ani called her the night before.

"Maria, can't you give her an excuse for me? I don't want to put myself in that awkward spot again. Once is enough... please..." Syakirah pleaded when Maria told her that Saleha wanted to see her again.

"Syira, I know. I did try. But this time it's not just Auntie and Mrs. Saleha, but her son too."

Syakirah was silent for a few seconds. "Her son? You mean Imran Hakim?" She asked and raised an eyebrow. "Really."

"I sure don't mean Hidayat," Maria joked. "So?"

"I can't...I'm going home today."

"Well, it's not today."

"No, I don't think so, Maria."

"Why not? Aren't you at least a bit curious? I sure am!"

"Why doesn't that surprise me?" Syakirah feigned exasperation.

"Simple, my friend. Because I love you and I want you to take a break."

"A break?"

"Yeah...a break from being so stubborn, maybe. And finally to let your guard down. You've been walling yourself off from life for so long. It's time to break down the wall. You told me you've been over Manaf for a long time and you're not being unduly picky when you reject marriage proposals… Here's your chance to convince me, Syira."

Maria felt bad but she knew someone had to say this out loud. And she was Syakirah's oldest friend.

Syakirah was silent again. She knew every word Maria said was true. It had nothing to do with Manaf; she simply could not accept the thought of someone dictating her future like this. She had always been independent. When her mother died, though, she had to listen to the needs of her family and gave up the opportunity to work at the country's most prestigious university, which had always been her dream.

"I know you mean well, my dear, but…" Syakirah stopped. She didn't know whether she should say what she had been feeling all this time. She didn't want to hurt anyone's feelings; she was hoping this whole thing would just slip away. She even thought it was a mistake to meet Saleha and Ani that weekend. But then again she remembered Allah (swt) knew the best.

"But what, Syira? You can tell me. I can see it's not just a simple no." Maria was curious as well as concerned.

"I…I don't…I don't like the feeling that I'm throwing myself into this. You know, like a woman without pride, desperate to find a man. Maria, I don't want people to think just because I'm thirty-something and single, I'm an easy mark."

Syakirah finished and took a long breath. She felt like a beggar when she wrote her last letter to Manaf confessing her feelings after he first hinted about a break-up. His reply was an offer to remain "just friends."

Syakirah closed her eyes, as this painful memory from her past suddenly emerged. She stared down at the telephone.

"Are you serious? Syira, you are plain stubborn, do you know that?" Maria laughed. "Since when do you care about what others think? You're my one friend who doesn't care about what people think, especially when you're not doing anything wrong."

Syakirah acknowledged what Maria had said. She recalled the Islamic story of Luqman and his son about thinking too much of what people said. You might end up being miserable.

"I did not say I care about what they think, but I don't like when people talk. And they like to talk about things like this. Don't tell me you wouldn't feel the same if you were in my shoes."

"You're right about that. But if you're going to let that cloud your decision, you're not being true to yourself either."

"Meaning?"

"Meaning that you're a fighter, not a coward."

"And what does this have to do with me not wanting to meet them?"

"Oh, Syira... it has everything to do with it. You never run away from a challenge. If they think they really can match-make you and you think they're wrong, prove it. Prove that you have your own mind when it involves your own future. After all, your destiny is in the hands of Allah Ta'ala."

"Wow! Since when have you been so wise and philosophical about love and life?" Syakirah teased her friend and laughed.

"Since I got married!" Maria joined the laugh.

"Well, you weren't match-made by your folks."

"I know. But I'm right, aren't I?"

Syakirah sighed. "I don't know, Maria."

"You do, Syira."

Syakirah took a deep breath. "Okay, now that you've triggered the fighting spirit in me, I guess I'll accept the challenge." Syakirah heard Maria chuckle.

"Good. I'll call you with the details tonight, insha Allah."

"Hey, why don't I wait till you come home? We can meet at your folks' house, insha Allah."

"I'm afraid not, because Aidil and I have just decided to go to Penang tomorrow. So we might stay for a while, and we won't be home until Sunday, insha Allah. You'll be gone by then, right?"

"Yeah…well, just call me tonight then."

"Insha Allah. Have a safe flight home!"

~

Syakirah was happy to be home. But it did not take long for her parents to start asking her about Imran Hakim. It was right after dinner when they started to grill her. She told them about the past meeting, but not the coming one.

It was around nine-thirty when Maria called. She said the meeting was on Sunday at three o'clock at the coffeehouse of Hillview Hotel. Saleha, Imran, and her aunt would first go to the college to drop off Hidayat. Syakirah kept telling herself that it would be their last meeting. She told Maria she would bring Yasmin with her and made Maria promise not to tell anyone about this meeting, not even Maria's mother, who wouldn't be able to resist discussing the subject with Syakirah's grandmother.

On her visit to her grandmother's home, Syakirah was asked about the 'issue.' She gave her grandmother the same story she told her parents. She was careful not to give her any indication that there would be a future meeting.

Syakirah went out with her sister, Nadhirah, one evening and almost confided in her. She decided against it, however, because she was determined to make this coming meeting with Saleha and Imran their last. Then this whole thing would end, and there would be nothing more to talk about. She just wanted to enjoy her holiday until Sunday came.

CHAPTER 12

After breakfast, Hidayat helped Saleha in her orchid garden. They were talking when Imran came out of the house. Hidayat walked over to him as he was leaving. Imram was pensive.

"Abang Imran, will you be home for lunch?"

Imran awoke from his daydream and smiled lightly. "Hmm? Lunch? Oh…sorry, Hidayat. I have a meeting at two-thirty. But we're still playing tennis today with Umar. I'll be home before five, insha Allah."

After Imran left, Hidayat pondered his brother's mood change. He was fine during dinner the night before. Hidayat went back to the garden.

"Mom, is something wrong with Abang Imran?"

"What do you mean, dear?" Saleha casually asked him.

"I'm not sure. But something is bugging him, I think. He didn't talk much this morning. There's something on his mind."

"It must be the meeting he's having today. Dato' Annuar is a very influential man," Saleha hoped this answer would stop Hidayat from worrying about his brother.

"Well…yeah, I guess. I hope it was nothing personal." Hidayat voiced his concern.

~

As he drove, Imran thought again about what Saleha told him the night before. He knew he had promised to go along with this idea, but the thought of actually performing bothered him. "What have you got yourself into now, Imran?" He whispered. After several moments of frustrating speculation, however, he resigned himself to the idea. In the end, he looked forward to getting it over with. "Why do I let this get to me? It's just going to be this one time after all!" Imran smiled to himself.

When he got to his office, his secretary reminded him of his meeting with Dato' Annuar at eleven o'clock. He performed his morning routine and checked the documents and contracts in preparation for his meeting. Umar called later that morning.

"Imran, I'm afraid I have to cancel the game today. My kid came down with flu, so we're taking him to the clinic. Please tell Hidayat I'm sorry."

"Oh, it's all right, Umar. He'll understand, insha Allah. I know it won't be fun for him to play without you. Hey, perhaps I could ask him to go bowling instead."

"Bowling sounds good! I wish I could go with you for that. Next time he comes home, we'll set another game date, insha Allah. At any rate, I'll try to see him before he goes back to college."

"Insha Allah. Err...and Umar, there's something I..." Imran hesitated telling Umar about the upcoming meeting with Syakirah. He would wait until after it. "Umm... never mind."

"What? You got something in mind, just say it. I'm all ears, buddy."

"Nah...it can wait. I'll see you on Monday at lunch then, insha Allah."

"All right, I'll see you then, insha Allah." Umar knew very well that this must be something personal.

After talking to Umar, Imran called Hidayat. They agreed to go bowling instead of playing tennis. Imran checked his watch. After calling his secretary to bring some files for the meeting that day, he left for Dato' Annuar's office.

He arrived fifteen minutes early. He was flipping through one of the magazines in the waiting room when Melissa walked in. She smiled at Imran and walked to the secretary. Then she approached Imran, who then got up to greet her.

"Assalamu'alaikum, Mr. Imran. We meet again."

"Wa'alaikumussalam, Miss Melissa. I guess we do. I have a meeting with your father."

"Yes, he told me. You know, I was going to sit in, but I have something urgent to attend to. Oh, I met your brother last week, at the dinner with my father."

"Oh, yes. I'm sorry I couldn't make it. Next time insha Allah." They both smiled.

"Insha Allah. Well, nice to see you again, Mr. Imran."

"So nice to see you, too."

The meeting with Dato' Annuar took an hour. When it ended, Dato' Annuar invited Imran for lunch. He told Imran he was supposed to have lunch with his daughter but she could not make it.

"Yes, I met her outside before I came in. She said something urgent had come up." Right then Imran's cell phone rang. He excused himself to answer the call. It was his secretary informing him that his lunch meeting had been postponed. "That was my secretary. I guess I can join you for lunch after all."

They left for the restaurant, conversing easily while Imran drove. Their discussion continued into the restaurant, as they waited for their meals. Soon, Melissa showed up, having finished her work earlier than expected.

"I thought I'd join you because I didn't want you to eat alone. But I see you already have Mr. Imran's company." She smiled at both men.

The men stood and motioned for Melissa to take a seat. After ordering for Melissa, Dato' Annuar explained that Imran's lunch meeting had been postponed. The meals were delivered while the three got to know each other better.

Imran learned that Melissa started working with her father a month ago. "I didn't think I would be working with Papa when I came back from the States. I wanted experience from a large company, so I went to work with J & J Corporation. I really enjoyed it, but it was time for a change. My brother had been urging me to come to the family business since I finished my graduate studies, and Papa said I could learn working here too."

"You're doing great, dear. For someone as young as you are, you're very good."

"Papa…" She smiled at her father, a little embarrassed. "Mr. Imran, I heard you're a successful businessman. I don't mean to pry but I've heard a lot about the history of your company. It must've been difficult taking over management after your father passed away."

"It was, but alhamdulillah I certainly haven't been alone. My family has always been a motivational source for me." Imran paused. "Iskandar is more than the company accountant, in spirit and in fact. We leaned on each other throughout the first year. And the same people who worked for my father have been very good since the first day we've been there. They've given us full support."

They continued talking about KS Holding. At the end of the lunch, Dato' Annuar asked if Imran bowled, because he and Melissa liked the game.

"Well, it so happens that I'm going bowling with my brother today. If you're free, maybe we can have a match." They agreed to join him and Hidayat.

~

It was four o'clock when Imran greeted Saleha and Mak Jah, who were preparing tea. Imran excused himself to get clean and do his Asr prayer before the game. Saleha was relieved that Imran seemed to be in a better mood. She assumed everything was fine.

On his way to his room, Imran poked his head into Hidayat's room. He greeted Raju and reminded Hidayat about the game. Hidayat said he would be ready by the time his brother finished his prayer. Half an hour later, they were all at the dining table having tea. After tea, Raju asked to leave and Hidayat and Imran left for the game soon after.

In the car, Imran told Hidayat that Dato' Annuar and Melissa were joining them.

"So how long have you known Miss Melissa?" Hidayat was keen to know.

"I've met her a few times. Once was during one of my meetings with Dato' Annuar and another time I bumped into her while I was having lunch with Umar. How come you're interested, Hidayat?" Imran teased his brother.

"Me? Why? I'm not…I'm just wondering because it's not like I always get to see you in public with…you know." Hidayat eyed his brother curiously.

Imran laughed at his brother. "With whom? A woman? Of course you haven't because that is not me, and it's not Islamic, and it's not business. Anyway I would bore a nice woman with my business talk."

Hidayat laughed with his brother. "But it would be nice for a change. One of these days you're going to meet someone and I'll have another sister-in-law besides Kak Marina."

After arriving at the bowling alley, they waited for Dato' Annuar and Melissa, who were late. After a while, the brothers decided to start bowling without them and enjoy their time together. Midway into their first game, Melissa came. She apologized for coming late and told them her father would not be able to come as he received an unexpected house guest at the last minute. Imran introduced her to Hidayat.

"You look a lot like Iskandar."

"And you look...white!" Hidayat told the woman with a grin. She wore a light gray scarf to match her white long-sleeve shirt, track bottom and sneakers.

Melissa laughed at Hidayat's comment.

"Mind you, my brother is a student of journalism and tells it like it is," Imran laughed.

"You've met Abang Iskandar?"

"Yes, at dinner last week with my father." She smiled at Imran.

After more small talk, Imran had the scores reset and asked Melissa to start the new game. "Let's go!" she answered enthusiastically.

"All right!" Hidayat cheered.

Melissa won the first game. Hidayat won the second one and Imran the third. All in all, they were evenly matched.

Before leaving the place, they decided to stop for drinks. Sipping her drink, Melissa asked Imran, "Were you being a gentleman and let me win, Imran?"

"You were good, that's why you won. But my brother here..."

"Your brother's right, Hidayat. You were good."

"Thanks! I go bowling with friends at the college whenever I have time."

"Where would that be?"

"Pine College, KL. I'm going back this Sunday."

"I've heard that's a good college and has a great writing program."

"It is. Is there anything you don't know, Miss Melissa?" Hidayat was impressed.

Melissa laughed. "I happened to read about it in a paper when I was in KL a few weeks ago. I don't know much about it. And what makes you think I know much about anything?"

"Well, you're good at this game, you know about Pine College and you're also a good businesswoman."

"And you learned that about me from Imran?" Melissa laughed.

Hidayat just smiled at Imran. Imran could tell what his brother was doing. He was trying to get Imran interested in Melissa. He checked his watch. It was after six-thirty.

The three of them left the bowling alley at a quarter to seven. Melissa invited Imran for another game the coming weekend. Imran said he would call her back.

"She's cool, Abang Imran!" Hidayat commented on their way home.

"Yeah, she's nice," Imran said casually.

"You told me that you met her a couple of times before. Do you like her?" Hidayat sounded very anxious for the correct reply from his brother.

"She's okay. I can see that you like her a lot," Imran replied in a teasing voice.

"Well, I think she likes you a lot too." Imran gave his brother credit; he *did* try.

"Is my little brother trying to be a matchmaker here?"

"What if I am? You two look very chummy, so…"

Imran interrupted him, "She's a good business colleague. End of story."

"You need to loosen up a bit or else you'll stay like this forever."

"Stay like what? Hey, I'm not complaining. My life is fine, alhamdulillah! And thank you for your concern, little brother." Imran grinned at his brother. Hidayat gave up. It wasn't easy talking to his big brother about commitment.

~

That night after *Isha'* prayer, Imran went to see Ani and Zaid. The couple was happy to see him. Ani guessed his reason for the visit.

"It's been a while since you came, Imran. It's so nice to see you," Zaid told Imran.

"I've been busy for the last couple of months. I'm sorry, Uncle Zaid."

"So how's the family?"

"Fine, alhamdulillah!"

"And you?"

"Business is good, alhamdulillah."

"Alhamdulillah, I'm glad to hear. Your father would be proud of you, Son. But that did not answer my question. How are you?" He smiled at Imran.

Ani came to join them with drinks.

"That's the reason why I'm here tonight."

"About tomorrow, right?" Ani asked and Imran nodded.

"I'm worried about Mom. I don't want to break her heart. I'm taking this meeting lightly, but I think Mom has set her hopes too high."

"Syakirah is a nice person as far as I could tell, and her parents are good Muslims, according to my niece," Ani explained.

"That's good, alhamdulillah. Honestly, Uncle Zaid, Aunt Ani…since Kaira, I've met some women who are good…good by the acceptable moral standard in our culture. But when it comes to the practice of Islam, I have doubts. I always remember what you once taught me. Being virtuous may not include the quality of being righteous. In Kaira, I saw both of these. She possessed good moral values, acceptable and respected by anyone who met and knew her. But, beneath all those was the shine of righteousness…a righteous Muslim living by her faith…shown in her every action …that made her different. In her I saw the difference between the two qualities. Honestly, I still miss her sometimes, especially when it seems like it's impossible for me to meet someone like her again. But don't worry. I've let her go years ago. Thanks to you and, most of all, I thank Allah, alhamdulillah."

Zaid answered, "For almost ten years I've watched you live your life for your family. When your father passed away, you devoted your time and life taking care of them. Subhanallah! How Allah Ta'ala can make a tragedy a turning point in His servant's life. Calamities in life bring people closer to Him. They become closer to Allah as they seek His help with patience and perseverance."

Zaid let that sink in before continuing. "It's excellent that you know the difference between being virtuous and righteous from an Islamic point of view. Nowadays the two qualities have become synonymous as more and more Muslims have come to accept the two as such by the standard of customs and beliefs in general rather than as prescribed in the Quran. I sometimes ask your mother if you'd like to remarry. She says only when you are ready and when you have met a righteous woman. See, even your Mom knows what's in your heart. So I'm sure she looks for this quality in this girl and sees it."

Imran answered, "One thing that I learned from Kaira was the meaning of belonging. I didn't put much thought into her deep understanding of this word until I thought I had 'lost' her. On that day I told her she was mine for life, and she said we belong only to Allah Ta'ala. It was only months after her death and after listening to your advice that I realized that since she was not mine...did not belong to me...I did not lose her. She returned to Allah Ta'ala, and insha Allah, we will be together again in the next life. Through her and later through you, Uncle Zaid, Allah Ta'ala made me understand the true meaning of marriage—that is, it is not a possession but a trust, an amanah. Most people I know see marriage as a possession."

"Imran, you're a good judge of people. Use this to find out what this person is like. Then just be honest with your mother. Tell her what you think of this woman, insha Allah. As for the rest, just leave it to the All-Wise Allah Ta'ala," Zaid advised Imran.

CHAPTER 13

They were about to leave for Hidayat's college when Imran's cell phone rang. It was Iskandar.

"Glad that I caught you."

"What's up, Iskandar? You want to talk to Hidayat?" Imran asked while checking the time.

"No, we had our goodbye last night. This won't take long. Mr. Reese called yesterday while you were out. Hayati transferred his call to me."

"He's not backing out of the deal, is he?" Imran asked anxiously.

"No, no. He's still with us. I forgot to tell you that last night. He told me that he would be in KL today. I thought you might want to see him there. I'll give you a call sometime today, insha Allah."

"Okay, thanks, Iskandar." Imran wondered if he would have time to see the client.

"Have a safe trip, insha Allah."

They left the house shortly after eight. During the journey Hidayat talked about his coming assignment for the *Daily Pine* and the Language Camp. Saleha and Ani just smiled and once in a while laughed at his excitement. Imran listened and occasionally popped in with a question that demonstrated his interest. Neither the women nor Imran mentioned the meeting with Syakirah and Yasmin.

It was after one o'clock when they reached Pine College. The meeting with the ladies was at three, so they hurried to Hillview Hotel to check in.

∼

Syakirah took the ten AM flight from KB, or Kota Bahru. Her housemate picked her up at the airport. After lunch, she called Yasmin about the meeting.

"Are you still coming with me, Min?"

"I'd never miss this, my friend. I'm looking forward to meeting this Imran Hakim!" Yasmin answered excitedly.

"Don't get too excited. As much as I look forward to seeing Aunt Saleha again, I think this will be the last time." She recounted her last conversation with Maria.

"She was right, you know. You can be so stubborn sometimes, but, like she said, why do you care about what other people say? This is not the old days. Who cares if you're forty and unmarried?"

"Yeah, right. As far as I'm concerned, the sooner this is over, the better. Then I can move on with my life! I'll pick you up at three, insha Allah."

"Insha Allah, I'll be ready! See you, Syira!"

Syakirah smiled after talking to her excited friend. It was hard to believe her friend was a mother of two, with her being cheerful all the time.

∼

Yasmin was waiting at the porch when Syakirah arrived at her house. Nik was playing with their children. Yasmin had filled Nik in about the meeting, too.

They arrived at Hillview Hotel a few minutes early. When they entered the coffeehouse surprisingly, Saleha and Ani were already there. As they approached the table, Yasmin noticed the seriousness in Syakirah's face.

"Syira, lighten up a bit. You don't want to show that somber face to those nice people."

"Well, if it weren't for them, I wouldn't be here, not even if someone paid me a thousand ringgit. For all I care, it doesn't matter how I look. I'm here to prove how wrong this matchmaking is. I feel like I'm forcing every fiber of my being just to be here. I can't wait to get this over and done with."

"Oh please. This is not an appointment for a lobotomy, for goodness sakes! Just let go of it for the next couple of hours, Syira. Be cool and try to be nice. Now smile…" Yasmin told Syakirah as the two elder ladies watched them approach.

"Asalaamu'alaikum," Yasmin and Syakira said in unison.

"Wa'alaikumussalam," Saleha returned their salams.

Syakirah introduced Yasmin to Saleha and Ani and Saleha explained, "Imran will be here in a minute. He stopped by a table to talk to his friend."

The waiter brought them their drinks. Saleha told them about the trip to KL, and Ani asked about Pine College. They all laughed when Ani recounted Hidayat's excitement about his writing job during the trip.

Upon entering the coffeehouse, Imran saw Saleha and Ani talking to Syakirah and Yasmin. He stopped short and studied the two younger women from afar. There was something familiar about one of them, yet he couldn't pinpoint it. The women did not notice him approach the table.

"Assalamu'alaikum, ladies."

Saleha introduced Imran to Syakirah and Yasmin. They exchanged greetings and Imran took his seat between his aunt and his mother. Imran tried not to stare at Syakirah, even though he wanted to find out what seemed so familiar about her.

"So was I interrupting something just now?" Imran asked.

"We were talking about the trip this morning," Ani answered.

Saleha added, "And about Hidayat." The ladies giggled.

"You all must be tired from the trip," Yasmin said with a smile.

"Not with Hidayat entertaining us along the way," Ani answered.

Imran responded, "Aunt Ani was right. With Hidayat in the car, the drive wasn't tiring at all. And I'm sure my brother would be happy to be here considering you two are here."

"That's very kind of you to say," Yasmin answered graciously. Syakirah had not spoken since they had exchanged greetings. Yasmin felt awkward with her friend's silence, and as she smiled and listened to Imran, she nudged Syakirah's knee to make her talk. Yasmin knew her being there was not a waste but a saving grace.

"So you taught him before?" Imran asked them.

"I haven't, but Syakirah did. I've come to know him this semester when he started writing for the *Daily Pine*, the college paper. He's really talented, Mr. Imran."

"Call me Imran, please," Imran urged and then looked at Syakirah. "What about you, Miss Syakirah?" Imran asked, studying her at the same time.

"I taught him once...his first semester last year. Like Mrs. Yasmin said, your brother is doing a good job." Syakirah finally said something. Yasmin was relieved.

"Of course when he has lecturers like you two," Saleha added and Ani agreed with her friend's comment.

"Alhamdulillah. We're just doing our job." Syakirah smiled at the two women and glanced at Yasmin. Then she caught Imran looking at her. Syakirah felt uncomfortable.

"That's what we're paid to do," Yasmin added with a small laugh.

"So you like teaching Miss Syakirah?"

"Syakirah, please. Yes, alhamdulillah, I enjoy teaching. It's a challenging job, trying to meet the needs of the students while at the same time learning about them."

"What do you mean? You study every student in your class, Miss Sya…er…Syakirah?"

Ani and Saleha looked at Syakirah with interest. Yasmin could sense that her friend was uncomfortable with all the attention. She had always known that about Syakirah.

"Absolutely. Each student is unique. I have never had a set of students with the same or even similar characteristics and attitudes. Learning about each student personally occurs as the semester progresses, which helps me gauge what they're learning and how I'm doing as a teacher. That's how I know whether I'm using an effective teaching approach, whether something else might work better, whether the students are actually interested… It really helps to pay attention to the students' responses and attitudes."

"Wow, that's a…really profound outlook, Syakirah. I wish all teachers had such a perspective. What a good place school would be," Imran stated respectfully.

"Are you saying that it is an idealistic view, Mr. Imran?" She appeared annoyed.

Yasmin was watching Syakirah now. She had never seen her friend acting like this. Syakirah could not care less about what other people think of her teaching perspective. What she always cared about was the teaching itself. That was more important to her and to her students. Yasmin looked at her watch. It was ten minutes after four. Now it was she who wished the meeting finished.

"Well, I just thought...." Before he could finish his sentence, his cell phone rang. "Please excuse me, I've to take this call." He turned to look at his mother. "It's Iskandar, Mom." Saleha nodded and he left the table to go to the foyer.

Syakirah was relieved and less tense but still very much disturbed. She was not sure why she had gotten annoyed so easily. She thought it could be because she was trying so hard to get 'the proof.' She was wondering what Imran was about to say when the phone rang. She looked at Yasmin, who then gave her a just-forget-about-it look.

"Would you like to have some more tea, Syakirah, Yasmin?" Ani asked to break the silence.

"I'm fine, no...thank you," Yasmin replied politely. Syakirah did the same. Just then they heard someone calling Saleha's name. They turned and there was Dr. Norman. Saleha got up. Syakirah noticed Saleha's surprise. He greeted both Saleha and Ani. Saleha was worried Imran might return to their table. She glanced at the foyer and saw that Imran was still on the phone with Iskandar. Saleha invited Dr. Norman to join them for a drink with them but he could not stay that long.

"What brought you here, Dr. Norman?" Saleha asked.

"Oh, I'm meeting a friend. And you two?" Dr. Norman asked looking at both Saleha and Ani.

"I came to send my son back to college, Pine College. We drove here this morning. I came with my other son. You've just missed him."

"So is one of these young ladies the future daughter-in-law you were meeting last time?"

Saleha was unsure how to respond to this and wondering at the same time what made the doctor ask that question. "Uh... yes...Syakirah. And this is her friend Yasmin."

Syakirah was trying to hide her disbelief.

"Nice to meet you, Miss Syakirah, Miss Yasmin."

"Mrs. Yasmin."

"I'm sorry, Mrs. Yasmin."

"So you'll be staying here tonight, Mrs. Saleha?"

"Yes. We're leaving tomorrow morning."

"Well, then I could invite you to my house. I'm giving a small party tonight...a thanksgiving party. I'd be honored if you all could come."

"Thank you, Dr. Norman. I'll have to talk to my son first." Saleha was glad Imran wasn't there. She hoped Dr. Norman wouldn't say anything about her health.

"Do come. It's a pleasure to have more friends over, and that includes you too, Mrs. Yasmin and Miss Syakirah...I don't have to mention. You're coming of course with Mrs. Saleha, right? That is, if she accepts my invitation." Saleha smiled at the kind doctor, still praying he would not mention her medical condition.

"I'm afraid I have plans with my family tonight," Yasmin excused herself. "But I'm sure Miss Syakirah is free."

Syakirah felt a knot in her stomach and said to herself, "I'll get you, Min, for this."

"Uh...insha Allah." That was all Syakirah could say smilingly, trying not to embarrass Saleha but at the same time trying to save herself from the invitation. She was also still trying to hide her disbelief at Saleha's answer to Dr. Norman's question just now.

"Just call me if you could come. You do have my card with you, right?"

Saleha nodded. As Dr. Norman was leaving, Saleha followed him.

"Doctor, my son doesn't know about..." Saleha began but was interrupted by Dr. Norman.

"Fine. Don't worry. A patient's record is confidential, remember? I addressed you as a friend, didn't I? After all, my wife loves Ms. Ani's clothing line." They both smiled.

"Thank you. And my salam to your wife. If we decide to come tonight, my son will know you as the husband of a regular customer at Ani's friend's boutique. Anyway that was the place I met your wife.

"And one more thing, Dr. Norman...about Miss Syakirah... well, actually my son has just met her today, so I apologize for giving you the wrong impression."

Dr. Norman seemed a little surprised. Then he smiled at Saleha. He could guess why Saleha would want to do that. It was a dying mother's wish, he thought.

"Any mother would wish marriage for her son, no need to explain, Mrs. Saleha."

"I appreciate that."

"Well, I hope to see you and your son tonight, insha Allah. Oh, and Miss Syakirah and your friend too. It's almost four-thirty. I'd better leave now." They said goodbye. As Saleha walked back to the table, Imran finished his call and walked over to his mother.

"Who was that man, Mom?"

"Dr. Norman. His wife is a regular customer at the boutique in KL," Saleha answered abruptly, hoping Imran did not suspect anything.

"Small world, alhamdulillah." Imran smiled. "I'm sorry about the interruption just now, Mom. Iskandar informed me this morning that he would call about our client who is in KL right now. I could not say no to him because then I would have to tell him about this meeting."

Saleha was not happy with the sudden phone call but noticed Imran was trying hard to please her. "I understand, dear." Saleha smiled. Everything had gone well, except for his comment to Syakirah just now. There were times that Saleha wished Imran could be less outspoken with his opinion. Today was one of them.

"Now, I have a meeting at six, but I promise you it would be a short one and I'd…"

"Imran…" Saleha interrupted and was a little upset. They stopped walking and stood facing each other.

"I promise I'll make up for this tonight. We'll go out tonight and have dinner…your pick, Mom." Imran tried to console his mother. Saleha's face still looked upset but then she thought of Dr. Norman's invitation.

"My pick, huh?" Saleha smiled now, and Imran nodded. They continued walking.

Meanwhile at the table Ani was trying to explain to Syakirah why Saleha introduced her to Dr. Norman as the elder woman's future daughter-in-law. Syakirah had a hard time swallowing this.

"I'm sorry, Syakirah. I'm sure she never meant to make you feel uncomfortable. She let it slip when she was talking to Dr. Norman the last time we met him in KL."

"Aunt Ani, I don't want to be impolite, but this is getting too much now. I just hope it won't get out of hand. I agreed to come because I like and respect her—and you too. She reminds me of…someone." Syakirah would not encourage Ani and Saleha by stating that Saleha reminded her of her mother. "But just because I'm willing to show up, it does not mean I'd be…you know…"

Ani nodded.

"Syira, I'm sure there is nothing to be concerned about." Yasmin tried to calm her friend.

"I promise it won't happen again, insha Allah," Ani added solemnly.

"Does Imran…"

Ani interrupted to assure her, "No, Syira, and he won't have to know, insha Allah."

"Thank you. I hope we won't have to deal with this again, insha Allah." Syakirah looked calmer now but still a little agitated. Yasmin was relieved.

As the three women were finishing their talk, Saleha and Imran reached the table. Saleha looked at Ani as she and Imran were sitting down. Ani gave her a look that said everything went well while she was absent.

"I'm sorry. I had to discuss something with Dr. Norman." Saleha gave a meaningful look at Syakirah.

Syakirah knew Saleha was apologizing for more than that. She smiled at the elder woman. "It's okay. We understand. He was nice to invite all of us to the party, but I really can't go." At that moment she just wished the meeting were over.

Hearing about the invitation, Imran asked. "An invitation?"

Saleha told him, "Imran, you promised that we'd go out tonight. So insha Allah, we'll go to Dr. Norman's house then."

"Well, if that is your pick, Mom, then yes, insha Allah!" Imran smiled at his mother. "What time is the party?"

"Eight-thirty." Saleha looked happy now. Ani, Syakirah and Yasmin watched the exchanges between mother and son.

"Okay. I'd be back before Maghrib prayer time, insha Allah. Now I have to leave to get ready for my meeting." Imran got up to leave. "Well, it was a pleasure meeting you, Miss Syakirah and Mrs. Yasmin. Sorry we could not finish our talk just now, Syakirah," he continued with a smile.

"Nice meeting you too, Mr. Imran." Syakirah was glad that the meeting was finally over.

"Maybe next time, insha Allah. And nice to meet you too, Mr. Imran," Yasmin said after Syakirah. The three of them exchanged polite smiles.

Suddenly Saleha made a suggestion, "Maybe you two could continue it tonight. Syakirah, what do you say? I'm sorry that Yasmin already had plans, but you could still come with us."

Yasmin looked at Syakirah. "Well, I don't really know Dr. Norman..." Before she could finish, Imran interrupted casually.

"Nor do I." Imran preferred that the meeting with Syakirah ended there. He had just fulfilled his promise to Saleha by coming to the meeting. Syakirah was a nice person, just like Ani and Zaid had told him, but that was all. To him, the meeting was like any business meeting, except at his mother's request. Now, with the invitation to Dr. Norman's house, he was afraid that his mother would have higher hopes about matchmaking.

"Are you sure, Syakirah?" Ani asked.

Syakirah felt uncomfortable with all of them waiting for her answer. Then Imran spoke.

"I'm sure Miss Syakirah has other plans, and, considering we've just met, I'd understand if she can't join us. Mom?"

Imran's comments seemed casual, accurate even, but Syakirah was annoyed. Could he be trying to keep her from going to Dr. Norman's house? She quickly erased her suspicion. Suddenly she felt awkward. "Uh...you know what...Mr. Imran's right. Anyway

I'd be busy tonight. You see, classes start tomorrow. I need to do some preparation."

"Are you sure?" Now it was Imran asking her.

"Yes. I think Mrs. Yasmin and I should leave now too." Then looking at the two women in front of her, Syakirah continued, "I'm sure Aunt Saleha and Aunt Ani will need some rest before tonight. And Mr. Imran has a meeting to go to."

The elder women could sense everyone was becoming a little ill at ease. Ani graciously spoke, "Oh, we'd love to have you and Yasmin stay a bit longer here and talk with us."

Syakirah felt she had to leave. "Thank you, but I really think we should be going now. Yasmin…?" Syakirah glanced at Yasmin as she was getting up to leave. Yasmin got up. She was unsure of what to say but agreed with Syakirah. Imran was watching Syakirah as she was saying this. The elder women could only smile.

"Well, again nice meeting you, Mr. Imran." Syakirah said in a business-like tone. Yasmin said the same but in a more cheerful voice, trying to make up for Syakirah's less-than-friendly way. After a salam the two young women left.

Imran excused himself for the Asr prayer. Then he would see Saleha before leaving for the meeting.

∼

Saleha had just finished praying in her room when Ani let Imran in. Ani left the two of them to talk alone.

Imran went to sit next to Saleha. "Mom, I'm sorry if the meeting did not turn out the way you expected it to be… interruptions here and there."

Saleha was quiet. Imran was right. It did not turn out as she had hoped.

"Besides the interruptions, don't you think you could have been a little nicer in your opinion of her teaching principle?" Saleha asked, knowing well how forthright her son could be, even in his polite and subtle way.

"Oh, that...well, I guess I should have shut my mouth and just paid attention to her," Imran joked and smiled.

"It's not funny, Imran. I think you should call and apologize to her."

"Maybe I should, but then..." He was interrupted by his mother.

"You'd do that Imran?" Saleha asked, looking excited.

Imran smiled and nodded. He knew it would make Saleha happy.

Saleha gave him Syakirah's phone number she got from Maria. "Do you think maybe we could still invite her to Dr. Norman's thanksgiving party?" she asked, hopeful.

Imran didn't really like the idea, but the look on Saleha's face made him agree. He left and promised to call Syakirah before the meeting.

~

Syakirah and Yasmin drove home without talking much in the car. At first Yasmin tried to say something about Imran, but before she could even finish her sentence, Syakirah stopped her. Yasmin understood Syakirah very well. Nobody should try to talk to her about anything when she was annoyed.

When they reached Yasmin's house, Syakirah seemed a bit more relaxed.

"Imran Hakim is quite a charming man."

"He's okay, but his bluntness, subtle as it may seem, bugged me in some ways."

"Well, he's entitled to his opinion."

"Of course, he is. It's just that at the end of the meeting, he seemed to be hinting that I should turn down the invitation to Dr. Norman's house. The look on his mother's face was a different story—she seemed hopeful."

"Well, don't you think that would make you and Imran alike...regarding a matchmaking, perhaps?" Yasmin said with a small laugh.

"Perhaps so!" Syakirah was not interested in thinking much about the meeting.

"So there's still a chance for you and Imran. Aunt Saleha wishes that something will click between you two."

Syakirah shrugged her shoulders and casually told her friend, "It will take a whole lot more than what I saw today for that to happen. Impossible!"

Yasmin smiled at her friend. Letting go a sigh, she dropped the topic.

"Well, I'll see you tomorrow, insha Allah!"

"Insha Allah! And, Min, thanks for coming with me."

"Anytime, insha Allah."

When Syakirah arrived home, her housemate, Lily, had not come back yet. Lily had told her that she might stay overnight at her friend's place because she was taking a day off the next day. Syakirah prayed the Asr prayer and sat on the couch afterwards. She thought about what had happened in the coffeehouse. Imran's forthrightness still annoyed her, but it was wrong for her to judge him, Syakirah thought. One thing for sure, only an obedient son would agree to such a meeting!

"Be careful, Syira! Don't set yourself up for a heartbreak again!" Syakirah said to herself. She knew she was over Manaf. It helped her a great deal to forget him the day she learned it was Islamically wrong for her to be in love with a man before marriage or a man who was not sure of choosing her as his life partner. She promised herself not to repeat the mistake. She never hated Manaf, but the consequence of his decision had hurt her deeply, and still hurt sometimes.

Syakirah grabbed the remote control and turned the television on. She was watching the news when the telephone rang.

"Hello, may I please speak to Miss Syakirah?"

Syakirah did not recognize Imran's voice on the other end of the line. "This is she. May I know who's speaking?" When Imran introduced himself, she almost hung up. She remembered his remarks about her teaching perspective and her own words that the meeting was to be the last encounter with Imran Hakim.

"Syakirah, I apologize if I offended you in any way at the coffeehouse today... I mean, my personal comments about your teaching view."

Syakirah paused. "Was that what your mother told you? Or did she ask you to call me to apologize?" She asked coldly.

"I speak for myself and my mother meant well with the meeting. Anyway, being Muslims, I believe we must as much as possible observe the ways of Rasulullah (saw). That includes asking for forgiveness when one realizes his or her mistakes. So again, I'm sorry, Miss Syakirah." Imran's voice sounded firm but apologetic at the same time.

Syakirah felt a little guilty, even embarrassed, for sounding cold earlier on. Immediately, she said 'Astaghfirullah' in her heart. "I accept your apology. And I'm sorry too for what I said to you just now. If there's nothing else, then Assalam..."

"Actually, there is. My mother still would like you to come with us to the thanksgiving party at Dr. Norman's house tonight."

Syakirah paused to consider that Imran did this at his mother's request. So he's not all that bad.

"I'd understand if you say no, but it would mean a lot to her if you could come." His voice sounded softer.

Syakirah thought for a while. "And how would I know what had happened earlier would not happen again?"

Silence.

"I give you my word, insha Allah." Imran replied firmly.

Syakirah thought of Saleha and how agreeable the woman was. There was something about the elder woman that she liked so much. She respected this woman even though she barely knew her.

Then she remembered what she had said to herself earlier about not setting herself up for heartbreak again. God forbid. Amen.

"Okay, but on one condition."

"Name it."

"I don't have to speak to you while we're there."

"Fine. Insha Allah, we'll pick you up at eight."

They hung up and Syakirah called Yasmin. "I've just talked to Imran Hakim."

"You what?"

Syakirah explained and Yasmin wished her luck.

～

They came to fetch Syakirah at eight o'clock sharp. After greeting everyone, she got into the car. Syakirah sat in the back with Ani. They avoided talking about what had taken place earlier. When they reached Dr. Norman's house, Ani and Syakirah walked in first.

Ani was glad that Saleha had clarified the matter about Syakirah with Dr. Norman. When she told Syakirah about this, the younger woman felt relief. As soon as they entered Dr. Norman's house, Ani and Syakirah were greeted by the kind doctor and his amiable wife. The party was small. Some of the people invited were Dr. Norman's patients.

Saleha was happy to have Syakirah with them at the party. She said this to Imran, who did not tell his mother about Syakirah's condition for coming to the party. Saleha introduced her son to Dr. Norman and his wife. As promised, Dr. Norman kept Saleha's secret from everybody.

Later Saleha and Imran joined Ani and Syakirah for a while before Dr. Norman's wife came and invited Ani to meet her friends. Imran and Syakirah barely spoke to each other but managed not to make it too obvious in front of Saleha. In order to keep his promise, Imran excused himself to mingle.

"So, Aunt Saleha, how long have you known Dr. Norman and his wife?" Syakirah inquired.

"Oh…about a year now. His wife is a regular customer at a boutique, which belongs to Ani's friend. Sometimes when I come to KL with Ani, I would meet her at the boutique." She didn't like having to hide from Syakirah her real relationship with Dr. Norman but thought that was how it would be for now. They talked about Ani's business in JB. While they talked, Saleha saw Dr. Norman approaching them.

"Enjoying yourselves, ladies?" He smiled at them. "Miss Syakirah, I assume you are not in the boutique business?"

"I teach English at Pine College."

"A lecturer. That's a good profession with many 'patients' too…the students in need of help and guidance," Dr. Norman joked, which made everyone laugh. They talked about her job at the college.

"Imran's in a good business, Mrs. Saleha, and he's a good son, I can tell." Dr. Norman commented with a smile. "I hope your wish for him will come true."

"Thank you, insha Allah." Saleha gave Syakirah a cue for her to leave so she would not feel uncomfortable. "Dr. Norman, I've been meaning to talk to you about something." Syakirah understood her intention and excused herself.

After Syakirah left, Saleha thanked Dr. Norman for keeping her secret and told him she would tell her family soon.

"I really meant it about your wish for your son and Miss Syakirah. She seems like a nice person. I am perhaps just your doctor, but I'm also a father of two sons. Alhamdulillah, they are both happily married now."

Saleha smiled and told him she appreciated his comment about Imran and Syakirah.

Syakirah went to refresh her drink. Suddenly she heard Imran's voice not far from her. She turned and their eyes met. She casually walked away. Imran excused himself from the people he was talking to and followed Syakirah. He knew he made the promise but he thought he would try anyway to make amends for what had happened at the coffeehouse.

"Syakirah."

She turned around. "You gave me your word."

"I did but I'm sorry to break it for a while." He grinned. "I think it would look awkward if we keep avoiding each other. So why don't we try to be friends temporarily?"

Syakirah was irritated by his statement but tried to be reasonable, considering the surroundings. She nodded in agreement. "Let's go back to our table."

"Not so fast. Don't worry, I won't bite you if we stand here for a while." He joked and laughed a little, but Syakirah just smirked.

"Keeping your promise would be better, I think."

He smiled but agreed, "I guess we should, then. Anyway it won't be proper Islamically for us to be in close proximity like this." As he was walking behind her, he whispered, "You're one tough lady, Miss Syakirah."

They walked to their table. Ani and Saleha were talking when they reached the table. Saleha smiled when she saw the two of them.

They left the party at ten o'clock, telling Dr. Norman they needed a good sleep for the next day's drive. Then they took Syakirah home.

"Thank you for the evening, Aunt Saleha."

"You're welcome, dear. I hope we'll meet again…I mean, maybe the next time when we visit Hidayat." Saleha smiled.

"Insha Allah." That was all Syakirah could say to be polite to Saleha. She hoped this was their last meeting.

"Mom, I'm sure our dedicated lecturer here will be busy. The new semester has just begun, remember?" Imran interrupted with a grin. He noticed Syakirah smiling at his joke. Saleha gave him a quick glance.

"It was nice knowing you, Miss…Syakirah," added Imran.

"Same here, Mr. Imran. Have a safe trip tomorrow, insha Allah."

They bade goodbye and left.

On the way to the hotel, Saleha wanted to talk to Imran about Syakirah but decided to wait until they got home. She thought it would give Imran some time to think. After all, she knew Imran would not say anything until she asked him first. The three of them talked about the party instead.

CHAPTER 14

Syakirah was walking to her office after class when Hidayat stopped her with a salam.

"Excuse me, Miss Syakirah, but do you have a minute?"

Returning his salam, Syakirah looked at her watch to check the time. She had an appointment with the Head of the Language Center at ten-thirty.

"Yes, insha Allah, Hidayat."

They talked en route to Syakirah's office.

"I heard from one of the Language Camp committee members yesterday that a meeting will be this Friday. So I was wondering if you could give me some info about it. I'd like to be well prepared."

"Yes, two of the committee members came by my office on Monday. The subcommittees finalized the activities. I guess they got together during the break." Syakirah smiled, thinking of the subcommittees' enthusiasm about the Language Camp.

"Do you know what the activities are, Miss Syakirah?"

"So far, yes, but Mrs. Yasmin and I suggested that they reduce the amount. We were told that the Head doesn't have any problem with the activities except that there are too many. So, I guess we'll hear from the committee this Friday."

The two-day camp was set to start in a week.

They reached Syakirah's office. Syakirah glanced at Yasmin's office, which appeared unoccupied. Hidayat followed her to her office. Syakirah filled him in on details of the tentative activities. He thanked her and left.

Syakirah whispered, "It's hard to believe that they are brothers. One is so reasonable, easygoing and the other…" She heard Yasmin's voice outside her office. She grabbed a file from her table and left her office to see Yasmin.

Yasmin saw Syakirah coming. "Syira, I've tried calling you a couple of times from the Language Center. Where were you this morning?"

"In class, of course. What's up?"

Yasmin told her that the Student's Affairs Department decided to allow a small number of outsiders to visit during the camp. Permission was limited to the students' immediate family members, and camp activities would not be communicated to the general public.

Syakirah and Yasmin agreed with the decision, based on the students' expectations. The students more than likely would feel under the microscope if the public were invited to participate.

Syakirah told her that Hidayat had come by and that she was on her way to her appointment.

"Any new news from Dr. Norman's party?" Yasmin asked. Syakirah had filled her in on the party several days before.

"Nothing! Which I think is a good thing. Talk to you later!" Syakirah replied cheerfully and left. Yasmin puzzled over her friend's response.

～

Saleha noticed Imran had not mentioned the coffeehouse or Dr. Norman's party since they returned from KL. Ani had advised her not to push him. Saleha had said her time was running out and she needed to know his answer. Ani suggested Saleha give Imran a couple of days before confronting him.

Two days after meeting Syakirah, Saleha brought up the issue. As she had expected, Imran gave no indication as to whether he liked or disliked her.

"Mom, remember what I said when I agreed to go through with the meeting?" Imran asked his mother politely.

"You didn't promise you'd commit to anything. I remember that."

Imran nodded with a smile.

"But Imran…"

"Mom, please. Okay, if you really want my opinion about her, all I can say is she was okay." He sounded calm and casual. That was his honest opinion.

"Okay? What does that mean?" Saleha asked in a dissatisfied tone.

"That she was nice and respectful…to you and Aunt Ani. But she was also…" He paused. Then, with a chuckle, he added, "Well, she overreacts and seems hardheaded."

"Overreacting and hardheaded? Well, Imran, as I recall she was being plain honest when you asked her about her job. Unlike your comment…a bit unpleasant, I should say. You embarrassed her, dear."

Imran laughed more and asked jokingly, "Are you defending her, Mom? Wow, that hurts…because I'm your son, remember?" He grinned at his mother.

"Well, you know what I meant, Imran."

"I do and I've just given you my honest opinion. So I hope we don't have to talk about this again, okay Mom?" Imran said with a smile.

Saleha reluctantly agreed. She remembered Ani had advised her not to push him.

~

Saleha's thoughts and breakfast preparation were interrupted when the telephone rang.

"He's still upstairs getting ready. Is everything okay, Umar? You don't usually call at this hour."

"Alhamdulillah, Auntie. I just want to ask him about something."

Saleha asked Umar about his family. As they talked, Imran came down the stairs and Saleha handed him the phone.

"Imran, sorry about Monday. I was out of town with some contractors...got back yesterday." Umar had cancelled their lunch on Monday and wanted to make it up to him. "How about today? Any business lunch?"

"No. So I'll see you at the usual, insha Allah?"

"Great. Insha Allah."

"And Umar, it's been a while since I went bowling with you. How about bowling this weekend?"

"Sounds good. And by the way, about what you said last time..." Umar recalled that Imran was about to tell him something the day he called to cancel the tennis game.

Imran interrupted, "I'll see you at lunch."

Umar understood Imran. He did not want his mother to hear what he had to say. They hung up.

Imran went to the kitchen for breakfast. Saleha was pouring their coffee. She seemed calm. That was a relief. He woke up that morning a little worried about his mother. Letting her down was one of the last things he would ever do. But he had to make his stand clear about Syakirah. He did not want to give his mother false hope. He hoped the sooner he made it clear, the sooner his mother would let go of the matchmaking scheme.

"Mom, about last night...I'm sorry if I've hurt your feelings in any way."

Saleha looked at him. "It's okay, dear."

"I'm sure, insha Allah, when the time is right, neither one of us has to search for my wife, whoever she may be. It'll just happen, insha Allah." Imran smiled.

Saleha smiled back at him. "I understand. I didn't mean to push you either dear. I just want you to be happy, insha Allah."

In her heart she was praying, *"Our Lord! Bestow on us Mercy from Thyself and dispose our affair for us in the right way."* (Qur'an 18:10)

∼

Dato' Annuar called Imran to invite him to go bowling with him and Melissa that weekend. Imran agreed, asking if he would mind Umar joining them as well. Later, Imran left the office for his lunch with Umar.

After a brief discussion of his new project, Umar changed the subject, drilling Imran about Syakirah. After hearing the details of the trip to KL, Umar asked him what he thought of her.

"You're just like my mother, Umar. Well, to be honest with you, she's okay. But I don't think I'm...you know."

"No, I don't know," Umar answered. "Do you like her?"

"As a Muslim to another, yes. I've nothing against her."

"I see."

Imran did not like the tone in Umar's voice. "What?" he asked, squinting.

"Kaira."

"What does Kaira have to do with this woman?" Imran looked puzzled.

"That she's not Kaira."

"Ah…you really think she's the reason why I can't accept another woman in my life?"

"If you've really closed that door to your life with her and walked away, you would have entered a new one by now to spend the rest of your life, insha Allah."

Imran smiled at his friend's frankness. He knew Umar cared about him. They had always appreciated each other's advice regarding most matters.

"It has to do with Kaira in a way, but not for the reason that you think, Umar."

"Care to explain?"

"I've closed the door to that life a long time ago, the short life I had with her. Good times I had with her are now moments I look back as Allah Ta'ala's gifts. That tragedy still does give me a shiver sometimes, but as Muslims we both know better than to let ourselves be run by emotions. It makes you weak and that opens the door for the devil to manipulate you. I'm sure you remember I was such a mess."

Umar nodded.

"Well, I'm glad, alhamdulillah, to hear this. I've known you are always good at hiding your feelings, Imran. I was just worried that, you know…"

"Well, don't. If I still remember Kaira, it's because in her I saw this model of a Muslim woman. And in my business world and yours too, it's a reality that we don't get to meet many Muslims with such characteristics. Quite many are virtuous, but righteous as well? I'd rather not judge people, but when I meet one with both qualities, it's a blessing, really!"

"I agree. So back to Miss Syakirah. If you are ready to enter a new door to a new life, does she have a chance to be the one you want to spend the rest of your life with?"

Imran laughed a little while lightly shaking his head. "You are never going to let this go, are you? Honestly, I don't know her that well. Like I said, she seems okay. When the right time is here and the right person comes into my life, you will see me enter that door, insha Allah."

"So, that means you have to know the person first, right?"

"Yes, of course!"

"So go and find out more about her then!"

"You make it sound easy," he laughed. "She doesn't even like me, and only tolerated me for my mother's sake."

"Ah... so she's respectful of a person's mother, masha Allah. Quality of a good Muslim, my friend."

"I just want to leave it all to Allah Ta'ala, Umar."

"But you won't get a chance at all if you don't even try. It doesn't have to be Syakirah, okay? It could be anyone as long as you're willing to take the chance. Take the chance then, and leave it to Allah Ta'ala."

"I don't know, Umar. I'm not up to it...not yet perhaps. Thanks for the concern. I appreciate it."

They both smiled and finished their lunch while talking about the coming game of bowling. Umar was a bit startled when Imran mentioned that Melissa and her father would be joining them. But he did not say anything.

CHAPTER 15

On Tuesday, Imran had a meeting in Penang with a potential client. Iskandar drove him to the airport. As they left the house, it occurred to Imran that his mother had not brought up the topic of Syakirah since their talk last week. Imran said "*alhamdulillah*" to himself and to Allah. He thought of talking to Iskandar about the subject, but changed his mind, figuring the matter would soon be forgotten.

Saleha needed to talk to Ani. She called her friend early that day, but Ani had gone to Singapore on business. Dutifully, Ani called upon her return.

"When is he coming back, Sal?"

"Thursday afternoon."

"That's tomorrow."

Saleha paused. She recalled Umar telling her that Dato' Annuar and Melissa were going bowling with him and Imran. Saleha noticed it was the second bowling game for Imran and Melissa, but tried not to read too much into that. However, on Monday night Imran had dinner with Melissa and her parents.

"Yes," Saleha finally spoke and told her friend about Imran and Melissa.

"Sal, sorry I wasn't here when you needed someone to talk to." She could imagine how Saleha was feeling earlier that week after listening to everything her friend had told her.

"You don't have to apologize, Ani. You have a business to run. I understand."

"You don't think it was more than dinner, Sal?" Ani realized her friend was down.

"Well, not from the impression he gave. According to him, it was a promised dinner treat for Melissa for having won the game. So it was more like a friend keeping his promise," she stated, unsure of herself.

"Then you don't need to worry. He would not lie to you, Sal."

"I know." She laughed a little.

"Even if he really likes her, I don't think it's wrong. We might think that Syakirah is the one for him, but who knows? Maybe Melissa is the one meant for him."

Saleha did not like what she had just heard. "Ani, you're backing out already?"

"I don't mean that. I'm with you all the way, as long as you need me. I've promised, remember? But I also remember you saying your intention was to see him happily married. And if it means to Melissa, then why not? Your wish would still be fulfilled. And Sal, Imran has grown into a good Muslim. He could lead any woman he marries to the right path, insha Allah. He has come a long way since Kaira passed away, alhamdulillah!"

Saleha paused before saying anything. She knew her friend was right. "I know that. It's just that deep in my heart I still believe Syakirah is the one for him."

"I'm sure you haven't forgotten what happened at Hillview. We tried to bring them together and the outcome was less than satisfactory."

"I'm leaving it in Allah Ta'ala's hands. But if I say I want to pursue this matchmaking, would that make me a bad mother, you think?"

"No, I would say you're a strong and determined mother who is doing everything for her son's happiness even if it means interfering with his life...which I'm sure he would not like." They both laughed. "For now I'd say, let's just see what's going to happen next. And Sal...Allah Ta'ala knows best!"

"I just hope it won't take too long, insha Allah. I'm running out of time." They were both aware of that. It was almost the end of March.

Saleha heard the sound of Iskandar's car. "Iskandar's here. I'll talk to you soon."

Iskandar arrived with Marina and the twins. They had stopped by each night that Imran was away. Saleha thought of asking Iskandar for details about Melissa but decided against it for the time being. She didn't want him to suspect anything was going on between her, Ani and Imran.

They all had dinner together that night. After dinner, Imran called. He informed Saleha that he had to make a stop in KL for some business and might drop by the college to see Hidayat. He'd be back Saturday instead of Thursday. Saleha smiled as she hung up the phone, then grimaced as she headed for the painkillers.

∼

Two buses carrying the campers left the college after Friday prayer. Their destination was Kanching Recreational Forest, in the Gombak district, which was about twenty kilometers north-west of KL. The language lecturers rode in cars. Yasmin and Syakirah shared a car with Mei Lin. They reached the camp site at four that afternoon.

The remote recreation park, cooled and isolated the surrounding jungle, was beautiful and peaceful. The park's most striking feature was a three-tiered waterfall, whose upper tiers cascaded magnificently into huge pools and rocky streams, eventually tumbling over the bottom tier and feeding a calm, clear river.

Gazebos were scattered all over the campsite, one of which the cooking committee used as a resting place for the food and cooking utensils they brought.

Syakirah and Yasmin set up their tent as the students set up their own. After that the students had a congregational Asr prayer followed by a short briefing. The first activity was a hiking trip that started at five and ended at sundown.

At seven-thirty they performed Maghrib prayer in congregation and then had dinner. The students later gathered for a campfire. They were divided into smaller groups for three activities—storytelling, poetry reading, and charades. Syakirah and Yasmin had fifteen students in their group.

As the activities went on, Hidayat walked around the campfire, observing and making notes for his upcoming article. It was around nine-thirty when Hidayat stopped by Syakirah and Yasmin's group. He was invited to take part and agreed to participate in a game of charades. Absorbed in the game, they were startled by a car entering the camp area. Mr. Aziz went to see who it was.

Syakirah, Yasmin, and Hidayat were surprised to see Imran walking with Mr. Aziz to the nearby gazebo. The two women continued overseeing the students' activities while Hidayat left the group to meet his brother.

"What are you doing here? Checking up on me?" Hidayat asked teasingly. They both laughed.

Mr. Aziz excused himself and left the two brothers alone.

"Hey, you can't say I can't! But no, I'm not. Do you want me to leave?" Imran pretended to look hurt. Hidayat punched him on the arm.

"Only if you don't tell me why you're here." Hidayat grinned.

"Hey, I rented a car and drove up here and all I got are questions from my little brother? Give me some credit for the effort!"

Hidayat looked at his brother with a big smile.

"I was in Penang for several days, and ended up having to run some errands in KL, so here I am. I arrived this morning. I thought of meeting you at the college after Friday prayer, but when I called they said you had already left."

"I did tell you about the camping trip."

"Yeah, but I thought you were leaving tomorrow morning. It must have slipped my mind. Anyway I'm here now!" Imran cheerfully told his brother.

"So you drove up here just to meet me? I thought you're a busy businessman," Hidayat teased his brother again.

"But never too busy for my brother," Imran grinned, flashing his dimples.

"So how's Mom?"

"Mom's fine. I told her I was coming to visit you. I didn't expect I'd meet you here."

"You shouldn't have driven up here, but I'm glad you did."

"Well, I was going to leave you a message at first and stay at the hotel. But then the thought of joining you at this campfire sounded like fun. I'll just take the later flight and get back tomorrow afternoon, insha Allah. Long and short of it, I'd rather be sleeping in a tent with you than be all by myself in the hotel room…that is, if there is room for me." Imran smiled.

"I'm afraid not." As Imran raised his eyebrows, Hidayat continued, "Just kidding, bro. But still hard to believe that you'd come here just to be with me, eh!"

"I was your age once, little brother. I love camping!"

"So let's go! We have about fifteen minutes before the late supper."

Hidayat glanced at his watch. It was almost ten. The two brothers approached the nearest campfire, Yasmin and Syakirah's. They sat near the group but did not join the game. Syakirah glanced at Imran, who happened to be looking at her as well. He shot her a polite smile, which she returned it with a nod.

The last activity finished at ten-thirty, and the students went to the canteen to have some light supper before going into their tents. Hidayat and Imran walked to Syakirah and Yasmin. Hidayat introduced his brother to the two lecturers. Syakirah and Yasmin played along as Imran acted as if he had never met them. They talked a little about the camp. Then Hidayat left them to join some of the students.

"Thank you," Imran said as they were walking to the canteen. "I mean, for not letting him know we've met before. My mother would've appreciated that."

"Well, I was surprised for a while but thought maybe it was some kind of a deal between the two of you," Yasmin looked at both Imran and Syakirah.

"No, Min. There wasn't any, but I could tell why Mr. Imran here would want to do that." Syakirah looked at Imran with a wry smile. She remembered his promise before they went to Dr. Norman's party more than a week ago.

"Please call me Imran." He smiled at both women. They reached the canteen. Imran excused himself to meet Mr. Aziz, who had welcomed him earlier. Syakirah and Yasmin took their drinks and joined the other lecturers.

By eleven-thirty, all the students had left the canteen except the few who were on the cooking committee. Hidayat talked to them while Imran got his personal items from the car. Syakirah and Yasmin were discussing the next day's activities with the other lecturers.

"So that's about it. Hope the treasure hunt goes well, insha Allah," Mr. Aziz ended the discussion. Gradually the lecturers left the canteen. Syakirah noticed Hidayat and Imran walking and talking to each other. The two brothers headed for their tents after saying goodnight to the lecturers. Yasmin and Syakirah helped the cooking committee clear the tables before retiring to their tent.

"You think this has anything to do with the meeting at Hillview?" Yasmin asked while they walked to the tent.

"I don't know, Min. Hope not. At least then I had Aunt Ani and his mother to buffer us. He'll be gone by tomorrow, insha Allah." Syakirah replied with mock confidence.

"Don't be too sure you won't see him again, Syira!" Yasmin teased her friend.

Syakirah shrugged her shoulders. But she had a feeling that Yasmin was right.

~

The treasure hunt started at eight o'clock sharp. Hidayat went with one of the groups to get a firsthand story for his article while Imran waited at the canteen with the lecturers. He joined Mr. Aziz, Yasmin and two other male lecturers. The lecturers were discussing the next activity—*Win, Lose or Draw.* Imran learned that Syakirah and Mei Lin would be supervising together.

Syakirah and Mei Lin were so busy talking to some students that they did not notice Imran looking at them. He wondered what made her agree to the meeting at Hillview. She seemed to be at ease among the students and her colleagues. He could tell

Syakirah was not someone who could be talked into something she did not want to do. Nor did she seem to be so traditional as to agree to be match-made by others.

Imran came back to reality when Syakirah turned her head toward him. She must have felt his stare, he thought. He smiled politely at her and she returned it quickly.

Imran looked at his watch. The time was eight-fifty. He had told Hidayat he would be leaving at nine.

Mr. Azmi noticed Imran checking the time. "Hidayat knows you're leaving at nine, Mr. Imran?"

Imran nodded. "I guess he didn't think hunting for the treasure would take this long." They both laughed at Imran's remark.

"Well, it's been almost an hour. They should finish anytime now. We didn't cover that much area for this game."

"I'll give it another fifteen minutes. Then I'll have to leave."

The groups soon trickled in, but Hidayat's group had not. Imran checked his watch again and told Mr. Aziz and the lecturers in their group that he had to leave. "Tell him I'll call him tomorrow, insha Allah."

Mr. Aziz promised to do so. They all bid him salam. He asked them to say salam to Syakirah and Mei Lin as the two lecturers were still talking with the students. Then he went to Hidayat's tent to pick up his things.

Syakirah and Mei Lin finished their discussion and joined Mr. Aziz and the group. They were told that Imran had to leave. Syakirah asked about Hidayat, and Yasmin told her that Imran could not wait any longer.

"Well, he won't get to watch the next activity. But then he could get a complete story from his writer brother, I guess," Mei Lin said with a smile.

"Now that reminds me I need to get the word cards for the game. They're in your car," Syakirah told Mei Lin.

"Here!" Mei Lin handed her the car keys.

As Syakirah walked to Mei Lin's car, she saw Imran putting his things away. He closed the door of the back seat and walked toward Syakirah. They both stopped at Mei Lin's car.

"Syakirah, can I speak to you for a moment?"

"I thought you were leaving." She spoke casually and proceeded to open the car door. She picked up a box containing the word cards.

"Oh, this won't take long."

"Okay." Syakirah closed the door. Holding the box in her hands, she stood facing Imran.

"I've been meaning to ask you this since..." Imran paused as Syakirah listened carefully.

"Yes?" Syakirah waited for his question.

"Why did you agree to meet us at Hillview?" *There, I said it,* Imran thought. He finally asked the question that had been on his mind since the day his mother told him about the meeting at Hillview. He wasn't sure why he asked her now, but he just wanted to know her reason.

His face was expressionless as he waited for Syakirah to answer. He thought to himself, Hidayat was right to doubt his intention of coming to visit him here. Perhaps he was hoping to meet Syakirah.

Syakirah was a little surprised but she was right, she thought. It was exactly like she had imagined. Imran had thought she had been amenable to matchmaking. She paused and appeared relaxed as well.

"Why do *you* think?"

"I asked you first." Imran studied the woman in front of him. She looked very much in control of herself, he thought. The good thing was, she did not appear to be upset by his question. This woman was different from the one he met at Hillview.

"It was your mother. I came for your mother. You may think that I don't know her well, and you're right. But I do like her and I respect her. She reminds me of my own mother," Syakirah thought that might sound trite, but it was a true statement.

"She's a sweet lady, Mr. Imran. I could not refuse when she asked me." Syakirah was contemplating telling him her main reason—the one that she had told Maria right before she agreed to the meeting.

"Well, that she is, alhamdulillah. But that doesn't explain it all." Imran realized he sounded like he was interrogating her now.

Syakirah felt her temper slowly rising. She told herself she was not going to let him get to her like last time. She would tell him her other reason. She had nothing to hide from him anyway. Syakirah took a deep breath. "I think I could guess what you're thinking, Mr. Imran. You're wondering why I would agree to a matchmaking, right?"

Imran nodded slightly.

"Well, the answer to your question, Mr. Imran, is that I didn't. Going to the meeting was my way of demonstrating how wrong the whole idea was. I proved my point, yes?" Syakirah finally said what she had been thinking.

Syakirah had never confronted a man that way before. But she felt relief that it was now all in the open. They both remembered the incident at Hillview. Syakirah noticed Imran didn't look surprised and neither was she as they stood there facing each other. He was composed. Syakirah held her ground.

"As Muslims we should believe that destiny is in the hands of Allah Ta'ala."

"I'm very aware of that, Mr. Imran. Allah Ta'ala does what He wills. Other people may not control my life."

Ouch, Imran thought.

"I'm sorry if I've offended you with my question. I was just looking for some explanation." Imran glanced at his watch. It was nine-thirty. Then he heard someone calling him. He turned around and saw Hidayat.

Imran's apology sounded sincere. Her anger slowly subsided. However, there was still a part of her that was angry with herself for getting involved in the first place. Another part of her was grateful because she finally got the chance to redeem herself. On top of it all, she remembered, this was planned by Allah (swt) to happen. But she would never, in a million years, let this man think of her as someone who would let others, especially a man, make decisions for her. She did let Manaf do that once and that was the last time ever, she thought.

"Well, so was I. Now that we're both clear about it, I think you could leave in peace." Syakirah told him casually.

"Peace. That's a nice word. It's the essence of our religion. I hope if we ever meet again, it would be in peace, insha Allah," Imran said honestly.

"Goodbye, Mr. Imran. Assalamu'alaikum."

After Imran returned her salam, she turned to leave. But Hidayat was in her path by then.

"Assalamu'alaikum, Miss Syakirah."

"Wa'alaikumussalam, Hidayat. Mr. Imran, have a safe flight, insha Allah." Syakirah smiled at both brothers and left.

"Hey, I thought you left already."

"I was about to." Imran smiled at his brother. His mind was still on what had just happened. There was more to Syakirah than met the eye. There was something else that would explain her odd methodology, he thought.

CHAPTER 16

It was almost two in the afternoon when Mei Lin dropped her colleagues off at their homes. They were all tired but happy because the Language Camp was a success, though they looked forward to hot showers, hot meals, and their own beds. During the ride, Yasmin and Mei Lin vocalized their longing for their families. Syakirah, somewhat surprised at herself, felt a small wave of melancholy as the others talked.

After ablutions and prayer, Syakirah told Lily all about the camping trip, then went to her room to rest. She picked up *Anis* magazine and settled into bed, forcing herself to enjoy the quiet. As she flipped through the magazine, she half-scowled remembering her conversation and confrontation with Imran. *Sometimes I surprise even myself,* she thought.

Syakirah wanted to believe that Imran was a closed book, a non-issue, a past tense, but she wasn't so sure. As she put the magazine down, Syakirah realized that he may have been outspoken to the point of irritation. Nevertheless, there was no denying that Imran Hakim's personality was infused with the spirit of Islam. She saw a little bit of it in KL and again at the Language Camp.

Her life was back to normal, though, thought Syakirah. Her parents and grandmother stopped asking about Imran when she told them that there was no possibility of marriage. And now that she had told Imran and her family what she thought about matchmaking, she felt so much better.

~

Saleha glanced at the clock. It was almost four. Imran was on the phone with Umar, planning their afternoon tennis game. Saleha was surprised but happy to find out that Imran had gone to the Language Camp. She asked him if he had seen Syakirah there. Imran answered that he had, but did not give details.

Saleha excitedly called Ani that morning to fill her in. Ani reminded her not to get too excited, because Imran had dinner with Melissa and her parents after coming back from the camp. Saleha remembered her promise to Ani to wait and see. However, she could not help but be hopeful after Imran told her about his trip.

Saleha was deep in thought when Imran joined her for tea.

"Assalamu'alaikum Mom…"

Saleha shook her head, startled.

"Daydreaming?" Imran teased her.

Saleha smiled. "About the Language Camp."

"Like I said, it was fun. You should have seen Hidayat. He was so excited about his article." Imran could tell his mother had more than just the camp on her mind, but Imran would not succumb to pressure—not even from his beloved mother.

"Umar is picking me up in about half an hour. I'm going to get ready now." Imran finished his tea and kissed his mother.

Imran and Umar left for the game after Asr. In the car, Imran told his friend about the camp.

"You should have stayed until today. You could use some relaxation, pal." Umar glanced at Imran with a smile.

"How's that possible?" Imran filled him in on what had happened between him and Syakirah.

"Can't say she shouldn't have acted the way she did, but you were asking for it. Fine, you were curious, but you shouldn't have asked such a loaded question if you weren't prepared for the answer. Rude, too, don't you think?"

"I guess so," Imran said without looking at Umar.

Curious, Umar asked, "So, I don't get it. Why did it bother you so much?"

"Well, I asked myself that same question before I had the conversation with her." Imran glanced at Umar. "But I guess I didn't get much by asking anyway. In fact, I apologized because I felt I had offended her." He concentrated on driving for a while before continuing.

"I mean, I now know we both detest matchmaking, but I still couldn't answer my own question...you know, on why I was making such a big deal out of it. All I had to do was to let it go, just like that. In fact, I already told Mom 'no way.'"

"Maybe you do like her after all, Imran." Umar smiled.

"Mom would be thrilled. But no, I don't think so. I mean, she is okay, but I don't think I'm interested in her that way, you know."

"Well, okay. No pressure." Umar laughed. "Take your time, though I think you've taken too much already. Now what about Melissa?"

"Melissa? We're friends. I stopped by the office yesterday and got a message that she called. I called her back and we went out for dinner last night—with her parents, mind you."

"Hmm..." Umar grinned, raising his eyebrows. "So why go out with them so often lately if you're not interested in her?"

"One word, Umar. Business. She is a colleague, and our businesses profit because of our relationship. On a personal note, I respect her father and spend so much time with him because he was my father's friend. Isn't it my Islamic responsibility to keep in touch with my parents' friends even after my parents have passed away?"

"I'm well aware. Doesn't explain why you're spending so much time with her." Umar continued, "This is progress, my friend. I mean, you having any kind of relationship with a female."

Umar paused. "So you want to marry her?" he teased.

"Let it go, Umar!"

"Not like Syakirah, who you have to tick off all the time?"

"All the time? I've only met the woman three times, Umar!"

"And you've seen Melissa more than that and she's not perpetually angry at you. Good sign. I'm not trying to pick for you, Imran, but I think it's pretty obvious. Your mother has chosen Syakirah for you, but you don't seem to agree. You like Melissa, so your mother may eventually, too, if you tell her you like the girl. In the end, it should be you making the choice, don't you think?"

"Why don't you stick to contracts and tenders?" Imran laughed at Umar. "I'm not at a point where I'm making a choice about anything. Syakirah is simply an acquaintance, thanks to my mother and Aunt Ani. And Melissa, like I said, is a business associate. End of story."

"But not the book?" Umar grinned.

Imran shook his head lightly.

"So," Umar paused thoughtfully, "why did you go to the camp, really? Just to meet Hidayat? Or to get the chance to meet Syakirah? You knew she would be there. You couldn't have gone all the way out there just to ask her that question."

"Oh, not this again, Umar. I thought we've finished talking about her. You sound just like my mother now. Meeting Hidayat, of course!"

Umar looked at Imran, unconvinced.

"Maybe...the chance to see and ask her that question too. Unfinished business."

Umar smiled with a twinkle in his eye. "Come on, Imran. You're a businessman. It's not over till it's over. Maybe you should ask yourself why you wanted to see her instead of why you asked her that question."

"You're reading too much into this, Umar."

"Look. You may believe you were there to find out why she agreed to the meeting at Hillview, but then perhaps you went there because you wanted to know more about her. I mean, what kind of person she is to agree to such a meeting."

"Why would I want to do that?"

"Because you could've called her to ask her that simple question, right? Instead you took the opportunity to see her for yourself. Without the pressure of your mother or aunt on the transaction. My question now is, why do you care if you're not interested?"

Imran shrugged his shoulders. Umar just smiled at him.

"Now that you've seen more of what she's really like, are you still saying she's just okay?"

"What do you want me to say?"

"Look, Imran. Here you have two nice women. One you like and the other, your mother likes. Maybe it's time to settle down, my friend!"

Food for thought, thought Umar. He let Imran digest his advice. As they approached the Sports Center, the two were silent.

"Umar, thanks," Imran finally said. He knew his friend cared about him but he didn't know what to do about it. He decided to let it be for a while. He would go with the flow.

"Anytime, pal, insha Allah!" Umar hoped that Imran would start thinking more seriously about his future.

~

Imran had lunch with Dato' Annuar and Melissa later that week. During the meal, Melissa invited Imran and his mother to a thanksgiving dinner, having completed a corporate project with Imran's help. As Imran conveyed the invitation to Saleha during breakfast the next morning, Saleha made a mental note to talk to Imran about Melissa prior to the dinner. However, Imran brought up the conversation then.

"Mom, do you have something that you want to ask me?" Imran recognized the look on his mother's face.

"Why, dear? I was just thinking about your father's friend's daughter. I mean if…"

Imran interrupted his mother, "We're just business colleagues. That's all, Mom!" He smiled at her.

Saleha could see he was telling the truth. She was glad in spite of herself that her son had not chosen Melissa. Maybe there was still some hope for Imran and Syakirah after all. But maybe not. She called Ani.

"Maybe I will never have the chance to see him married. He doesn't like Syakirah and he doesn't seem interested in pursuing Melissa either," Saleha expressed her worry and disappointment.

"My dear friend, Imran knows what he's doing. Whatever he thinks about these women, it must be guided by Allah Ta'ala. Kaira was a good example of a Muslim woman…a Muslim wife for him, though for only a short time. So he's taking his time in waiting for such a person, or one better than her, to come into his life, insha Allah."

Saleha relaxed a bit. "I pray so too."

"By the way, Sal, are you saying that now you wouldn't mind if he chose to marry Melissa?"

"Maybe…I don't know. What I know is I want to leave this world knowing that he has someone to look after him. And right now it doesn't seem like it's going to happen anytime soon."

Ani hated to hear her friend sounding worried and depressed, but she didn't know how to help her. Maybe Saleha would like to go with her on her next trip to KL. It would take her mind off Imran's future for a while, and they could visit Hidayat too.

CHAPTER 17

Saleha agreed to accompany Ani to KL for a Muslim women's fashion exhibition, Busana Muslim, on Tuesday. Ani also had to run some errands for her boutique. They reached KL at two o'clock and checked in at the usual hotel. They planned to stay overnight in KL so they could visit Hidayat the next day. After Ani finished her errands, they went shopping at the mall.

Before dinner they took a taxi to KL's oldest mosque—Jamek Mosque. Built in a traditional Arabian style, the mosque was located at the junction of the Klang and Gombak rivers, KL's birthplace. Though located in the heart of the chaotic city, its palm tree surroundings offered a quiet and peaceful retreat from the bustling city just outside its red brick walls.

As Saleha and Ani walked inside the mosque area, they saw a few people taking ablution at the pool in its courtyard. The view gave such an air of tranquility to the place. To Saleha, this was a beautiful greeting that welcomed her every time she set foot in this place of worship. It also brought back lovely memories of her husband.

She and Kamal visited Jamek Mosque whenever they were in KL. Three years before his death, they had gone for *Hajj*. Saleha noticed and was grateful to Allah that her husband had become a more conscientious Muslim after the experience.

After prayer Saleha and Ani went to dinner at their favorite place at Jalan Benteng's car park. The décor was not expensive or fancy, but it offered an ambiance that no restaurant downtown could match. The food was even better. They were about to leave when Ani started talking about Imran.

"You haven't mentioned him all day, although we're here— the town where Syakirah lives."

Saleha smiled. Ani saw confidence and hope on her friend's face when they talked about those two.

"I know, but when we were at the mosque, I did pray for them...like always."

"The last time we talked, you told me he was going out with Melissa and her parents. Has anything changed since? You still think there's a chance that something will happen between Imran and Syakirah?"

"Have I told you that I changed my mind?" Saleha smiled.

"No. But Sal, don't you think perhaps we should give him and Melissa a chance? I mean, what's the point of hoping for him and Syakirah if Imran has already found someone else? You've never told me that he doesn't like her."

"He's never told me he's interested in her either. He said they are friends." Saleha sounded confident. "Ani, I'd know if he really cares about her. I can still remember how he acted when he was in love with Kaira. He's not in love with Melissa. So I have hope."

"But he sees Melissa regularly. I know you'd like to see him with Syakirah, but looking at things right now, I wouldn't be surprised if he asked Melissa to marry him."

Ani paused then continued, "What I want is for you to be happy for the time you are here, insha Allah. I don't want you to be heartbroken, Sal. And if you continue with this, you are setting yourself up for it."

Saleha saw the truth in Ani's words. She should be hoping and praying for Imran and Melissa. She should be happy that her son finally seemed to show an interest in his own future. But deep down, she simply did not believe Melissa was the best choice for Imran—Syakirah was. That was what her heart had been telling her since the first time she met her.

"I understand, Ani. To be honest, part of the reason why I came with you today is to get away from that fact. You know me well. I'd never hide anything from you. I want to be happy for him, but I just can't. Perhaps I'm being stubborn, but I can't help it."

Saleha's mood change was palpable. A few minutes ago Saleha was strong, but now she was breaking down. She was holding on to the small hope and what little confidence she had. She was fighting to face the fact that her wish might not come true after all.

Saleha added, "The only thing that keeps me going is my faith in Allah Ta'ala, that He, the best Planner of all, is taking care of everything."

"Alhamdulillah, that's the best thing to do in this situation. But remember that fighting Allah's will is not good for you, Sal." Ani looked at her friend with concern. "You know I'd do anything to help you get your wish, insha Allah, but this is not something we can get by simply going after it. We cannot force it. It's a matter of the hearts, feelings and commitment. We've done what we could. It's in Allah Ta'ala's hands. Only His will can bring those two hearts together. If it is to happen, it will, insha Allah. If not, you've got to let it go."

Saleha listened quietly and recalled a verse in the Qur'an that, in a way, reflected what her friend had just said. *"And moreover He hath put affection between their hearts; not if thou hadst spent*

*all that is in the earth couldst thou have produced that affection
but Allah hath done it; for He is Exalted in might, Wise."* (Qur'an
8:63)

Reluctantly, Saleha agreed with Ani. She knew that although
she had Imran's best interests at heart, she was being selfish.
Imran's happiness was her happiness, and if he had found it, she
should be happy for him. She liked Syakirah a lot. She could not
explain, even to herself, why she did. She only wished that Imran
liked her as much.

Saleha and Ani went back to the hotel. They decided to drop
the subject and concentrated on the next day's meeting with
Hidayat and the exhibition.

~

Saleha woke up at five o'clock with a throbbing pain in her
chest. She called for Ani, who was shocked to see her friend pale
and sweating. Ani helped her take the medicine and asked her to
lie down as she dialed Dr. Norman's number. Saleha stopped her,
however, and explained that she suffered similar attacks before
and that she would recover within a half hour.

Ani thought of calling Imran but decided to wait a little longer. Later Saleha was fine and performed her *Fajr* prayer. Ani was
relieved to see her friend well again, but continued to worry.

"Are you sure you're up for the exhibition, Sal? You could
stay and get some more rest if you want. You still look a little
tired." The opening ceremony of the exhibition was to start at
ten-thirty.

"I'm fine now. I just need to lie down for a while and I'll feel
better, insha Allah. It's still early." Saleha looked at the clock on
the chest beside the bed. It was almost seven.

At ten, the two women took a cab to the exhibition. Every once in a while Ani would glance at her friend to make sure she was really fine. Ani was worried that Saleha's concern about Imran's future prompted the attack that morning. Saleha seemed particularly quiet after her call to Imran last night after dinner. Saleha might have gone to bed feeling heartsick.

They arrived twenty minutes early, but there were already many people waiting in the grand entry. They took their seats and waited for the opening ceremony. While the crowd rumbled and chattered prior to the exhibition's commencing, Ani noticed that Saleha looked uncomfortable and seemed to be in pain again. Ani suggested they went to the hospital. This time she agreed with her friend.

They walked out of the building so as not to make a scene and left for the University Hospital. While waiting for the cab, Ani called Dr. Norman on her cell phone. Dr. Norman met them at the emergency entrance.

~

Syakirah received Aunt Ani's message at eleven just after class. The office boy said it was urgent. She left a message for Yasmin, asking her to take care of things. When she arrived at the hospital, Syakirah ran to the emergency room and spotted Ani. She was nervous by the worried look on the elder lady's face.

"Thank you for coming on such a short notice, Syira. I'm sorry if I troubled you."

Syakirah couldn't conceal her panic. Being in the emergency room reminded her the night she brought her neighbor's bleeding son. Most of all, it brought to her mind the night her mother was taken to the emergency room in University Hospital in KB, a week before she passed away.

"Aunt Ani, what's going on? Why are you here? Who are we waiting for?"

Ani took Syakirah's hand and walked to the chairs in the lounge. Syakirah studied the woman's face. She was composed despite her obvious worry.

Taking her seat, Ani faced Syakirah. "Saleha asked me to call you when I brought her here." Ani looked down at her hands on her lap. Ani knew she had to tell Syakirah about Saleha's condition.

Saleha had decided to inform Syakirah of her prognosis. She could have asked her to call Imran, but she had chosen Syakirah instead. Ani considered the words she'd use with Syakirah. She shook off feelings of resentment for having this task. It was only the second week of April. Saleha still had two to three more months, according to Dr. Norman. But Allah (swt) knew best.

Syakirah was unable to mask her impatience. Deep down, she realized her genuine concern for this woman. It was like reliving her final moments with her late mother. Syakirah didn't know what to think. Suddenly she had all these questions and she blurted them all out, "Is she all right? What happened to her? Where's her family? Where's Imran?"

Ani held Syakirah's hand and began telling her about Saleha's illness and why she did not contact Saleha's family. She told Syakirah about Saleha's call the night before and that she thought it could have led to this attack. Syakirah was speechless after listening to Ani's explanation. As Ani finished her story, Dr. Norman approached.

"How is she, doctor?" Ani made a gesture to Dr. Norman that it was all right to discuss Saleha in front of Syakirah.

"It's probably nothing to worry about, but I'd like to keep her overnight for observation."

The answer brought a look of relief to Syakirah's face. Then immediately she asked, "So what caused the pain?"

"I'm guessing that she has been under pressure and feeling too worried lately. Her blood pressure was high and blood sugar low. But don't worry, her heart is fine, alhamdulillah. I'll keep an eye on her. I'd say she'll be fine tomorrow, insha Allah."

Both Ani and Syakirah felt better and thanked Dr. Norman. After the doctor left, Ani invited Syakirah to come with her to see Saleha. As much as she wanted to see her, Syakirah hesitated. She felt it was not her place to be there. She had told herself after the party at Dr. Norman's house that was the last time she would see Saleha.

"Human beings plan, but Allah (swt) is the best Planner of all." These words rang in her thoughts. If Saleha had thought this much of Syakirah, then she was foolish not to give the woman her care and support. Even so, she was not sure why she was there. She refused to entertain the thought invading her mind that this was a matchmaking scheme, but did hope that she would not come into contact with Imran again.

They walked into Saleha's room. She smiled when she saw both of them. Saleha apologized for asking Syakirah to come.

"I wanted to come."

"I'm sure you're busy, dear. I'll be fine now, insha Allah." Saleha paused. "I guess now you know that Dr. Norman is more than an acquaintance to me."

"Yes."

Ani immediately added, "But his wife is indeed a regular customer at my friend's boutique."

"Dr. Norman said I could go home tomorrow, insha Allah."

Syakirah smiled politely. "Yes, he told us. Alhamdulillah, I'm glad that you're fine, Aunt Saleha. Is there anything you need, or anything I could do?"

"No, thank you, dear. I'm fine. I've been such a fuss. I know you need to get back to the college."

"I'll come again tomorrow, insha Allah."

Saleha thanked her for coming. Syakirah said goodbye to the ladies and left. As she walked to her car, she considered her relationship to Saleha and her family. Only two weeks ago she was sure she had seen the last of these people. But now she was again in their lives, like it or not. She would be meeting Imran again, she was sure of it. "Ya Allah, whatever is reserved for me in this whole thing, I pray and seek your guidance," she whispered.

∼

"Sal, I told her about your illness and that you like her very much. And you were worried sick about Imran…that this might have led to the sudden attack."

Saleha listened to her friend attentively. "And what did she say then?"

"She didn't say much."

"I never thought it would turn out this way, Ani. But at least now she knew why I insisted on the meetings. I just hope she doesn't have any hard feelings toward me."

"I doubt it. She said she'd come tomorrow, right?"

Saleha nodded.

"Why Syira? Why her, Sal?" Ani looked at her friend questioningly.

"Just in case I have to…say goodbye…I want to apologize to her and…" Saleha paused.

"And?" Ani waited.

"And to ask her to take care of Imran," Saleha said, almost whispering. She looked sad.

Ani felt tears in her eyes.

~

Syakirah reached her office at one-thirty. She was still thinking about the hospital visit when Yasmin dropped by.

"Syira, is everything all right? What was the emergency about?" Yasmin sat opposite her friend.

Syakirah told Yasmin everything except Saleha's decision to tell Syakirah about her underlying illness. "When I saw her, all I could think was how relieved I felt that she was fine. I felt like hugging her. It's weird to think that I could feel so close to her, like there's a bond between us. She's so real, Min."

"She reminds you of your mother."

Syakirah nodded.

"I can understand how you feel, Syira. But then, why did she ask for you? It's not like she was dying. And where are her children? She could have asked for Hidayat and yet she chose you? Still wishing for you and Imran?"

"I don't want to think about that, Min. By the way, I've promised her that I'd come again tomorrow, insha Allah."

"Do you want me to come with you, Syira?"

"No, I'll be okay by myself. At least now I know the truth. And that makes a difference in a way."

Yasmin didn't question Syakirah further.

~

Imran was in the study when Saleha called to tell him that they would come home the next day.

"I was having a meeting when you called, Mom. I got worried when the message said you were not coming back today." Saleha left a message from the hospital a few hours after Syakirah left. She told Imran's secretary that she would call him that night.

"Nothing to worry, dear. I hope we have time to see Hidayat tomorrow."

"So you haven't been to the college yet?"

"Not yet. Maybe tomorrow after your Aunt Ani gets everything done. If not, I'll give him a call. He'll be disappointed, but he sure will understand, insha Allah. Anyway there's always next time, insha Allah, when your Aunt has to go to KL." Imran didn't suspect anything.

After the call, Imran was about to resume his work when a thought crossed his mind. "No, can't be," he said to himself. Could his mother be planning to meet Syakirah again? He remembered his mother not saying much when he told her that he and Melissa were just friends. Could his mother be keeping hopes of him and Syakirah? With that thought, he opened the drawer and took out Kaira's picture. He smiled before putting it back.

"I wish I could say yes to Mom's request. But I can't. At least not until I'm sure she's a good Muslim like you, Kaira, or perhaps better, insha Allah."

Suddenly he remembered something. He took the picture out again. Then softly he said to himself, "The white hijab!" He recalled seeing Syakirah for the first time at Hillview. There was something about Syakirah on that day that seemed familiar. Syakirah was wearing a hijab similar to the one Kaira wore in that picture! A smile appeared on his face as he remembered their encounters at Hillview, Dr. Norman's home, and the Language Camp.

"Subhanallah!" Imran spoke, realizing why he went to the Language Camp. Umar was right. He did not go there simply to ask her why she would agree to a matchmaking plan, but also to know more about her. The hijab made him want to see more of this person Syakirah Sulaiman. He was compelled to see for himself if she was indeed a good Muslim!

~

The next day, Syakirah left the college after her morning class. She arrived at Saleha's room as Dr. Norman greeted her on his way out of the room.

"Thank you for coming again, Syira."

"Alhamdulillah, I'm happy to see that you're better today, Aunt Saleha." In reality, she was more than glad to see the elder lady looking better and healthier than the day before. At the same time, she was annoyed that she was betraying herself in her attempts to remain detached from Saleha.

"Yes, alhamdulillah. She sure is. The doctor said we could leave now. You came just in time. A little later, you would have missed us," Ani joined in.

"Well, I'm glad you've been discharged." Syakirah smiled at both ladies. "I could give you a ride to your hotel. Or are you two leaving for JB now?"

"No, we're going back to the hotel first. The flight is at four." Saleha thanked Syakirah for her offer. On the way to the hotel, Saleha invited Syakirah to join them for lunch. Syakirah agreed.

As they ate, Syakirah asked Saleha, "Does Imran know about the hospital stay?"

"I told him that I was detained, but did not tell him why. I told him truthfully that Ani had some last-minute errands to do and we'd be back later today." Saleha paused. "And Syakirah, about what Ani told you…"

"It's okay," Syakirah interrupted. "I understand. Everything will work out fine, insha Allah. And insha Allah your secret is safe with me." With that she changed the subject.

CHAPTER 18

Imran noticed his mother seemed different after coming back from KL. He caught her lost in thought several times. When he asked, Saleha would dismiss his concerns with some excuse. Now he was worried. He asked Ani but Ani told him not to worry. She said Saleha must have been missing Hidayat. But he could tell it was more than that; his mother was unhappy.

After a few days at home, Saleha was sick again. Imran brought her to the clinic and the doctor said she had a fever. Ani was getting more worried and wanted to tell Imran, yet Saleha asked her to wait until Imran was closer to choosing a wife. However, she gave Ani permission to tell Zaid about her illness.

When Ani told her husband about Saleha, Zaid was surprised. He understood why Saleha wanted to hide it from her children, but he would have preferred it if they were told now before it was too late. Marriage was a destiny that was in the hands of Allah (swt). To wait for Imran to be married first before breaking the news was not a wise thing to do. However, like his wife, Zaid respected Saleha's wish. He and his wife would always be there for Saleha's children if anything happened, he thought.

Ani told her husband how they could help Saleha, and Zaid agreed, but only if the people involved gave their full consent and commitment. There would be no turning back once it was done, he reminded his wife. It was either this or nothing, and she knew they had to do something to help Saleha.

Zaid had to leave for Melaka so he left it to Ani to talk to Imran and Syakirah, the two whose consent she needed if her idea were to have any chance of working at all. Once agreed, the four of them would meet. Ani contacted Syakirah first.

~

"Syakirah, I'm sorry to call you about this again. I'm so worried about her."

Syakirah was silent for a while. "I don't know what to say, really. I would just tell Imran, if I was you, but then that may not help much either. What she needs is to learn to accept what is happening. I'm sorry to say this, Aunt Ani. I'd do anything to help, insha Allah. I know she doesn't have much time left. But I don't know how to help."

"I think, insha Allah, I have a way to make her happy for the remaining time she has, but I need your help."

"In any way I can, Aunt Ani, insha Allah," Syakirah reassured the elder woman.

"I want to make her dream for Imran come true, insha Allah."

Syakirah was shocked; Aunt Ani wanted her to marry Imran? She was being put on the spot. Both Syakirah and Ani realized the younger woman's growing affection for Saleha. Syakirah would do practically anything to make this dying woman happy. She was so much like her own mother.

However, at the same time, Syakirah was reluctant, especially on realizing how little she knew about Imran. Her first encounters with him were not exactly pleasant. Yet, she could not help but smile when she recalled Imran's last remarks at the Language

Camp: "I hope if we ever meet again, it would be in peace, insha Allah." That glimpse into Imran Hakim had so touched her heart. But could she legitimately think that he was a good Muslim man that she could trust, better than Manaf, perhaps?

"I'm not sure I can do that, Aunt Ani."

Silence.

"Syira, I have a question to ask."

"Yes?"

"What do you think of Imran?"

Again she felt like being put on the spot.

"To be honest with you, Aunt Ani, my encounters with him haven't been particularly pleasant experiences." Syakirah chuckled. "The last one at the Language Camp almost led to an ugly argument."

"His mother told me he went to the camp, but couldn't tell me what happened there."

"Well, he actually came to see Hidayat at the camp. I guess he didn't tell Aunt Saleha what happened. That tells me that he has no interest in matchmaking or in me. So do you still want to go on with your plan, Aunt Ani?"

"You haven't answered my question, dear."

"Well, to be honest, despite the unpleasant meetings with him in KL, at the camp, I thought I saw a decent, Muslim side of him, if I may say so."

"And?" Syakirah could picture Ani raising her eyebrows.

"He's not such a bad guy after all, I thought, but..."

"It's not enough for you to like him."

"I didn't mean it that way. I don't like to be prejudiced. Being suspicious of one's brother or sister in Islam is wrong."

"That's not what I meant. And Syira, you are a good Muslim woman. I appreciate you telling me your opinion of Imran, and

I respect your need to know him better before you decide to marry him. From what I understand, Imran approaches Saleha's matchmaking attempts the same way you do…except maybe he's so concerned with everyone he's responsible for, he refuses to discover what it is that he really wants.

"Believe me, I'm not trying to trick you into anything. I'd never take advantage of your growing affection for Saleha. If you don't agree, I won't force you. It's all up to you."

"Give me some time to think, insha Allah." Syakirah felt herself being convinced in spite of herself.

"You know we don't have much time?"

"I do. Can I discuss this with a friend?"

"Please do. This is nothing to take lightly. I won't say anything to Imran until I've heard from you," Ani promised.

"Thank you and I'll call you soon, Aunt Ani, insha Allah."

~

Ani was relieved after her conversation with Syakirah. She felt good that she had gotten a somewhat favorable opinion regarding Imran. Now she knew there was hope after all, though those two might not think so. She thought this would be the time for her and Zaid to do something to help the couple.

Allah willing, Ani's idea would make everyone happy. Saleha would get her wish. Imran would make his mother happy for her time remaining. Syakirah would help the woman she had grown to love like her own mother.

Whatever the consequences, Ani knew she had to place her trust in Allah (*swt*) to make the plan work. Only He knew what the future held, Ani thought, as she remembered the meaning of a verse "…*And whoever puts his trust in Allah, then He will suffice him. Verily, Allah will accomplish his purpose. Indeed, Allah has set a measure for all things."* (Qur'an 65:3)

~

Imran had not seen Umar for several days. After taking Saleha home from the clinic, he called Umar from his office and made plans for lunch.

During lunch he told Umar what he thought Saleha might have done in KL because of her seeming so distracted after coming back from KL. Umar suggested that he talked to Ani.

"You think that's a good thing to do?"

"Well, how else are you going to know?"

Umar had a point, Imran thought. "Well, I'll think about it. I don't want my mother to know if I were to see Aunt Ani."

"Good. Now what are you going to say to Aunt Ani if this has to do with you and one of the...you-know-who?"

Imran shrugged his shoulders.

"You'd better get ready with some answers, pal!"

Imran thought about Umar's question for a while. "I'll figure it out, insha Allah."

~

Imran had been postponing a business trip to KL since the day his mother was sick. Saleha learned that from Iskandar.

"Imran, I'm fine now, alhamdulillah. You have other responsibilities besides your mother," Saleha urged, smiling. She did feel better today.

"Mom, I can wait another day."

Saleha lightly shook her head, still smiling.

"Okay, so I'll leave first thing tomorrow morning, insha Allah."

"Do you think maybe you could visit your brother?"

"I'll try, insha Allah. Why? You have something to send to him, Mom?"

"Just my salam and tell him I miss him. And ask him if he could call sometime."

"I will, insha Allah."

CHAPTER 19

After his meeting and taking care of a few business matters, Imran drove to Pine College. By the time he arrived, it was almost four. Imran left his brother a message to meet him in the parking lot near the Language Center.

Ten minutes later, as Imran waited at a table under some shady trees, he saw Hidayat walking with his friend. There was another person with them—Syakirah. Imran was surprised to see her again. She must be going home, he thought.

"Assalamu'alaikum, Abang Imran," Hidayat greeted, followed by his friend and Syakirah.

"Wa'alaikumussalam."

Hidayat introduced his friend Jamal to Imran. "Nice meeting you, Abang Imran, but I really need to catch the lab before it's closed." Then he turned to Hidayat. "I'll bring the printout to your room later, insha Allah."

"Okay, insha Allah."

They watched Jamal rush in the direction of the computer lab. Imran turned to look at Syakirah, and they exchanged friendly smiles. Syakirah was about to ask to leave and go to her car when Hidayat told Imran that she was one of the English Club advisors.

"She's been helping me and the team at the *Daily Pine* with our articles." He smiled at Syakirah.

"You are a good writer, Hidayat. I don't help you so much as I enjoy reading your work."

"So, what's your hot topic in the next *Daily Pine*?" Imran asked his brother.

"Zero Coupling Campaign, organized by Muslim Students Association!"

"That's interesting!"

"Hidayat, perhaps you could ask for your brother's opinion on it." Syakirah caught a quick glance from Imran.

"Yeah, that would be cool! I could use some quotes from the students' families and you could provide me with my first quote for this article, Abang Imran, insha Allah!"

"If I could be of any help, sure, insha Allah."

"Miss Syakirah, do you mind staying while I do this?"

Syakirah agreed and took a seat at the table.

"So Abang?"

"Well, ten years ago, I'd probably have a different view, but now I agree with the campaign. With the increasing number of cases where Muslim students are caught in close proximity in secluded areas, in and outside campuses, it's high time we had such a campaign. Now we also have more cases of abandoned babies, which could also be linked to premarital sex. It's our duty as Muslims to do "*'amar ma'aruf wa nahi mungkar*," enjoining the good actions and prohibiting the bad actions!"

"What about non-Muslims who are involved in such actions?"

"Almost all, if not all, religions promote healthy relationships between males and females. Premarital relationships, especially for young people and while still studying, might lead to an unplanned future, such as early parenthood. Dropping out of high school or college sometimes happens too. Islam provides clear guidelines when it comes to relationships between a man and a woman, whatever your age."

Hidayat was jotting down what Imran said in his notebook. Imran and Syakirah smiled at the young reporter.

"May I add one more thing?" Imran asked.

"Go ahead!"

"A person's college career is an opportunity to obtain as much knowledge as possible, not a time to be wasted 'studying' intimate feelings. The time for that will come eventually. And for Muslims, particularly, that time should come after the couple is married. I may sound old-fashioned, but take my word, I was young once and I know how wasteful it is to spend time dreaming of an uncertain future with your so-called special partner."

Syakirah watched how Hidayat handled the interview. At that moment she had never felt so proud of a student. Imran too seemed agreeable and cooperative. It was good to see this side of Imran, thought Syakirah. His Islamic view of the topic paralleled hers.

Suddenly Ani's plan came to her mind. She wondered if this was the Imran Hakim that would sway her into agreeing with Ani's proposal.

"Why do you think premarital relationships happen among Muslims?" Hidayat asked, probing.

"Many reasons I could think of, such as the influence of the Western lifestyle that practices such a relationship. But I believe the main reason is they let themselves be guided by the mind, instead of by faith in Allah Ta'ala." Imran spoke confidently.

"What can be done to curb the problem?" Hidayat asked seriously.

"Faith! Like I said, Islam is not the only religion that preaches good moral values. Premarital relationships can lead to many unhappy consequences. I'm sure you could dig up a lot of information on that.

"In Islam, one should first be in love with Allah Ta'ala. Know what pleases and displeases Him. Then you pray that you will meet a good Muslim to spend the rest of your life with. Once you find her, you spend your life with her, leading a life that pleases Allah.

"Of course one way of finding your spouse is by getting to know about the person first. There are Islamic ways to do this. And until you are sure of her faith in Allah Ta'ala, any feeling of love must be withheld. I believe other religions share more or less similar perspectives."

"Thanks, Abang Imran."

"Anytime, insha Allah!"

"Now I will try to talk to some non-Muslim students and their parents too if possible, insha Allah."

"He's not going to include my name in the article, is he, Miss Syakirah? I'd like to be anonymous if that's okay," Imran asked Syakirah playfully. She had been paying such close attention to the interview that his question took her by surprise.

"You have the right to tell him to keep your name out of it," Syakirah replied. "That's the end, right? I really have to go now. It's almost Asr prayer time. Nice meeting you again, Mr. Imran, Hidayat."

Hidayat thanked her. They exchanged salams. Imran made a 'peace' sign to her when Hidayat was not looking. They both smiled as they recalled his remark at the Language Camp about peace. Syakirah left the brothers and headed for her car.

"She's one of the best, Abang Imran."

"I could tell from your high regard of her opinion."

They walked to Imran's car.

"Yeah…and she's single too, you know," Hidayat told his brother in all seriousness.

"Oh really! You're trying to be a marriage broker now, Mr. Journalist?"

"Well, can't help trying."

"Well, don't quit your day job!"

They both laughed. Imran told Hidayat they would perform Asr prayer first before going out to eat.

"Mom sends her salam to you."

"Wa'alaikumussalam. I'll call her tonight, insha Allah."

"Do that, please, insha Allah. She misses you, Hidayat."

∽

It had been two days since Ani's phone call when Syakirah told Yasmin of Ani's proposition. Yasmin raised her eyebrows in surprise.

"I'm not sure what to say, Syira. Weeks ago I was thrilled when you first told me about a man named Imran Hakim. I thought there would be a getting-to-know-you period, and a possible wedding, months down the line. Now you're getting married? To a man you don't particularly like?"

Yasmin recalled Manaf. Despite Syakirah's assurance that she had moved on, Yasmin always felt that she hadn't. Syakirah might not love him anymore, but her personal life was certainly influenced by her relationship with him.

Syakirah told Yasmin about her recent meeting with Imran when he visited his brother at the college.

"Min, you know I hate the idea of matchmaking, but…"

"But now you think it's not such a bad idea anymore?"

"I don't know. Allah Ta'ala has His ways of doing things. In *Al-Baqarah* we are reminded that sometimes what is good for us is hidden in bad experiences."

"Be honest with me, Syira. Have your feelings about Imran Hakim changed? Do you now like him better than before? This is important for me to know if you want my opinion about Aunt Ani's idea."

"And don't compare him with Manaf, please!" Yasmin added seriously.

"I'm not, Dearie. Honestly? Okay. After meeting him at Hillview and at Dr. Norman's house, I had no reason to even consider giving him a chance. But at the Language Camp, I saw something in him. That was when I began to give him the benefit of the doubt. Now I didn't say I like him after the confrontation at the camp. I just thought…hmm…he's a good Muslim—and *that* I like. And today I saw more of this side of him. This really means something to me. It tells me something about his faith in Allah Ta'ala…his love and devotion to Him."

Yasmin smiled as she listened to her friend. "Hmm… interesting!"

"What?"

"Perhaps seeing this other side of Imran made you want to accept Aunt Ani's idea?"

"I thought of saying no, but my fondness for Aunt Saleha and after seeing this side of her son… The 'yes' is there, but the 'no' answer is still strong!"

"Well, you're considering marrying a man in order to make a dying woman happy. No wonder. But you know what? I know you don't want me to say this, but I think I like what I'm hearing. It makes me so happy to hear you talk about your future after so long."

"It's nothing definite, Min. I've got a lot to learn about him if I say yes. Also I don't know if Imran is even interested in this scheme, or his motivation."

"Hey, remember I once said maybe in your case, love will bloom after marriage, the old fashioned way, kicking and screaming, insha Allah," Yasmin told her with a big smile on her face.

Syakirah stared at Yasmin, envying her enthusiasm.

"I hope what you know about Imran is enough to help you go through this, if that is what you want to do, Syira. Remember this is marriage we're talking about. You have to be really sure before you agree to commit your life; marriage is meant for a lifetime, insha Allah. I hope the engagement period will allow you to really get to know him. Then you can decide if he's the one."

"I haven't made my decision yet."

"Well, when you have, may Allah Ta'ala watch over you, Syira." Yasmin paused. "Pray *Istikharah* prayer and ask for His guidance before giving Aunt Ani your decision."

~

Ani stared at the telephone on the desk in front of her. Syakirah had called with her consent. Ani was thinking of calling Imran. She recalled her last conversation with Saleha during her last visit.

"Ani, I think I have to accept and be grateful with what Allah Ta'ala has blessed me with. My children are all healthy and happy. They are all doing fine with their lives. What more do I want, right?"

Ani could read the disappointment on her friend's face. "What about Imran?"

"Well, I made my wish but we know that a wish doesn't always come true. As long as he's happy, Allah Ta'ala will look after him for me. Anyway I have you. You'll look after him and see that he marries the right one, insha Allah."

"Insha Allah," Ani had answered.

She was startled when the telephone rang. She was surprised to hear Imran's voice on the other end.

"I'm sorry if I caught you at a bad time, Aunt Ani."

"Oh no, in fact I was just thinking of giving you a call."

"Oh, really? Well, that's good. Now you can tell me what you have in mind. Ladies first?" Imran laughed.

"No, you first, Imran. What can I do for you?"

"Well, Mom seems so distracted lately. Any ideas? I was wondering if something happened in KL recently."

"And what exactly would that be, Imran?" Ani was curious to know.

"Aunt Ani, I'm sorry if this sounds a bit blunt, but did you two meet Syakirah again? Or are you two planning to have another meeting for all of us again?" Imran finally asked what he had in mind.

Ani was silent for a few seconds when she heard this. She thought now was the time to explain her plan.

"Imran, you know how much I love your mother and all of you children, right? I would do anything if it would make the whole family happy, insha Allah." Ani paused.

"So you did see her in KL then?"

"Yes, but not for the reason you think. We didn't plan for another meeting. We just met and talked. I guess your mother really likes her but she also respects your decision. As for Syakirah, she likes your mother, but like you, she doesn't want to be set up. I guess in that way, you have one thing in common with her. A marriage arrangement wouldn't work for either one of you."

Imran listened silently. He thought Ani was going to convince him that his decision was wrong. However, he was hearing exactly what he had wanted to hear. Alhamdulillah!

So it was settled. Imran felt a pressure being lifted from his shoulders and relief course through his body. At the same time, he felt heaviness in his heart knowing that he had disappointed his mother. He knew his being unmarried worried her and he loved her all the more for her misplaced efforts. No wonder she seemed sad lately. He guessed the last meeting that his mother and Ani had with Syakirah amounted to a closure.

"Aunt Ani, thank you."

"For what?"

"For helping her through this. I never meant to disappoint her. As much as she wants to see me happy, I also want the same for her. She means the world to me."

"You're a good son, Imran. But listen. We really need to talk face to face. Tomorrow. Lunch. Insha Allah."

Cryptic message, Imran thought, but Ani would not say more. He agreed to lunch the next day.

~

Imran kept looking at his watch until it was finally lunchtime. He was both curious and worried when he recalled the urgency in Ani's voice. She had never spoken to him in such a serious tone. He tried to think what she could possibly want to tell him, but he was at a loss. He told himself to relax until lunchtime.

Ani was sitting at a table near a corner of the restaurant when Imran showed up. He knew Ani all of his life, and knew that only something critical would make her ask to see him personally. Suddenly, Imran knew that something was wrong with his mother. That revelation filled him with dread.

"Aunt Ani, I'm sorry to have kept you waiting. I thought I was early… Now I'm really nervous," Imran began after taking his seat. Imran's anxiety was obvious to Ani in spite of his best efforts to put on a pleasant appearance.

With a sad smile, Ani spoke, "You know that I love your mother like my own sister, right?"

Imran nodded in agreement.

"Well, what I'm about to do is what any sister would do. Imran, there is something that she has been keeping from you, your brothers and your sister." Ani paused as she studied the worried look on Imran's face, the young man who was like her own son.

"Your mother is dying, Imran."

Imran suddenly felt his heart stop beating and time stood still. His whole world changed in that split second. He could not believe what he was hearing. He gazed at Ani and wanted to ask Ani for details, but he could not speak a word. He was numb. He slowly moved his gaze across the table, as if searching for words to speak.

"*Innalillahi wa innailairaaji'un* (To Allah we belong and to Him is our return)," Imran recited the verse in a whisper. Those were the only words he could utter, an expression any Muslim should say when receiving bad news.

"Imran, I'm sorry to be the one to tell you this. But I have no choice. She has asked me not to tell anyone, especially you. She didn't want to worry you."

"What is she...?" Imran could not finish his question after he had finally gotten the words out.

"Cervical cancer." Ani could see Imran's eyes glistening with tears.

For several minutes they didn't say a word. Ani understood Imran very well. He would shut himself off like he had when Kaira and Kamal died. The waiter brought the drinks Ani ordered. Neither of them would eat lunch. Ani just watched Imran.

Finally Imran spoke, "What should I do, Aunt Ani?"

"Make her happy for the time we have with her, insha Allah."

"How long?"

"Three months, insha Allah."

Imran bent his head as he ran his fingers through his hair. He closed his eyes. Part of him was blaming himself for not learning about this sooner, though he knew that his mother would never let him worry unnecessarily.

He accepted this unwelcome news with redha, being pleased with Allah's (swt) decree. That was his duty as a Muslim, to welcome all things and events, even those associated with distress and fear. He took a deep breath and looked up. The thought of Ani seeing him like that did not embarrass him a bit. He only knew that he had to be strong for his family, his mother, and himself. He needed Allah's (swt) help and guidance more than anything at that moment.

Ani told Imran of her plan, including Syakirah's knowledge of Saleha's illness and assent to the marriage. He looked hesitant and uncomfortable with the idea. He recalled every incident since his mother proposed matchmaking in the first place. He was sorry he took the whole thing lightly when it mattered so much to her.

Saddened by the thought, his eyes were welling up with tears. Now he wondered how to make Saleha believe that he would marry the very person he had convinced his mother he did not have feelings for. There was a long pause before he finally spoke.

"I'm not sure if I can, but I will try, insha Allah," Imran said with a heavy heart.

It was not the thought of his mother's death that made his heart so heavy. He would miss her when she left this world, as he did Kaira and his father. However, the pain he felt from his perceived failure in fulfilling his responsibilities was almost unbearable.

Surah Luqman suddenly came to his mind, "*And We have enjoined upon men concerning his parents. His mother beareth him in weakness upon weakness, and his weaning is two years. Give thanks unto Me and unto thy parents. Unto Me is the journey.*" (Qur'an 31:14)

Ani studied Imran's sad face and responded, "Insha Allah. And I'm sure you would make her very happy, Imran. Insha Allah you will."

Imran assented to the marriage. From there, Imran let Ani do the talking. Thankfully, he had little else to do but agree with her. Ani made plans for them to meet Syakirah at Hillview the coming week. Ani would talk to his mother; the particulars of the arrangement would be hidden from her in order to maintain Saleha's health, insha Allah. After Ani talked to Saleha, she and her husband would meet Imran and Syakirah for counseling before the wedding.

CHAPTER 20

Syakirah was out shopping with Yasmin when Ani called and left a message the next day. Syakirah and Yasmin pondered the call.

"Why do you think she called?"

"I don't know, Min, but I have a feeling my life is about to change."

"It's still not too late to back out, right?"

"I already gave my word."

"She'd understand, Syira."

"No. I've made my promise and I'm going to keep it. And it's not just a matter of keeping a promise, Min. I want to do this. And I've been praying Istikharah since the day Aunt Ani told me about this idea. Though the whole thing scares me, I am at peace with the decision I'm making."

"You know what makes me not so worried about this plan, Syira?"

"What?" Syakirah raised her eyebrows.

"The fact that you've begun to like Imran Hakim," Yasmin told her friend with a caring smile.

Though Syakirah was reluctant to admit it, there was truth in what her friend said. She had become hopeful that perhaps Imran was the person with whom Allah (swt) meant for her to share a life. Though the fear of another jilting could not be

completely eliminated, she felt good with her decision. She put
her trust in Allah (swt) for the good intention she felt within her
and recited a prayer in Arabic, *"And put thy trust in Allah and
enough is Allah as a Disposer of affairs."* (Qur'an 33:3)

~

Syakirah just finished her Isha' prayer when Ani called and
confirmed her suspicions.

"Aunt Ani, we all know that Imran and I are against arranged
marriage. Do you think she would believe it if we both suddenly
change our minds?"

"If you make it convincing, insha Allah!" Ani chuckled. She
told Syakirah that she and Saleha were coming to KL on Tuesday.
She was going to encourage Saleha to try matchmaking one more
time, then Syakirah would have to make Saleha believe that her
agreement was not pressured. "Can you do this, Syira?"

Syakirah doubted her decision for a second.

"Syira, are you there? Are you okay, Syira?"

"Yes..." *This was really an old fashioned matchmaking,*
Syakirah thought. *Would love bloom after marriage for her and
Imran, like Yasmin always teased? Too soon to think about that,* she
answered herself. Allah (swt) would take care of that as long as
she was honest with the decision she made. After all, she would
always have Allah's (swt) love to help her go through anything.

"Syira, like I said, as much as I need you in this, I don't want
to force you into anything," Ani said, wanting to reconfirm and
to see that Syakirah was truly sure of her decision.

"I do want to help her, insha Allah, Aunt Ani." In her heart
Syakirah was repeating, *"And put thy trust in Allah and enough is
Allah as a Disposer of affairs."*

~

On Monday morning, Ani dropped by to visit Saleha on her way to the boutique. She called Saleha before coming and said she wanted to talk to her about Imran and Syakirah. Saleha was surprised at first because she had all but decided to drop the issue. However, she maintained some excitement at the prospect.

Ani noticed Saleha seemed more cheerful than she had over the last couple of days. This somehow made Ani a little uncomfortable. She felt guilty for breaking her promise, yet she knew she had to do what she thought was best for Saleha. Though Ani was more confident than not that an arranged, planned marriage was the way to go, she could not help but fear her plan might not go according to plan. She prayed that Allah (swt) would help it go smoothly.

Imran left for the office as usual and the ladies had the house to themselves. Looking at her friend, Ani casually told her that she was going to KL the next day and would like Saleha to accompany her. Then she told Saleha about meeting Syakirah.

"Why all this again? I was just thinking of backing out." Saleha smiled.

"Well, I think we should give this one last try. I'm going to call Syakirah and set up a meeting with her tomorrow. And you could try to talk to Imran about your wish for him and Syakirah." Ani could tell that Saleha was a little surprised and skeptical. They had been through this before. What would be different this time?

"Ani, what are you saying here? As I recall, you said I should stop getting my hopes up. Not that I like it, but it's better than setting myself up for disappointment." Saleha was puzzled.

"Yes. I understand you want to accept things as they are right now. But it breaks my heart to see you unhappy." Ani smiled to give her hope. "I don't think it would do any harm if we take another shot at this. I'm not saying that we are going to ignore their feelings. We know how they both feel about matchmaking but what we don't know is how they actually feel about each other," Ani said sensibly.

"Nothing much has happened so far. Ani, I would be very happy if they clicked, but I have my doubts."

"We won't know until we've tried."

"I really don't want to make Imran feel like his mother is forcing him to get married. He has already told me how he felt about her."

"I know. But we should ask him again. There's no guarantee that he'll give us the answer we want to hear, but whatever his answer may be, we'll just accept it. This will be the last time we'd ask him…perhaps ever, insha Allah."

Saleha seemed thoughtful as she paused before giving any response to what Ani said. Then, taking a deep breath, she spoke, "I guess I could do that, insha Allah. I could ask him again, but the thought of him giving the same answer is…" Saleha couldn't finish her sentence.

"Try not to think about that until you hear what he has to say. Just tell him honestly how you feel, insha Allah."

～

Ani asked Imran not to tell anyone about her idea, but he insisted on telling Umar, who was shocked. "Your mother? If there's anything I can do, pal…"

"Wait, there's more…" Imran continued as he recounted the plan to marry Syakirah.

"Are you sure you want to do this, Imran?" Umar looked at Imran with concern.

"I know marriage is not something to be toyed with. And as much as I would prefer to get to know her before marrying her, I don't have much time. My mother only has three months left, insha Allah."

"Perhaps during the engagement time, you two could get to know each other better."

"Insha Allah. That's what I'm hoping." Imran let go a sigh. "This really comes out of the blue, Umar. Only a few weeks ago I met Syakirah. I never thought it was going to be like this. Allah Ta'ala has His own plans as always. He knows best!"

"Seek help from Him. That's the best thing to do. What about Syakirah? How could she agree to marry you just to help a woman she has known only for a short time?" Umar was curious and perplexed.

"I don't know. Aunt Ani didn't give me details about Mom's and Syakirah's relationship. I only know that she has agreed."

"That's very noble of her, considering the situation. I hope she likes you enough to have agreed to marry you, Imran."

"I guess I won't know until I talk to her."

"Maybe she's come to like you after all," Umar teased.

"I don't know," Imran responded seriously, "We really need time to know each other first," Imran responded seriously.

"Well, in the old days, that usually happens during the engagement period and, with some couples, after marriage!"

"I know that too. Frankly, to enter a marriage this way would be my best hope, pal! Once I marry her, she would be my *amanah*, a trust from Allah Ta'ala for me to take care. May the Almighty Allah bestow upon me *mawaddah* and *rahmah* for her, a foundation for a happy marriage."

"Since you both have agreed, I think you two just need time. I like the thought of seeing you getting married again. I hope you have what you had with Kaira, insha Allah." Umar was sincere.

"Thanks, Umar. I will marry Syakirah because she's my mother's choice. I may not have the feeling of love for her yet, but I do like her. We could be good friends, given time. And she could be what I'm looking for in a wife, insha Allah."

Melissa came to Umar's mind. He hated having to bring up the issue, but he believed he was doing so to try to help his best friend.

"OK, so what about Melissa?" Umar tried to read Imran's reaction but failed. He waited for his response.

"What about her? We're friends, Umar. She's a nice person and we get along well. And you know I respect her father. He's an old friend of my father," Imran spoke casually but with no conviction.

"Broken record, Imran." Umar voiced his skepticism. "Try again."

Imran closed his eyes and shook his head. "Before Dad passed away, or maybe I should say before I married Kaira, I remember my father used to mention...well, he used to tease me...wanting us, me and Melissa...you know. She was very young then," Imran told his friend with a slight smile.

"You, too. So what happened?"

"Nothing. After I married Kaira, and after her death, I never really thought about it again. Dad understood, and we just didn't talk about it. Of course these past couple of months I've been seeing a lot of her. But mainly for business reasons, and to maintain the family friendship."

"Nothing serious then," Umar added.

"It was just like the-old-friends-getting-together-again kind of thing. And forgive me for being repetitious, but Dad was really close to Dato' Annuar."

Umar let go a sigh. He felt reassured hearing this. All his worry about Imran and Melissa was for nothing after all. "I'm glad to hear this, pal."

"Pray for me, Umar."

"I will, insha Allah."

~

Imran came home at five and met his mother in the garden while she watered her orchids. Every moment with her was a blessing from Allah. Her serenity in the garden was something he would remember for the rest of his days.

"Seeing you doing this reminds me of Hidayat, Mom." Imran thought this would help bring up the topic of visiting Hidayat the next day. Ani had told him that his mother was happy when she suggested using the excuse to visit Hidayat for going to KL.

"Yes. These last few days I really miss him, Imran. Maybe we could visit him soon, insha Allah."

"I like that thought. Maybe tomorrow we could drop by the college, insha Allah. I have to do some business in KL. I could drop you off at the college before my meeting."

"Insha Allah. But this won't trouble you?"

"Of course not, Mom. You could ask Aunt Ani to accompany you." Imran smiled.

Saleha's face lit up at the mention of Ani's name. Now was the time, she thought. She walked toward the bench nearest the flowers and sat down. Imran followed.

"Imran, there's something else I want to do tomorrow, insha Allah."

"Yes?" Imran was trying to act as clueless as possible, knowing what Saleha was about to say.

"I'd like us to meet Syakirah one more time. I know how you feel about matchmaking... But who knows, perhaps this time you both could find a way to get along. Insha Allah."

"Mom…I don't know." Imran faked reluctance.

"I promise you won't have to see her again after tomorrow. I'm sorry if my asking this is too much. It's just that since we both don't know what the future holds, let Allah Ta'ala decide."

With a smile, Imran responded, "Okay, Mom. No more meetings after this. Promise?"

"Yes, I promise, insha Allah."

∼

As scheduled, they left JB early and reached KL at noon. After checking in at Hillview Hotel, Ani called Syakirah.

"We just got here."

"Alhamdulillah. Aunt Ani, Yasmin is coming with me."

"Whatever is comfortable for you, Syira. I'm grateful enough that you agree to be with me on this. All Saleha knows is that you will come at our request."

"I remember that, insha Allah."

"Imran will drop us off at the college at two before his meeting. He said he'd pick us up at around three-thirty."

"Hidayat will be happy to see his mother," Syakirah commented.

"I'm sure he will, insha Allah. After that we'll excuse ourselves to go to my friend's boutique."

"Okay. I'll meet you at five as planned, insha Allah."

∼

They went to the college to meet Hidayat, who was happy and surprised to see them. Saleha explained that Imran had a meeting in KL. Hidayat had classes but spared time to have drinks and talk with the two ladies. Imran then came to pick them up and had the chance to talk to his brother before they left for the boutique.

At five, the three of them were waiting when Syakirah and Yasmin came. Imran was all polite in greeting the young women, which made Saleha happy. They talked casually about work.

"Thank you for having me at the Language Camp," Imran spoke to both Yasmin and Syakirah.

"I'm so happy you could come. This was the first year the college allowed family or relatives to visit," Syakirah told him. Yasmin nodded, agreeing with what her friend had said.

"So maybe I could join the Language Camp again?" Imran joked with a smile that showed his dimples.

"Insha Allah. Make it strictly emergency. We don't want it to be a family outing-cum-camping instead," Yasmin said with a laugh. The others joined her laughter.

"All this time I've never asked about your business, Imran," Syakirah changed the topic.

"I didn't think language teachers would be interested in business."

"Well, for your information we do teach English for business students at the college." Syakirah smiled.

"Yes. Maybe one of these days we could invite you to lecture our students," Yasmin chipped in. They all laughed.

"Excellent idea," Ani laughed, with Saleha voicing her agreement.

"Well, to answer your question, Syakirah, we produce and supply home and office furniture," Imran went back to Syakirah's query. Imran was glad to see how friendly and agreeable she was.

Suddenly he remembered what Umar had said. How noble of Syakirah to consent to this. *Maybe it's not such a bad idea, and who knows? I could really like her. Only Allah Ta'ala could bestow love in two people's hearts."* He also noticed how his mother was enjoying herself in the conversation.

Yasmin was impressed to hear the kind of business Imran was in. "A good business I would say, Mr. Imran. Not many Malays succeed in this business."

"It's a family business, I guess, from the company's name, KS Holdings?" Syakirah asked.

"Yes, Kamal and Sons. But my Mom here and my late father were the founders of KS Holdings." Imran smiled proudly with a glance at Saleha.

"Aunt Saleha?" Yasmin was surprised.

"Well, dear, I didn't do much…just lent my ideas. All the hard work was done by Imran's father," Saleha responded in a humble manner.

Imran smiled. "You're being modest, Mom."

Saleha told them briefly the history of the factory and growth of the business, and Imran chipped in a little here and there.

The conversation continued and everyone was at ease. Saleha beamed with happiness. Syakirah and Imran learned about each other's educational backgrounds and work experiences. Later, at about six, Syakirah and Yasmin excused themselves. Saleha thought of inviting the young women to have dinner with them, but she didn't want to ask too much from Imran. But to her surprise, Imran made the invitation.

"Would you ladies care to join us for dinner tonight? I know this special place at Jalan Conley…or maybe you've heard of this place called Seri Melayu. They serve all traditional cuisines." Imran invited Syakirah and Yasmin, sounding very sincere and hopeful that they would accept. Saleha and Ani smiled at the younger women, waiting for their answers.

"I can't. I've already made plans with the kids. Thank you anyway, Mr. Imran."

"Next time perhaps, Mrs. Yasmin, insha Allah." Imran turned to look at Syakirah. "How about you, Syakirah?"

"Syira?" Ani asked while Saleha was looking at her anxiously.

"I… " Syakirah hesitated. She glanced at Saleha. "Well, I guess I could come and join you all, insha Allah. After all, it's not always that I get the opportunity to dine with a successful businesswoman and her son." She smiled as did everyone else. She glanced at Imran who seemed to nod in agreement.

Imran promised to pick her up at eight. Shortly after, Yasmin and Syakirah left. Saleha turned to Imran. "Thank you, Imran."

"For behaving, Mom?" He joked.

"That, and for inviting her to dinner."

"Well, that's my treat. You did say this might be the last meeting we have with her. So I want to make it special for you." Imran said politely, but he knew it wasn't something that Saleha wanted to hear. However, he also realized he couldn't show a complete change of heart, for she might suspect something.

"Yes. But we can't take that as definite. All is in Allah Ta'ala's hands, dear," Saleha continued cheerfully. Imran wished the happiness on his mother's face would last forever.

∼

Imran came with Ani and Saleha to fetch Syakirah. The four of them enjoyed their dinner and conversation. They were almost done when Ani noticed Saleha was not looking well.

"Sal, you look kind of pale. Are you feeling alright?"

Imran and Syakirah were worried but tried to hide it, for they didn't want Saleha to suspect anything.

"We've had a long day, Mom."

"I'm fine, dear," Saleha responded politely, but she felt suddenly weak.

"You need to rest, Aunt Saleha. I really enjoyed the dinner, thank you. But I think we should all go now," Syakirah told Saleha as casually as possible in order not to show the worry she was feeling inside.

"I agree with Syakirah, Mom."

"I'm just a little tired, that's all. I don't want to spoil the evening."

"You're not, Aunt Saleha. I have thoroughly enjoyed myself with you all tonight," said Syakirah brightly.

"I think we have all had a good time tonight, Sal," Ani agreed.

"And it's almost ten. Tomorrow we have a long trip to take. Syakirah's right; we should call it quits for tonight," Imran told his mother and smiled knowingly at Syakirah. Saleha finally agreed and they left the restaurant.

Imran was worried. He wanted to do more to attend to Saleha's sickness but tried not to make it obvious that he knew more. Saleha took her medication and rested.

When Saleha was asleep, Ani told Imran about Saleha's increasingly frequent, yet short-lived attacks. Imran, with a myriad of emotions, wanted to tell his mother everything. Ani, however, advised him to carry on with the plan. She thanked Imran for the good time they all had that evening. Then both of them thanked Allah (swt) for it. With His will, Saleha's wishes would come true.

~

The trio left KL at ten the next morning, but not before Syakirah called Ani to ask about Saleha, who had recovered. Syakirah wished them a safe trip home and promised to talk to Saleha again when the family reached JB.

It was noon when they arrived home. After prayer and lunch, Imran left for his office while Saleha continued to rest.

Imran was worried and could not concentrate on work. He wanted to stay at home but did not, or Saleha might suspect he knew the truth of her condition. He came home earlier than usual, however, his mother assuming incorrectly that he was tired after the trip to KL.

Syakirah called as promised and Imran answered.

"Assalamu'alaikum."

"Wa'alaikumussalam," Imran returned her salam and asked who she was. Then he apologized for not recognizing her voice.

"That's okay. How's Aunt Saleha doing?"

"Alhamdulillah, she's fine. Do you want to talk to her?"

"Yes, insha Allah, if she's up."

Syakirah talked to Saleha. Imran watched his mother, animated in conversation with Syakirah. He realized he too felt comfortable talking to her. He figured that might be because he wanted so much to please his mother.

After the talk, Saleha told Imran that Syakirah was nice to care about her. Imran smiled. Seeing how much Syakirah cared for his mother proved her sincerity. She was being honest when she told him that she liked and respected his mother. Somehow this fact brought him peace.

Fleetingly, he wondered if Syakirah would marry him for who he was rather than for his mother's sake. He erased the thought as he realized it was too early to go into that. He himself needed to learn the Muslim side of this woman more. For now, he liked her as a Muslim friend and he would marry her for his mother's sake. At least they both shared two things in common—they both detested matchmaking and loved his mother. Imran smiled lightly to himself at the last thought.

Syakirah called Saleha again during the weekend and several times over the following weeks. Saleha and Syakirah grew closer as they stayed in contact, a fact not lost on Imran. On one of Saleha and Ani's visits to see Hidayat, they accidentally met Syakirah. Hidayat was happy to 'introduce' Syakirah to his mother and Ani. *Alhamdulillah*, Ani observed, *everything's going well*.

～

Imran unexpectedly came to see Hidayat after one of his business dealings in KL. Unfortunately Hidayat had gone out with his friends. While passing by the parking lot of the Language Center, Imran saw Syakirah and Yasmin. He stopped the car and they talked for a while.

Yasmin noticed Imran's attitude toward her friend had changed. She was surprised but thanked Allah (swt) for the change and for making these two people not dislike each other anymore.

Syakirah smiled at Yasmin. "Alhamdulillah, I can stand to be around him much better now. I almost forget that I had a hard time dealing with this man."

Yasmin smiled and could not help praying to the Almighty Allah that Ani's plan would end with something wonderful for her friend.

~

About a month after proposing her plan to Imran and Syakirah, Ani came to see Saleha to talk about the couple. Saleha hadn't looked too healthy lately. Ani suggested that Saleha ask Imran about Syakirah again. Ani noticed the two of them had become friends, and she thanked Allah (swt) for that.

After Maghrib prayer, Saleha went to Imran's room. She found him reading *Surat Al-Baqarah*. She let him finish the verse he was reading: "*Allah is the Protector of those who have faith; from the depths of darkness He will lead them forth to light; Of those who reject faith, the patrons are the Evil ones; from light they will lead them to darkness. They will be the companions of the fire to dwell therein (forever).*" (Qur'an 2:257)

He stopped reading as he saw Saleha standing in the doorway. He was not surprised to find out that she wanted to talk about Syakirah.

"If you really believe she could make me happy, then yes, Mom." Imran meant what he said. He did like Syakirah, though he had not fallen in love with her. He would not hesitate marrying her, though, if it would make his mother happy. "I will, insha Allah," he added.

Saleha was surprised to hear Imran's answer.

"Imran, why the change? Are you sure you want to do this, Son?"

"Yes, Mom. Absolutely sure… and nothing has changed except me, I guess. Allah Ta'ala knows best, Mom. And He is the best Planner of all." He smiled peacefully at Saleha, and she left the room content, whispering "*alhamdulillah*" under her breath.

After she left, Imran prayed the Istikharah prayer again, asking Allah's (swt) guide to reaffirm his decision. He wanted to be completely sure he was making the right decision. He realized he could not offer Syakirah his love now because he needed to know her more, but it would not be impossible for him to love her in the future.

This thought brought peace to Imran. It meant that even though he would be marrying Syakirah for his mother's sake, he would enter the marriage with complete willingness and honesty. He wondered how Syakirah truly felt about the marriage.

~

On his way home from Isha' prayer at the mosque, Imran stopped by Ani's house. He wanted to discuss the marriage with Ani and Zaid.

"I've been following the progress of this plan through your Aunt Ani. And I'm glad that you came tonight. I've been meaning to talk to you since your Aunt told me that you and Syakirah agreed to fulfill your mother's wish. Alhamdulillah, tonight Allah sent you here." Zaid smiled at the last words he said.

Imran smiled back and told the elder man the reason for his visit.

"I wish I could be open with Mom and tell her I know about her sickness. But I want her to be happy, Uncle Zaid. Honestly, the first time Aunt Ani told me about this idea, it was hard for me to agree. But after contemplating and praying, I am at peace with my decision, alhamdulillah."

"What do you think of Syakirah? From what your Aunt has told me, I believe she's a good Muslim woman." Zaid waited for Imran's response.

"I like her and yes, she seems like a good Muslim woman. But to be honest, that's all I feel. We are friends who are getting to know each other. What matters most right now is my mother.

I will learn to love Syakirah if that's what it takes to make my mother happy. I will, insha Allah."

"Well, alhamdulillah, good to know that you do like her. To enter a marriage, that would be a start. Next you should look for the characteristics set by Islam in the person who is to be your spouse. First and foremost is her faith! Here's where virtuous versus righteous qualities come into play. Love can be nurtured after marriage, when you both are in a *halal* state, or Islamically permissible relationship." Zaid smiled at Imran. "I know it doesn't sound like love and marriage of the modern day, but believe me it's blessed by Allah Ta'ala and more beautiful this way, insha Allah."

Imran nodded in agreement. He smiled at Ani when the elder woman came to join them in the living room. She served them tea before she finally said something to Imran.

"Imran, when I first told your uncle about this plan, he strongly disagreed with me because he was afraid that you and Syakirah might end up with a temporary marriage. The solemnization of a marriage, the 'Aqad, is a sacred covenant with Allah Ta'ala. You can't pretend to be married because that would be a mockery of Allah Ta'ala's law. So he asked me to talk to both of you. Once you agreed, I tried to bring the two of you together so that you can get to know each other. Alhamdulillah, I think it's going well."

"So now the next thing is the marriage proposal. But I need to speak to Syakirah first, insha Allah." Imran told the couple in front of him.

"Are you going to tell her what you've just told us? That you'd marry her for real and assume all the responsibilities of a husband, except you need time to consummate the marriage? A waiting period?" Zaid asked bluntly.

"Yes, I guess I'd better. But more importantly at this point, I need to hear her assent. I don't want to feel like she's being forced into something repugnant."

"Of course, Imran, but I think you'll be satisfied with her motivation. Be sure, though, to tell her about the waiting period you are proposing. She knows you're marrying her for your mother's sake. You do not want to leave her unprepared," Ani added.

"Yes, insha Allah, perhaps when we have that meeting, the one with me, Syakirah and you both?" Ani had told him about this meeting when she told him about the plan.

"Yes, I will inform you when the time comes, insha Allah." Ani confirmed.

"I still hope and pray that I could tell Mom I knew the truth before the marriage takes place, insha Allah."

"Allah Ta'ala will see to that," Zaid told Imran with a smile. "And I hope you will find what you're looking for in Syakirah. I still remember you want to marry someone like Kaira or even better, insha Allah. The engagement period will allow you to know her better. If that's not enough, you will have plenty of time to do that after marriage, insha Allah... seek help from the Most Loving to grant you love for her."

Zaid repeated what Imran had told Umar, "Al-Qurtubi quoted Ibnu 'Abbas about *mawaddah* and *rahmah*. He said a happy marriage is based on mawaddah, the tender love Allah Ta'ala grants a man for his wife. Rahmah is his gentle care and treatment of her so that she would live in comfort with him."

Ani turned to look at her husband. He sounded confident, though she herself still had doubts. She knew how much Zaid loved Imran, and like any father would do, he offered a lot of prayers to Allah (swt) for Imran's happiness.

~

The next day Imran called Syakirah to talk about the marriage. "I love my mother and I know you love and respect her, too."

"That's true." Syakirah was listening attentively to what Imran was saying. She noticed he sounded solemn.

"We both know that she's dying," Imran, in a controlled voice, said sadly.

"Yes."

"Syira..." Never before had he addressed her like this.

"I'm here." Syakirah was trying hard to hold back her tears. In her heart she was crying. She didn't like to be reminded. It was like facing the death of her mother again.

"You're okay?" He asked, while clearing his throat.

"Yes, I'm here."

"It's about her last wish," Imran began and paused. Syakirah detected hesitation in his voice.

Even though she had agreed to the plan, Syakirah knew this was the part where Imran would ask her himself and that she was not sure she would respond as planned. Could she really agree to marry him knowing it may not guarantee her happiness?

"By now we both know how much she wanted you to be my wife. So please be honest with me, Syira. Will you be my wife and help me fulfill her wish?"

Syakirah paused. She debated with herself momentarily, and quieted a sudden panic that welled up inside of her. She remembered her promise to Ani and had to admit that she liked Imran though she doubted he felt the same toward her. He could be marrying her only for his mother's sake, for all she knew.

"Syira?" Again Imran had to call her after her long pause.

"Yes."

"Yes, you agree to help? Or just yes you understand what she wanted?" Imran wanted to confirm.

"Yes…for both. I will do it for her, insha Allah."

"Alhamdulillah. Thank you. Only Allah Ta'ala can repay you."

～

Saleha woke up at four-thirty for her *tahajjud* prayer. Later in the morning, she called Syakirah to talk about the marriage proposal. She told Syakirah that, as was customarily done, Imran's family would go to her house to meet her parents in KB for the proper marriage proposal. Since it was Thursday, Syakirah agreed to have them come over on Sunday.

Syakirah's parents were very happy for her when she informed them about the marriage proposal over the phone. They *might not have been so happy if they knew the whole truth*, she told herself.

Syakirah explained the engagement process to Yasmin.

"Syira, I never thought you'd do this."

"Me neither, Min. I really love Aunt Saleha though, and I can grant her wish, insha Allah. I know she likes me, too. When I said yes to Imran, I really meant it because I came to the decision after praying Istikharah. And you know what? Whatever the outcome is after the marriage, I will just accept with redha, and be pleased with Allah Ta'ala's plans. I'm leaving it all in the Almighty Allah's hands."

"Imran is a good man, alhamdulillah," Yasmin said. She had not known anyone who would sacrifice his own future to make his mother happy. In Islam the one most deserving of a man's love and attention would be his own mother.

Syakirah suddenly recalled the three year relationship with Manaf. She had thought she had known him well and could not have been more wrong. Now she was marrying Imran after knowing him for mere months. She wished she had more time to get to know him. She reminded herself of Saleha's illness.

"Too early to go into that, Min. We're just starting to know each other. Marriage is a matter of the hearts. True, I've seen some Muslim qualities in Imran…enough to say he's a good Muslim." Syakirah paused. "But his heart may not welcome my presence."

"The engagement period will be a good time to get to know him. Who knows, he will eventually want this marriage for himself and not for his mother's sake."

Syakirah smiled at Yasmin's hopeful face. Deep down in her heart, she too had begun to hope for the same thing. But what if Imran decided to end the marriage once his mother was gone? Would she be dumped again?

"*Wallahu'alam.* I put my trust in Allah Ta'ala." Syakirah recalled the verse, "*Allah, there is no god but He; and in Allah (swt) therefore let the believers put their trust.*" (Qur'an 64:13) Then she added, "He knows best and He's the best Planner."

~

The engagement ceremony took place according to the Malay traditional custom, with Islamic values not forgotten. Syakirah's family was very strict in observing Malay traditional customs in accordance with the Islamic guidelines. It was a small ceremony attended by a few close relatives. Saleha came with Ani and Hanim, accompanied by Imran and two of their relatives. Imran came to the house, but in observance of Islamic tradition, he neither watched nor took part in the ceremony. Saleha placed the engagement ring on Syakirah's finger.

They had a small family gathering after the ceremony. Imran watched his happy mother with Syakirah from afar before Syakirah left to finish out the semester. He was not displeased with what he saw. He could be comfortable with her, insha Allah.

The whole family and Imran's friends were happy for him. He received congratulatory calls from close friends who had learned about the engagement from Iskandar and Umar. After the ceremony, the two families agreed that the engagement would be for two months. They decided on a small wedding in late June, a week after the new semester.

Imran received separate calls from Melissa and her father, who both also congratulated him. Dato' Annuar politely inquired about Syakirah and the sudden move to marry, and Imran confided in the man, getting his blessing for the coming nuptials. Imran also received his assurance that he would say nothing about Imran's motivation to anyone.

CHAPTER 21

Imran and Syakirah stayed busy throughout the engagement period. Imran worked on a new project while keeping tabs on Saleha. Daily he hid his heartbreak from her. Syakirah spent her time grading papers as the end of the semester approached. They talked occasionally to discuss Saleha's health, knowing that there was not much they could do for her now except pray.

One night, Imran and Saleha went to the college to visit Hidayat before his final examinations began. The three of them went out for dinner with Syakirah. The next day Syakirah dropped by Yasmin's office after her class to tell her about her enjoyable evening.

"Min, I really love this family," Syakirah said matter-of-factly.

Yasmin smiled at her friend. "Didn't I say that you should give it a chance? Alhamdulillah, they're nice people, and Imran's not bad either, is he?" Yasmin spoke analyzing the matter. Syakirah nodded in agreement.

Yasmin recalled all the couple's encounters. What a change from the beginning of their relationship, when Syira could barely stand to be in the same room with him. The change in her friend and in the couple's relationship was beautiful to witness. *The miraculous work of Allah Ta'ala*, she thought.

Syakirah realized the longer she knew Imran, the more she liked him. From what she had seen, he might not have all of Saleha's wonderful traits but he was a good Muslim son, brother, and businessman. He acted professionally at work, responsibly towards his family, and above everything he was a good practicing Muslim. During their conversations, he regularly touched on the importance of keeping faith in Allah (swt). From the way he spoke, she could tell he hadn't suddenly become religious due to his current circumstances and his mother's failing health. He was certainly not hypocritical or disingenuous. He had been a good Muslim man for a long time. She thanked the Almighty Allah for the opportunity to learn about him rather than to think ill of him for the rest of their lives. As she read in the Qur'an: *"O ye who believe! Shun much suspicion; for lo! Some suspicion is a crime. And spy not, neither backbite one another. Would any one of you love to eat the flesh of his dead brother? Ye abhor that! And keep your duty (to Allah) Lo! Allah is relenting, Merciful!"* (Qur'an 49:12)

"As I recall, last time I said Imran was a good man, you said you both were just starting to know each other. So, what's new there?" Yasmin studied Syakirah's face for her friend's reaction.

Syakirah averted her eyes and picked a book from her friend's table. Flipping through the pages, she contemplated telling Yasmin about the growing affection she felt for him.

"These past few weeks, I've gotten to know him better, and yes, there are things about him that I never expected. And I'm impressed. He's a good Muslim: good to his mother and his family, he's a shrewd and fair businessman, decent and kind to his friends, including me…" she trailed off.

"But, he's not Manaf?" Yasmin had to ask this. She could not help suspecting Syakirah might still think of Manaf after all these years.

Syakirah faced Yasmin with a questioning look. "Why did you bring that up?"

"Is that true, Syira?" Yasmin replied with another question.

"I will not compare the two, insha Allah. I like Imran for who he is." Syakirah continued mechanically, "True, Manaf was a good man, too. But, even with all of those qualities, we failed to overcome something and we lost what we had."

"But you say that you've got past all that and him, Syira." Yasmin was not of the opinion that Manaf was the good person her friend said he was.

Syakirah nodded and continued in a detached and distant voice. "I have all but forgotten about him in that way. He's no more than just my brother in faith now. When we broke up, though, it took a lot from me...I was so young... I was almost left with nothing, except for my faith in Allah Ta'ala...it was what revived me and cured me...made me a stronger and a better person after that. Alhamdulillah," Syakirah ended strongly.

Yasmin understood. She never asked Syakirah the details of the break-up with Manaf to save her friend the agony of reliving it. The wound had healed, but a scar remained. Even scars fade, however, with the right treatment.

"I pray that Allah Ta'ala has a gift for you in Imran...a compensation for what you lost years ago, insha Allah," she said grasping her friend's hand across the table.

"Insha Allah. Sometimes I'm afraid of being hurt again. The only thing I'm sure of is Allah. There is nothing in my life except Allah that is perfect. Trust is so hard to give to a human being when humans are so fallible, so sometimes you just stay alone with the purest and most everlasting love of all...with Allah's love, the ultimate love. Allah Ta'ala's love should always be your first love. He will never leave you or disappoint you...you just have to love Him for the rest of your life...you love Him by doing what He enjoins and avoiding what he forbids...you fear Him, but you hope for His blessings and love because Allah Ta'ala, the Most Loving, will love you back unconditionally."

Yasmin watched her friend talk. It was clear to Yasmin that Syakirah no longer loved Manaf; it was proven by her fondness for Imran now. Yasmin could only hope and pray that Allah (swt) would give Syakirah and Imran love for each other after they were married.

~

It was Friday, the last day of the examination period. Hidayat came to Syakirah's office to say goodbye before going home for the semester holiday. He had been so happy to see her engaged to his brother. Since he was away from home during the ceremony, he called Imran after the engagement to congratulate him. He asked him when Syakirah and he had become serious in the relationship. Imran didn't give him a definite answer. He also congratulated Syakirah for the engagement. Syakirah continued to help him with his writings for the *Daily Pine*. The new status in their relationship helped them work more comfortably together.

"Soon you'll be my sister-in-law, Miss Syakirah ... I mean *Kak* Syira." Hidayat ended their short talk at her office.

"Insha Allah, Hidayat, insha Allah. But let's keep it profes-sional," Syakirah answered, laughing, thinking that in five weeks he would be her brother-in-law.

~

Syakirah went home only after preparing her lessons for the coming semester and for the coming English workshop at Pine College. She spent the first two weeks of the semester holiday preparing for the English courses they had been assigned to teach with a team of British lecturers.

"Syira, for someone who's getting married in a few weeks, you sure don't look anxious." Mei Lin told her. She was among a few friends who knew about her engagement to Imran. Syakirah had chosen to be discreet about the matter and threw herself into her work rather than spending time preparing for, or for that matter, even talking about the wedding.

"Really? Well, I must be a cool bride-to-be!" Syakirah joked with Mei Lin. She remembered talking to Saleha the night before about being a busy bride. Whether a busy bride-to-be or a busy lecturer, she stayed in contact with Saleha regularly. Earlier in the week, Ani and Saleha dropped by her apartment after Saleha's monthly medical checkup.

"No, seriously when are you going home?" Mei Lin asked.

"Well, now that we've completed this work, I still have some stuff to take care of before the workshop starts." Syakirah was referring to the workshop at the end of the week.

"Wow! You are a busy bride indeed, Miss Syakirah!" Mei Lin commented and they both laughed.

Imran called Syakirah a few times and she would ask him about Saleha. She was not sorry she was not able to see Imran much during their engagement time. Islamically, that was appropriate. Yasmin had been teasing her saying that she was falling for Imran. Syakirah told her that it was too soon.

I simply don't trust him enough for that yet, Syakirah told herself.

∼

When the English workshop ended, she took a week off to help her family prepare for the wedding. They were happy to have her there and asked her to stay until the wedding. She couldn't because she had to return for the new semester. She told them she would be home two days before the wedding, which was on Friday.

The day before she left for the wedding, Syakirah had asked Yasmin to help her with some shopping for the ceremony. They were leaving the shopping mall when they saw Imran with Melissa and Dato' Annuar. Syakirah hadn't known that Imran was in KL.

"Don't you want to go and greet them?"

"No." Syakirah said flatly. "Min, remember he agreed to marry me for his mother's sake."

"Well, yes, I know that…but there's nothing wrong in talking to Imran's friends."

"I can't. For all I know the beautiful lady beside him could be his real choice!" Syakirah remembered Ani telling her about Imran and Melissa, which had caused Saleha to worry.

"Well…you have a point, but I have a feeling they are just business colleagues."

"You and your feelings again…" Syakirah smiled while shaking her head. "Not my business to interfere, Min."

"I also have a feeling that you're falling for him… You should be honest with yourself, you know."

Syakirah looked at her friend and shook her head. "I like him, yes, but falling for him?" Nonetheless, at that moment she did feel different. For a split second, she doubted herself. Maybe Yasmin was right. Is she lying to herself? Suddenly a strong determination overcame her and she decided to guard herself against feelings of love that might be budding for Imran Hakim. She could not trust him.

CHAPTER 22

Every other night leading up to the wedding, Syakirah talked to Saleha, both of whom were busy preparing for the wedding. As the day approached, Syakirah grew more anxious. She sought Ani's advice, Ani advising her to keep faith in Allah (swt). She prayed to the Almighty Allah days and nights for Saleha to live long enough to witness the wedding. Several days before the wedding, Ani called her. She would be coming to her house with Zaid. Imran would join them too.

It was after Asr prayer when Syakirah received the visit from Ani, Zaid and Imran. Ani and Imran introduced her to Zaid for the first time. After some small talk, Zaid brought up the topic of the gathering.

"In a few days time, you both will be entering a relationship that will bind you, insha Allah, for the rest of your lives." Zaid told the couple in front of him. He studied Imran who then nodded in agreement. Syakirah, sitting next to Ani, looked at the elder woman for guidance. Ani took hold of her hand and smiled at Syakirah who smiled back nervously.

Zaid continued. "Marriage gives you tranquility so that you may have better focus to serve Allah Ta'ala. It is said to complete one's religion. Marriage is a trust, 'amanah', from Allah (swt). Imran, Syakirah...you both will assume the responsibilities of a husband and a wife. How you carry them out, in the end, you have Allah Ta'ala to Whom you both will answer. For you, Imran, your mother will always be the second to obey after Allah Ta'ala and you, Syakirah, your husband will always be the second after Allah Ta'ala to whom you obey. My question here is, how do you really feel about marrying each other? Imran?"

All eyes were on Imran. He was quiet for a second before replying.

"My mother is very important to me. Like you said, she will always be the second for me to please after Allah Ta'ala. This marriage is her last wish and as her son I'm willing to fulfill it… her happiness is mine, just like my happiness is hers." Imran paused and turned to look at Syakirah. "So, I will marry you, Syira, because we both know that would make her happy."

Syakirah appreciated the honesty in Imran's answer. However, she wondered if she was destined to live in a loveless marriage for the rest of her life. Is that what Allah had planned for her?

As if realizing the effect of his words on Syakirah, Imran turned to her and said, "And may Allah bring us happiness as well, insha Allah. Our future is in His hands." He smiled at her encouragingly. Syakirah nodded.

Zaid, then, turned to Syakirah. "How do you feel about this marriage, Syira?"

"I love Aunt Saleha, Uncle Zaid, and I know she loves me too. Sometimes being with her, I feel like I'm reliving the last months of my own mother's life. She was hospitalized for about a week before her death and I was there up to the last moment. So when Aunt Ani told me about her plan, I felt some kind of a need to agree to it…to make her happy for the last time…my late mother had a similar wish, but I could not fulfill it for her." Syakirah paused. Then she turned to Ani, grinned, and continued.

"At first, Aunt Ani, I questioned your sanity about such an arrangement. I'm sure you and Imran..."—Syakirah turned to Imran—"...remember our earlier meetings in KL."

They smiled at Syakirah's words. She turned to Zaid.

"But since then, I've come to know and respect Imran, which certainly supports my decision to marry him, even if only for his mother's sake, insha Allah. It's hard to explain, Uncle Zaid...she is someone I am not even remotely related to, yet I feel a strong bond with Aunt Saleha."

"It's a gift from Allah Ta'ala, Syira," Ani told her.

"Ani's right. When Allah (swt) loves His servant, He will bestow love in others to love that servant." Zaid recited from *Surah Maryam*: "*Verily, those who believe and work deeds of righteousness, the Most Beneficent will bestow love for them*" (Qur'an 19:96).

"Pray Istikharah to reaffirm the decision you have made... to be sure that the decision is guided by Allah Ta'ala." Zaid told both Imran and Syakirah. "After that put your whole trust in Him."

"I'm glad that you both know where the other stands now. There's just one more thing I need to remind both of you. We talked about this before, Imran...about the waiting period?"

"Yes."

"Well, have you both discussed it?"

Syakirah turned to look at Imran and he shook his head. When he had tried to broach the subject during his telephone conversations with her, his modesty got the better of him, and he decided to wait until he had Ani and Zaid to fortify him.

"Not yet. I guess now is the right time, insha Allah."

"Insha Allah. Well, you both are aware that there is no such thing as a temporary marriage in Islam. You either enter a marriage with the intention of keeping it, or you don't enter one to begin with. What I mean is your heart must be in it. You must be honest with yourself and above all with the Almighty Allah. The decision is based on your willingness, honesty to Allah Ta'ala. Sometimes, a couple needs time to make the marriage work …to be emotionally ready. So, for reasonable grounds, a waiting period before the consummation of marriage is allowed in Islam."

Ani picked up where Zaid left off. "What your uncle is saying is, you both have this option once you're married. At this point you are getting married to make Saleha happy…and you are doing it willingly and honestly… and trusting in Allah's decision. However, your Uncle and I also hope and pray that you will, in time, find happiness in each other… have a real and happy married life, insha Allah. So, if you need time, you both have it."

Zaid continued, "Just remember that Islam allows a waiting period provided both parties agree, redha, with the decision. The consummation of a marriage is the right of both married parties. If one wants his or her right to be fulfilled and the other denies it, the one denying the right would be committing a sin."

$\sim$

Saleha was admiring Imran who was putting on his *songkok* after he had finished getting ready for the wedding. The rest of the family was waiting for them to leave for the bride's house. Realizing they were alone, Imran thought it was the right time to tell his mother the truth before the ceremony took place. He had discussed this with Zaid the night before. Ani preferred he wait, as she continued to be concerned about Saleha's feelings of responsibility for Imran's and Syakirah's possible unhappiness.

What Imran's decision to disclose boiled down to, however, was the realization that he was deceiving his mother, and he could not continue, no matter how good his intentions.

"I never thought I would go through another wedding, Mom."

Saleha, who was sitting on the bed behind him, smiled happily. "I was never able to see the first one, dear."

Imran looked at his mother and respectfully spoke to her. "I know. That's why this one is so special, Mom."

"I'm so happy because my wish for your happiness, insha Allah, will be fulfilled in about an hour."

"Insha Allah, it will."

They smiled at each other. Imran's smile was mixed with some sadness. With love and respect, he began to tell her what was in his heart.

"Mom, I know…"

Saleha looked puzzled.

"Aunt Ani told me about the cancer. She couldn't keep it from me any more."

Imran sat next to Saleha on the bed. His mother was speechless. Suddenly it dawned on her why the marriage proposal and the engagement went so smoothly.

"So, the wedding…"

Imran immediately interrupted her. "No, no… it's not what you think, Mom. Syira and I willingly agreed to get married. I would be lying if I say we didn't do it for you, because you were the reason that brought us together in the first place."

"But, Imran I never meant to…"

"No, you didn't. You didn't force either of us into anything. At first it was hard for me to propose to her…our journey in getting to know each other was kind of a bumpy one." Imran smiled. "But these past couple of months we've come to like each other, and she's quite a good Muslim. In fact, Mom, I could not have chosen a better woman to marry and I have you to thank for this... She's cute, too," Imran teased.

Saleha's eyes glistened with tears.

"Alhamdulillah. I think Allah Ta'ala has granted me with more than what I've asked for."

"Alhamdulillah...And, Mom, please forgive me for pretending not to know you were sick...I had to hide it from you..."

"I understand. You're a good son, Imran. Alhamdulillah. Now, be a good husband, insha Allah."

"Insha Allah."

Imran and Saleha spent the next hour discussing Saleha's illness. Saleha felt her own burden lifted as she described the diagnosis and progression of the illness, the pain she'd suffered, the "business trips" with Ani, and the elaborate deception for the purpose of finding Imran a wife in time. Throughout their conversation, the mother and son wept and laughed and reassured each other. Each thanked Allah for the other, and faced the wedding with strength and peace in their hearts.

~

The house was full of people talking and laughing cheerfully when the groom's party arrived. By three-thirty, all were seated in the living room waiting for the procession to begin. Syakirah waited in the bride's room, which was just across from the living room. Yasmin and her sister, Nadhirah, were with her.

Before the ceremony began the *imam* and Syakirah's father entered her room to ask for her agreement in the marriage. She glanced at Yasmin. She felt like saying something and was about to open her mouth when she heard the imam asking for her signature in the marriage certificate. She signed it in front of the four of them. When the men left the room, Syakirah grasped Yasmin's hand. Yasmin noticed her friend's hand was cold. Yasmin smiled at her and, with a wink and a nod, silently told her friend that she had done the right thing.

Everyone listened to the imam's wedding sermon and advice about marriage. Then, the time came for the a'qad, the solemnization of the marriage. The bride was asked to witness the ceremony, so, Syakirah stepped out of her room. Yasmin and Nadhirah accompanied her out and taking their seats close to the bedroom door, watched the groom who was facing the imam. As Imran recited the a'qad, she wanted to see Saleha's face but tears of happiness blurred her vision. She hid them by looking down, as any shy bride would do. Then it was done. She heard happy voices from the witnesses of the wedding. She was about to wipe her tears and lifted her head when someone shouted for help. Somebody had collapsed. Syakirah heard Imran shouting, "Mom!"

CHAPTER 23

*"*He is the Irresistible (watching) from above over His worshippers and He sets guardians over you. At length when death approaches one of you, Our angels take his souls and they never fail their duty."* (Quran 6:61)

There was still daylight outside but the hallway of the ICU of the Hospital University of Science Malaysia was gloomy. Sad faces with teary eyes waited outside Saleha's room. The members from both sides of the new family were there. Imran, Zaid and Ani had come in the ambulance with Saleha; the rest packed into cars and followed.

Hidayat's sad face just broke Syakirah's heart. It reminded her of her brother, Ashraff when her mother passed away. Sensing Syakirah's presence, Hanim looked up. Syakirah sat next to her and offered her a hug. They held each other while Hanim cried softly on her shoulder.

Yasmin watched her friend with her new in-laws. Syakirah was a member of this family now. As she studied the new closeness between the three of them, she hoped this would be permanent for Syakirah. Saleha was the bond between Syakirah and Imran. Now they were bonded by marriage. She prayed hard for Saleha and that Allah (swt) would bestow love in this new couple's hearts.

The door to Saleha's room was opened. Imran walked out somberly, his eyes red. Iskandar, Hanim and Hidayat rushed to their brother, Syakirah slowly following behind. Yasmin could tell they had lost Saleha. Imran held his siblings, whispered something to them, then they walked in to see Saleha, leaving Imran in the lobby.

Imran found a chair and sat. With his elbows on his thighs he leaned forward and cradled his head. Syakirah watched him, unsure of what to do. Yet wanting to be there for him, she walked to him and sat on his right. She surprised herself in feeling so calm and comfortable sitting next to him. It was as if this was the most natural thing for her to do. She placed her hand on his shoulder and softly said to him, *"To Allah Ta'ala we belong and to Him we return* (Qur'an 2:156)." Syakirah paused. "I'm here if you need me."

Imran straightened his back and turned to face Syakirah. He looked into her eyes sadly. He smiled weakly at her. "Thank you, Syira."

Syakirah nodded.

～

After taking care of everything at the hospital, Imran and Hidayat went to the mosque nearby HUSM. Among their prayers for Saleha was, *"And Lord! Bestow on them Thy mercy even as they cherished me in childhood."* (Qur'an 17:24) Zaid, Iskandar, Marina, and the kids took a flight home, the adults to arrange for the burial.

Ani and Hanim stayed at Syakirah's house with Yasmin. Sitting with Syakirah's family, Ani finally told all of them about Saleha's cancer. They were surprised, but understood now why the wedding day was hurried. Yasmin returned to KL to take care of things for Syakirah at the college. Syakirah's parents followed their daughter to JB.

Later, Syakirah took Ani to the bride's room. Surveying the beautiful room, Ani thought how happy Saleha would be if she were there with her new daughter-in-law.

"She was beautiful, Syira. Her final moments were beautiful." Ani began as they sat on the bed. She looked around. "She'd love this room." Ani stopped, choking back tears.

Syakirah held the elder woman's hand. She was also trying to hold back tears. "I know she would have, Aunt Ani."

"She was happy, Syira. She didn't talk much. She was not in as much pain as she used to be when she had an attack like that. She broke out in a cold sweat... a good sign, your Uncle Zaid once told me...when someone dies with faith in Allah Ta'ala."

"She was a good person, alhamdulillah *Rabb al-Alamin*." Syakirah said and Ani nodded.

"She smiled at me and at Imran. And Allah Ta'ala's name was ceaseless on her lips. Imran saw how happy his mother was that her wish had come true."

Ani paused and looked at Syakirah. "Thank you, Syira. Thank you so much. Now, the wedding will be in remembrance," Ani whispered through her tears.

Syakirah was in tears. She knew what Ani had said was true. She was grateful to Allah (swt) for helping her with the decision to marry Imran. Syakirah prayed that the Almighty Allah (swt) would help her and Imran find love for each other to make the marriage work. That was what Saleha had wanted them to have, a happy marriage!

"You know, she even bought the two of you a gift. It's somewhere in her room at home. She wanted to give it to the two of you when you come to JB."

~

As they reached the house in JB, families and relatives were waiting. Iskandar, Marina, Zaid, and the older relatives managed to get everything ready for the burial. Iskandar noticed that his brother looked exhausted. Imran had not slept a wink at the hospital and instead spent the night praying and reading the Quran. Hidayat, who was with him, had fallen asleep.

When the body was attended to, Zaid led the prayer for the dead. Then the crowd left for the burial. Syakirah accompanied Hanim, Marina, and the kids to the cemetery. Syakirah witnessed how close Saleha's children were to each other. The bond between them was obvious. Their relatives were nice and sincerely sympathetic but the four siblings seemed to rally around each other more support. The bond they shared was enough to give them strength to face the death of their beloved mother.

It was almost noon when the burial was complete. Imran told Zaid that he did not want to hold the traditionally practiced *tahlil*, which involved inviting all relatives and the whole neighborhood to the house to say prayers for the dead and ended with serving them food. The older man smiled in agreement knowing that in Islam, foregoing that practice was preferable to practicing the innovation that was neither prescribed in the Quran, nor practiced by the Prophet and his companions. Imran and his siblings were too physically exhausted and emotionally drained to handle such a gathering with the hustle and bustle of food preparation. It would be enough for them to pray for their mother privately. The mourners respected Imran's wish, some of them to go home and pray privately.

Hanim showed Syakirah Imran's room - their wedding room. As she entered the room, she was so touched and felt the presence of her late mother-in-law. Everything in the room had a feminine touch. The pastel theme reflected Saleha's personality, and Syakirah was momentarily overcome. Later, Ani came to join them.

"Abang Imran left everything to Mom and Aunt Ani." Hanim explained about the room. Ani smiled sadly in agreement. "She was so happy with the preparation. She loved you so much, Kak Syira."

"I loved her too, Hanim."

Hanim nodded.

Ani watched them. Hanim left after explaining a few things about the room to her new sister-in-law. Syakirah told Ani that her parents wanted to leave the next morning. She, on the other hand, would stay for two more days. Since the semester had just begun, she could not take a long holiday.

It was almost three when Imran was overcome with exhaustion. He forgot that his wife was in his room. As he entered the room, he saw Syakirah standing near the window looking out. She was wearing her praying clothes and holding the Holy Quran in her hands.

"I'm sorry. I don't mean to interrupt. I must have forgotten. Hanim told me you…"

Syakirah interrupted him. "Don't apologize, please. I was about to go out anyway." Imran had been through a lot since the last twenty-four hours. Respecting his wish to be alone was the least she could do.

Imran nodded lightly. He was too tired to talk or to argue. He needed sleep. Syakirah went to the bathroom. When she came out, Imran was fast asleep on the bed. She quietly left the room.

It was almost Asr prayer time when Syakirah re-entered Imran's room. He was in the bathroom. Syakirah waited outside. When he came out, he saw Syakirah and smiled at her. "I'm going to the mosque."

Syakirah nodded and entered the room. As she was closing the door, Imran turned. He told Syakirah that he would be in the study room that night and the rest of the nights Syakirah was there. She nodded again with a light smile.

~

The house slowly became quieter as the relatives and friends trickled out. The day had been a long one for everyone. As soon as their relatives left, Hanim, Hidayat and Syakirah's parents retired for the night. Iskandar and his family were the last to leave the house. Imran and Syakirah saw them out. Marina whispered to Syakirah. "Take good care of him. You're the only woman he's got now."

As they walked to their separate rooms, Imran stopped. "Syira, thank you."

"You're welcome, Imran. But please stop saying that. I'm just doing what I'm supposed to do. Alhamdulillah, all went well today."

They stood in the empty living room.

Imran closed his eyes and nodded lightly. "Are you still leaving on Monday?"

"Yes. I'm sorry, I wish I could stay longer..." Syakirah said apologetically.

"I understand. What you have done is...so much already. I'm grateful, alhamdulillah," Imran smiled.

"I'll see you tomorrow morning, Imran, insha Allah."

"Insha Allah."

~

Imran had been in the study room since after Fajr prayer. He went to Hidayat's room to talk to him. Hidayat had been very quiet since they came back from the cemetery the day before and Imran thought he needed time to deal with their mother's death. Iskandar came that morning. Imran asked him to talk to Hidayat and suggested that their youngest brother spend time with the twins. They agreed Hidayat was still in shock and it would be good to get him out of the house for a while. Hidayat agreed to go with Iskandar.

After Syakirah accompanied her parents to the airport, she helped Hanim run some errands for the family. Syakirah noticed how much like Saleha her new sister-in-law was. The easy bonding she had felt for Saleha continued with Hanim, and she really enjoyed her company.

~

Syakirah said goodbye to Hanim, Hidayat, Iskandar, and Marina. Ani called her to say goodbye and promised to see her soon. Imran drove her to the airport. They were both quiet until they were half way there.

"Syira, I've something to tell you."

"Yes."

"About our marriage…well, you agreed to wait."

"Yes, I did."

"The marriage is a bond to my mother," Imran explained.

"In memory of her," Syakirah added.

Imran nodded. "We both know that I was fulfilling her wish."

"Yes, me too, Imran. You heard when I told Uncle Zaid that I agreed to this marriage more for her sake than for myself."

Imran nodded. "And we came to the decision with Allah Ta'ala's help...His guidance. That means this marriage is His choice for us. We may not have had enough time to get to know each other well enough to want this marriage for ourselves, but I believe we can be friends until we are both ready emotionally, insha Allah."

Syakirah agreed.

For the first time she saw peace in the man who was now her husband. She studied him and was touched by what he said.

"Being friends sounds great, I think." She meant that.

Imran smiled at her.

"So, you're okay with this?" Imran asked to confirm.

"Yes, insha Allah."

"Thank you, my friend." Imran teased her with the name and smiled. Syakirah returned his smile. They felt a subtle change in their relationship.

"You're welcome."

CHAPTER 24

Sykirah was grateful for the normalcy of the college environment and dove into her work with relish. The emotions of the wedding and Saleha's death could be put on the backburner while she worked. After getting back the day before, she busied herself with preparation for the new semester. She thought about Saleha constantly while she wasn't working and prayed for her. The conversation she had with Imran on their way to the airport somehow helped to keep the heaviness in her heart at bay.

Syakirah was heading for the Language Center when she saw Yasmin's car pulling into the parking lot. Her friend signaled her to wait.

"All went well in JB?" Yasmin asked as they walked to the Language Center.

"Yes, alhamdulillah. Everything was beautifully done. The family is taking it well, all things considered, though I feel particularly sad for Hidayat. He's the baby of the family after all, and he's been hit hard and without warning."

"How is Imran? What's going on between you two?" Yasmin asked what she had wanted to ask.

"He's doing well. Tired and sad, but he'll be OK, insha Allah. We talked… Imran and I. And we agreed to wait…to get to know each other better, insha Allah."

Yasmin was surprised to see Syakirah so calm as she explained this. "So, you're okay? You seem so serene."

"Yes. I surprised myself too. But I have faith in Imran. In fact, in a weird way, I was comforted by his presence. He needs time and I've nothing to lose by giving it to him. I need time myself… the marriage was a rush."

Yasmin listened attentively. "In other words, you're prolonging the engagement period…I heard this is practiced in some Muslim countries."

"Well, yes, if you want to put it that way." Syakirah said, smiling at Yasmin.

"But, you know what? This kind of engagement would make close proximity permissible," Yasmin teased.

"Mrs. Yasmin…I'm okay with the way things are right now. The rest I'm leaving to Allah Ta'ala. Remember that *hadith* in my office?"

Yasmin nodded as they recalled what the framed hadith said: "*If you put your whole trust in Allah (swt), as you ought, He most certainly will satisfy your needs, as He satisfies those of the birds. They come out hungry in the morning, but return full to their nests*" (Tirmidhi).

Yasmin wondered about this change of heart in her friend. She recalled their conversation about trust. Syakirah tried hard to ignore Imran and refrained from having any affection for him. That was before the wedding and before Saleha passed away. Had Syakirah let herself feel love again? Yasmin silently thought so.

～

Imran checked to see if Hidayat was ready. They were leaving that morning for KL. Ani had asked Imran to give her a lift to her friend's boutique. They could also meet Syakirah together.

"I'm ready to go." Hidayat told his brother.

Imran noticed Hidayat had lost weight since their mother's death a week ago. Hidayat told him not to worry, but Imran decided to ask Syakirah to keep an eye on him nonetheless.

They reached the college at around two. After leaving Hidayat at his hostel, Imran took Ani to the boutique. They promised to meet at Syakirah's place later in the evening before Imran left for JB.

~

Syakirah was helping Lily move her belongings to her car when Imran's car pulled up. When Lily found out that Syakirah was engaged, she made plans to move, against Syakirah's protests. An old friend of Lily's had recently moved to town, so the timing was perfect, as Lily said.

Syakirah introduced Imran to Lily before she left, her car loaded with boxes. The newlyweds made small talk as they entered the living room and got comfortable. Imran took a seat on the sofa while Syakirah went to the kitchen to prepare drinks.

Imran studied the décor of the living room as he took a seat on the sofa. The last time he was there, he was too occupied to notice. His wife's preferences, it turned out, leaned toward the warm and welcoming (and, perhaps unexpectedly, structured) rather than ostentatious and extravagant. He liked it. Cornflower blue and cream checkered curtains adorned the windows and complemented the furniture, which was tastefully arranged. The curtains perfectly matched the tablecloth and the cushions on the sofa. Behind him, against the wall, was a red apple-shaped clock. Two full bookshelves stood side by side against the wall near the twin windows looking out to the garage. The wall opposite the windows was decorated with a framed picture of a waterfall. He smiled when he saw two Scrabble boxes on the small table below the picture. They reminded him of the Language Camp. He walked to the bookshelves and saw a set of Quran commentary by Sayyid Qutb titled *In the Shade of the Qur'an*. He picked up one of the volumes. Standing by window, he flipped through the book. On the inside of the front cover the name *Syakirah* was written.

Syakirah entered the living room with a tray of drinks. She looked at the man standing in her living room. That was the first time they were together alone in that house. Sensing her presence, Imran placed the book back on the shelf and returned to his seat.

"This is a nice home, Syira," Imran complimented.

Syakirah sat across Imran before responding to his compliment.

"Alhamdulillah. I like it because it's a bit far from the noises. Peace and quiet are valuable commodities in KL," Syakirah smiled thoughtfully.

Imran nodded and smiled back in agreement with her explanation. Their eyes met and Syakirah quickly moved her attention to the drinks. She poured tea into the cups and invited him to drink.

"Hidayat's changed a lot since Mom died. I'm worried about him." Imran changed the subject.

"Did you talk to him about it?"

"Yes. He said he's okay. Iskandar thinks we should keep an eye on him. He was very close to Mom, so her death must have hit him hard."

"I guess so. The same happened to my brother Ashraff when my mother died."

Syakirah told Imran about the circumstances surrounding her mother's passing and how the family coped. Neither had ever mentioned much about Syakirah's family since they had known each other, but now seemed a great time to catch Imran up about his new wife. The new friends found themselves comfortable getting to know each other over tea.

They were engrossed in conversation when Ani gave a salam at the door. She was happy to see the couple enjoying each other's company. *Saleha would have loved to see them together,* she thought. Syakirah invited her in and asked how she was doing.

"I tried to get here sooner but you know how things are at a boutique, Syira."

"Do you have to be back tonight too, Aunt Ani?"

"No, dear. I'm leaving tomorrow afternoon. I've another meeting tomorrow with a friend."

"So, you could stay here tonight. Lily won't be back until tomorrow to pick up the rest of her things."

"That sounds like a good offer, Aunt Ani." Imran added.

Ani smiled at Syakirah. She had thought of asking Syakirah if she could stay overnight at the house, so she gladly accepted.

Having the couple there by themselves gave Ani an opportunity to gauge the couple's feelings about the wedding and marriage. "I just want to make sure you both are okay since everything happened so fast." Ani wondered if this couple would have proceeded with the wedding if Saleha had passed away before the wedding day, and their looks between each other gave no hint as to their thoughts.

Imran started, "Aunt Ani, I think we're both fine with this." Syakirah watched Imran and glanced at Ani. "Mom has given us something precious and we plan on taking care of it, insha Allah."

"Imran and I are both okay with the way things are now, Aunt Ani."

"I'm happy to hear that, alhamdulillah," Ani told Imran and smiled at Syakirah who was sitting to her right.

"We both need time to get used to the idea of being married," Syakirah said earnestly, "and we're both willing to give each other time to sort things out."

"And I like Syira very much," Imran said matter-of-factly.

"And I like him, too," Syakirah finished, nodding at her husband.

Ani watched their friendly exchanges. The two of them seemed so at ease with each other. She believed this couple would find a way to each other's hearts, sooner than later, insha Allah. They only need time and Allah (swt) would see to the rest.

As Imran was leaving, he repeated his request that Syakirah keep an eye on Hidayat. Syakirah agreed to call him if she noticed anything worrisome. After he left, Syakirah busied herself with her class preparation while Ani rested in Lily's room. Just as Syakirah was about to retire to bed, Ani came out of her room.

"Syira, there's something I should have told you earlier about Imran." Ani told Syakirah about Kaira.

CHAPTER 25

A few weeks had passed since Saleha's death. Imran and Syakirah talked to each other every now and then about Hidayat, who was adjusting to Saleha's departure. Syakirah told Imran that his brother looked better now than he did the day he returned to the college.

Iskandar and Umar both asked Imran when Syakirah would move to JB. He told them some details of their relationship, including the couple's self-imposed waiting period. Imran and Syakirah decided to reevaluate their relationship and marriage at the end of the semester. The relationship was constantly on Imran's mind, however, and Umar found himself defending Imran's decision to wait.

"How possibly can you think that you're ready to make it permanent?" Umar asked.

"Sometimes I think I'm more than ready, pal. I just wish I had married her sooner."

"There's a good cause behind everything Allah Ta'ala made," Umar reminded his friend. "So where are you going?"

"The place with the beach," Imran answered.

Umar nodded, thinking that Desaru Resort might be just the place for Imran to sort out his relationship with his wife.

"May Allah show you the way, insha Allah."

"Insha Allah."

~

Before going to the resort, Imran was in KL for a meeting. He visited Syakirah and was glad to learn that Hidayat was doing fine. The three of them went to dinner and talked about Hanim's upcoming wedding, which would take place during the semester break. After sending Hidayat back to the college, the couple drove to Syakirah's place.

When Imran's car stopped in front of her house, Syakirah turned to him. "Thank you, Imran, I've enjoyed our dinner."

Imran smiled and said, "Me, too."

"I guess, you're leaving tomorrow morning?"

"Around eight, insha Allah, to Desaru Resort."

"Business?" Syakirah asked, a little surprised that he was not going home.

Imran smiled. "No."

Syakirah felt ill at ease.

Studying her face, Imran's face turned serious. "I need to sort out some things about us."

Syakirah nodded slightly. She did not want to ask further. "So see you then, insha Allah."

"Insha Allah."

As she was about to get out of the car, she remembered something. "Imran, I've decided to tell my parents about our relationship."

The timing was just right, Imran thought, since he himself was determined to return from the resort with a decision. He nodded in agreement.

"You're okay with this?"

"Yes, and thank you, Syira, for asking my opinion. That's part of how a marriage works, I believe." He grinned.

Syakirah nodded with a smile. Imran was right. At that moment, she felt good about their future.

Imran added, "They're the only parents we've got now, so let's be honest with them."

Syakirah looked at him, wanting to believe there was more to what he was saying, but she kept her mouth shut.

"I'll call you soon, insha Allah."

She nodded, "Insha Allah."

Syakirah sat her stepmother and father down to inform them about her marriage. Her stepmother was totally overwhelmed by the truth of the circumstances. Her father was less visibly upset, but understandably concerned. The couple had so much wanted their daughter to be married, but they did not expect it to happen *that* way. At the same time they tried to understand why their daughter would agree to such an arrangement.

"Syira, we just want to see you happy. Are you happy now?"

"Mom, I've done my best to fulfill a dying woman's wish. She wanted to see her son married before she died. And she thought she had found the right choice for him. So, we did it...for her."

"But what about you? Your feelings, Syira? How do you feel about Imran?" Her father asked.

"Honestly Dad, when I agreed, I didn't consider my own feelings...I didn't even think much about how you all might feel... forgive me for that. My focus was to make her happy for the last time...I loved her, Dad."

Her father articulated his realization, "It was like doing it for your mother." His wife looked at him. "She wanted to see you married... So, your marriage was like a gift for your mother..."

Syakirah nodded her head and let it sink in.

Her father was touched by her deep love for her mother. The three of them were in tears. Her stepmother hugged her.

"Oh, dear...I'm sorry if I've said anything hurtful just now..."

"No, Mom, nothing to apologize for. Nobody knew except me." She paused and with a light smile she added, "... and Yasmin."

"Dad, you taught me never to take Islamic teachings lightly. Imran feels the same way; you'll like that about him. We both performed Istikharah prayers—a lot of them—before agreeing to marry. This means that we married each other believing that we were chosen by Allah Ta'ala for each other.

"But," Syakirah continued, "We were rushed. We hardly know anything about one another. So we've agreed to wait until we are both emotionally ready."

Her stepmother wondered how Syakirah really felt now about Imran. "After almost three months in a relationship, how do you feel about him?"

Syakirah smiled at her stepmother, then turned to her father. "We're friends now. I used to have problems even talking with Imran Hakim...but not anymore now. We genuinely like each other and enjoy each other's company. We both want to keep this marriage, but we need time...we don't want to rush."

Her parents' silence Syakirah took as doubt.

"Dad, Mom...I know your concern about my feelings, but I'm fine, alhamdulillah. Whatever the consequence, I will accept it as fate from Allah Ta'ala. I will, redha, be pleased with His decree. But I still need your blessings and your acceptance. And pray for us. We never meant to hurt anyone. I was just keeping the secret because I already gave my word to Aunt Ani and Imran.

But Imran and I recently agreed to tell you both. Dad, Mom...I love and respect you both."

"We just want you to be happy, dear." Her father told her.

"Yes, Syira, we do," her stepmother added.

"I know." Syakirah smiled. "I love you both. Thank you for understanding."

CHAPTER 26

Syakirah received a call from Imran who was coming to KL the next day with Ani. Syakirah was happy to hear from him as he had not called her since he left for the resort. He invited Syakirah to a thanksgiving party in JB, the day before Hanim's wedding.

~

Syakirah was about to pray when she heard the sound of a car pulling up in front of her house. She peeped through the window and saw Imran and Ani getting out of a cab. She welcomed them and they prayed Dhuhur together before eating lunch. After lunch and some conversation, they left in Syakirah's car to pick up Hidayat for a visit to Bukit Cahaya.

Hidayat was happy to be in the company of the three of them. Imran teased him for having too much fun.

"Of course. It's not like everyday I get to be together with you and Kak Syira," Hidayat answered, smiling at Syakirah

"And me?" Ani pretended to feel neglected.

"It goes without saying, Aunt Ani, it's an honor and privilege," Hidayat replied gallantly.

The conversation started with Hidayat's writing, then turned to Hanim's wedding.

"Mom would be happy to be here with us… and to see Kak Hanim married." Hidayat sounded a little sad.

"Yes. But she'd be happier to see you happy with us and at the wedding, insha Allah."

Hidayat smiled, conceded, and changed the subject "You're right… so where are we going tomorrow?" he asked.

"Our flight is at three in the afternoon. Wherever you want to go in the morning… that is, if Sunday isn't your sleep-in day," Imran teased.

The next day, Syakirah and Ani were reading the Quran in Syakirah's room when Imran and Hidayat came back from Fajr prayer at the *surau* nearby. Hidayat had insisted on sleeping on the couch the night before, but didn't argue when Imran suggested they stay in Lily's old room together while Ani stayed with Syakirah. At ten, they left the house to go sight-seeing in the country. Hidayat was happy that they did this especially for him.

～

"How long will you two wait?" Yasmin asked, worried. Yasmin closed the door and sat across from her friend.

"When we're both ready, insha Allah." *Imran should have made a decision by now,* Syakirah thought, disappointed.

"I just pray that it won't be too long."

"Really." This was a statement and not a question.

"I know you both agreed to wait, but somehow the longer the wait, the more I'm beginning to see something in you…"

Syakirah interrupted, trying to mask her feelings. "What do you see?"

Yasmin took a deep breath. "I see that you're hurting, Syira. I think you care about Imran much more than you're letting on. You seem so sad lately. At first I thought you were missing Aunt

Saleha so much, but now you look like you're about to lose your best friend. Are you afraid that Imran might leave you, Syira?"

Syakirah stood silently, not wanting to answer.

"Syira, are you?" Yasmin asked again in a gentle voice.

"I don't know Min... He has really grown on me. I care so much about him now...Allah Ta'ala made it happen...before the marriage I tried so hard not to love him...until I was sure I could trust him," Syakirah said while tears welled in her eyes.

She continued, "But I do love Imran...his commitment to his family and work, especially to his faith...I've witnessed all these since the day we got engaged. I can't help it the way I feel. Yes, I do love him... in Allah," Syakirah admitted and paused. "But, I don't know whether he even wants me. He was supposed to give me an answer last week, yes or no, but he hasn't. How can I possibly care about a man who cannot commit to staying married to me?" Syakirah voiced the concerns she'd kept in for too long. "Subhanallah... make dua'a for me to have patience, because I certainly don't trust him!"

Yasmin was happy to know that her friend was in love with Imran, and was somewhat more optimistic than she about Imran's feelings towards her. However, she remained guarded in voicing her opinion as she had very little to base it on except instinct.

"Does Imran know how you feel?"

"No. We both acknowledge that we like each other better now. We even call each other 'my friend.'" Syakirah smiled through her tears as she considered the irony.

"Don't you think he should know how you feel now?"

"I'd rather wait until he's ready. I do want to make this marriage work...to please Allah Ta'ala because I gave my consent on the wedding day and the marriage was solemnized before Him."

"But, you are afraid it won't work out..." Yasmin pointed out.

"I pray that I don't have to go through that... again. I want to be married and to love my husband... But oh, Min, Allah Ta'ala is enough for me! *Hasbi Allah wa ni'mal wakil* (Allah sufficeth me)... *"There is no God but He; On Him is my trust—He the Lord of the Throne (of Glory) Supreme!"* (Qur'an 7:129)

~

Syakirah was happy to receive a call from her parents. Her stepmother told her that Nadhirah had *finally* given birth, masha Allah, and that they planned an *'aqiqah* ceremony for the baby boy. Syakirah made plans to come home after Hanim's wedding and promised her parents to invite Imran to their home and to the ceremony.

When the last class before the break concluded Syakirah rushed home to finish packing for her trip to JB and back home. She looked forward to the flight, which would be much more peaceful than the bus full of college students that Hidayat chose for transportation.

Later that afternoon, Yasmin picked her up to go to the airport. Their conversation turned to Syakirah's marriage. "Syira, this is not just a waiting period before a consummation of a marriage. It's about your future. At this point, dear, I'd think he would have made a decision one way or the other," Yasmin said, concerned. She was worried that the little trust her friend had begun to have for Imran would vanish if the waiting period prolonged. "I hope that when you come back from break, things will be settled either way, insha Allah."

Syakirah had hoped as well. Imran had all but promised that he would talk to her about their relationship after his trip to the resort. It was unsettling, not knowing her future as it was determined by Allah and this man. She was in love after all, whether or not he felt the same. "Insha Allah," she said, agreeing with Yasmin.

"I just want my friend back. The one who is happy and high spirited to start the second half of the school year."

Syakirah smiled at Yasmin. "Insha Allah. I've missed her, too."

CHAPTER 27

On the way back from the airport, Imran and Syakirah caught up on each other's news. Hanim, it turned out, wanted Syakirah to be her bridesmaid. Syakirah felt it an honor to do that for her and looked forward to the experience. Syakirah's mood was elevated on the drive, and she pushed thoughts of her marriage to the side. It did no good to dwell on their unfinished business on such a beautiful day, when he apparently was not ready and limited their conversation to enjoyable, pleasant, easy topics. Neither was she prepared to discuss her marriage in a car, away from home, and without emotional support when the conversation could result in its termination. Better to enjoy the trip, the company, and be thankful. *Alhamdulillah*, she thought, *what a glorious day!*

Hanim was happy to see Syakirah and the two spent the rest of the day preparing for the thanksgiving party and the wedding. It was after Maghrib and Syakirah just finished her prayer when Imran came to their room. *Now it would get serious*, she thought as she looked at his calm but pained face.

"I'm not sure how to begin. But I guess I'll tell you something that you should know, which may explain the decisions I've made," he began, telling Syakirah about Kaira.

Syakirah listened and nodded her understanding. She did not interrupt, or tell him that Ani had already told her about Kaira. She wanted to hear it from Imran himself.

"You still miss her. I can tell that. Whatever you decide, I'll accept and try to understand, insha Allah."

Imran nodded.

"I was very young then. And I held on to her memory for some time until Aunt Ani and Uncle Zaid helped me see reality again. But, she's my past and you're in my life now, my 'amanah', a trust from Allah Ta'ala. Syira, I....." Imran was interrupted when Hidayat called him.

"This can wait, insha Allah. When we are not interrupted." Syakirah smiled while her brother-in-law continued calling Imran's name.

Imran smiled in agreement. After he left the room, she sat on the bed wondering what Imran was about to tell her just now. Had he make a decision at the resort or hadn't he?

~

The thanksgiving party ended around ten. Some of the guests stayed to clean up and to make a few last arrangements for the wedding the next day, but eventually, they went home to their families. There remaining were family members. Imran asked them all to gather at the living room.

"This is something that I should have done sooner but alhamdulillah, better late than never," he grinned. Imran picked up a small box. "This was left by Mom as a gift for our wedding." He turned to look at Syakirah. "At first I wanted to share it only with Syakirah. But Mom left a small note and after reading it, I realize she wanted to present this gift in front of the family."

"Syira, come here please." Imran signaled for Syakirah to come to his side.

The family and relatives who stayed behind were now watching them. They all smiled expectantly. Syakirah was nervous about what was about to happen. Imran hadn't told her about this. Could he be announcing his decision about their marriage? Did he want to honor Saleha's wish for real and finally make this marriage work? This thought crossed her mind, but she quickly erased it.

"She wanted you to have this. Thank you for being with her during her last days. She loved you very much."

Imran placed a sapphire ring on Syakirah's finger. She was touched by the gift. Tears welled up in her eyes as she looked at Imran. He returned the look with a tender and loving smile. Syakirah was embarrassed for crying, but she was not alone; Hanim and Marina were in tears too.

"I'll keep this as a memory of her. Forever, insha Allah." They looked into each other's eyes. Imran nodded with a smile.

It was late and Hanim was to be married in the morning. As the men left, the women gathered around Syakirah to admire the ring. Syakirah looked around for Imran but he was escorting relatives to their cars.

Half an hour later, Syakirah went to her room and changed into her nightgown. She wondered what Imran was going to say in their room earlier. Allah (swt) knew the best, she thought.

~

Hanim's beautiful wedding reminded Syakirah of her own. As Syakirah's mind visited the past, she caught a glance from Imran. When the 'aqad was complete, they caught each other's eyes again and smiled.

Hanim was beaming and looked so beautiful. Syakirah congratulated her with a big hug and kiss. They both had happy tears as they remembered Saleha who would have been the happiest had she been there. Syakirah promised Hanim that she would stay another day but had to get home to see her own family and the new baby. The two women had grown very fond of each other.

Imran accepted the invitation to the 'aqiqah ceremony at his in-laws' house but said that he would have to come back on the same day. Syakirah understood. Between the business, caring for his siblings, and running his home, he must have had a million things to do. She thought it gracious and generous that Imran accepted her parents' invitation despite his busy schedule.

Imran drove Syakirah to the airport. He didn't mention anything about their talk the night before and Syakirah didn't want to push it. As much as she wanted to know what he was going to say, somehow she wanted to put off hearing it. She was still touched by what had taken place after the party, and looked at the ring in remembrance. Imran noticed her admiring it.

"She had it all planned," Imran said.

"Yes and she'd have been happy yesterday to see Hanim."

"But we should be grateful to Allah Ta'ala for allowing her to do as much as she had done for us."

Syakirah looked at him. She could not really understand what he meant. Was he referring to their marriage?

Before Syakirah boarded the plane, Imran promised to meet her in KB the next day. He looked at Syakirah with affection and they parted with a smile.

~

Imran sat in the big chair in the study room, his favorite chair by the window. He thought about his mother, Kaira, and Syakirah. His mother had loved both women: Kaira for her son's sake, and Syira, independent of him. Imran admitted to himself that Syakirah shared some of Kaira's qualities. Her passion for work, her gentleness, and her faith all reminded him of Kaira. Perhaps these traits influenced Saleha in choosing Syakirah for his wife? *Syakirah, though, is certainly not Kaira,* Imran thought with a smile. Syakirah was not afraid to voice her opinion. She was outspoken when defending herself, and if she was ticked off, you did not want to be near her. Imran laughed out loud. He missed seeing the feisty side of her, which he had not seen lately.

~

As promised, Syakirah met Imran at the airport. As they discussed the details of the 'aqiqah ceremony, Syakirah warned him that none of her family except her parents knew the circumstances of their marriage.

"Thank you for being patient, Syira."

Syakirah nodded.

"I must be the most selfish man you've ever met." A small laugh escaped Imran's mouth.

"For asking me to wait?" Syakirah smiled.

"Yes."

"I did it because I want to…as Uncle Zaid said, as long as we do this in good faith and for Allah's sake, insha Allah, the best will come out of it, whatever that is. I respect your feelings, Imran, and cannot ask more."

"Am I entitled to that respect, having asked so much from you… for taking months out of your life?"

"I've not much to lose by giving it to you, Imran."

Imran was silent for a moment then said, "I'm asking you again here, Syira."

"Yes?"

"Remember about us being friends?"

Syakirah nodded.

"I hope to keep your friendship no matter what the future holds for us in this marriage, insha Allah."

Syakirah wished he would be less vague. She was determined more than ever to hide her feelings for Imran, but she doubted if she could do it for much longer. She could not help her feelings at this point; she loved Imran. She loved his family. She wanted a life and a future with him. She simply didn't trust him not to break her heart.

"If we're both okay with it, we leave it to Allah Ta'ala to decide the rest," Imran said, sounding convinced that he wanted to make it work. If they were meant to be in the marriage, Allah (swt) would grant them love and affection for each other. With this thought, he smiled as he also recalled the verse, *"And He hath put affection between their hearts; not if thou hadst spent all that is in the earth could thou have produced that affection but Allah hath done it; for He is Exalted in might Wise."* (Qur'an 8:63)

CHAPTER 28

Since meeting at Syakirah's parents' house, Imran and Syakirah kept in touch more, keeping the other informed about work and their families. Imran came to KL a couple of times for business and to see Hidayat and Syakirah. The couple progressively showed more affection toward each other.

Syakirah just finished her last class for the day when Imran called her at her office. He said he wanted to meet her to discuss their marriage. She agreed to see him after finishing her classes on Thursday. Syakirah suddenly was nervous thinking of Imran's final decision about their marriage. She kept reminding herself, whatever his decision, she would have to accept it. At least, she thought, this isn't coming out of the blue, like Manaf's rude awakening had. He had made the decision for both of them without her being let in on it. Manaf ended everything with her to marry someone else.

On the day they promised to meet, Syakirah received a call from Imran's secretary just before going to her last class, canceling their meeting. Syakirah was relieved and her nervousness largely gone.

However, when two days went by and she still had not heard from Imran, she began to wonder if he was trying to avoid telling her that he wanted to end their marriage. Again she reminded herself to trust that Imran would not make such a cowardly decision. She whispered to convince herself, "You're overanalyzing this, Syira. He must be busy with work!" But what if she was wrong?

~

The next day Imran called just after Isha' prayer, while Syakirah was debating whether to call Imran herself.

"I apologize for not making it there. I spent two days cooped up in the office working on an emergency. Even calling you slipped my mind. I'm sorry, Syira."

"Imran, really you don't owe me any explanation."

"I do, though. I'm sorry for breaking our date."

Syakirah smiled. "I guess we have to find another time to meet, insha Allah."

"Insha Allah, we will. But this week I don't think I can spare the time. I'm sorry."

"I guess I'm busy too. We have a Language Camp this weekend, insha Allah. So perhaps after this week, then. Anyway I'm sure whatever we're going to talk about, it's just a simple matter…a matter of technicality I assume…" She laughed a little, trying to cover up her nervousness, thinking about their marriage.

Imran was quiet and that made Syakirah feel awkward.

"Syira, do you trust me?" Imran asked in a serious voice. After a several seconds of awkward silence, he asked her again.

"What would make you think I didn't?" Syakirah asked, her voice shaky.

"I don't know… I have a feeling that you don't really trust my decision regarding our marriage… as if I'm taking the marriage, our futures, and our respective feelings too lightly. Is that true?"

"I think we're doing fine. We're friends and being friends, we're building trust in our friendship, insha Allah," Syakirah answered, avoiding the question.

"You haven't answered my question. What's going on here, Syira?" Imran persisted.

By this time, Syakirah was on the verge of crying and was grateful that Imran was not there to witness.

"Syira?" Imran's voice was gentle and caring.

"I'm sorry, Imran," she blurted as the tears came relentlessly in spite of her.

Imran was unsettled by her crying. The matters of the heart had always been a very personal topic with him. He'd always thought that feelings should be no one else's business other than the owner of the heart. Somehow, this was different. Whatever his wife was feeling, it was hurting her deeply, and it pained him to know this.

"I know I haven't been an easy guy to deal with, Syira, but I think we know each other well enough, and like each other well enough, to confide in each other. Please talk to me…"

Imran could be trusted for that, insha Allah, Syakirah thought. She started the story of Manaf. "There was a man in my life… many years ago…I was young, but I believed and trusted that we were meant for each other. My mother knew about him and gave us her blessing. My Dad never knew…this was kind of a secret between my Mom and me…and it died with her…"

Syakirah told Imran everything about her relationship with Manaf. She omitted nothing— whereas she had not even confided in Yasmin the most painful details of their relationship.

"I trusted him completely…no secrets between us, I thought. When I left Malaysia to go to school in the States, he came to the airport with our other friends. He eventually would go to Australia for school, too.

"She was there at the airport...the woman he eventually married. I always knew her as his sister. She was the daughter of the couple who adopted him after his biological parents died. She and Manaf grew up in the same house, and became engaged before he left for Australia. But he never told me about the engagement—not even when we realized we had fallen for each other while he was in Australia.

"He could have told me sooner...I wouldn't have let myself love someone who's engaged to another woman, but for some absurd reason, he wanted to keep the engagement a secret from me. He said he felt indebted to the family that raised him.

"I felt so betrayed. I *was* betrayed. I could have still loved him if he had chosen me after telling me the truth, and I would have respected him if he hadn't...instead, not only did I lose him...I lost trust in him, in myself, and in finding love again."

She paused. "With that last phone call, we parted as friends. We did write twice to each other before I returned to Malaysia. That was when I learned the details about him, his family and the engagement. But really... whatever hopes I had about my future with him, or any man... were gone by the time I came home. I remember the day I tossed all those expectations out the window, I felt so empty inside and so alone...I cried because it hurt so much... the only words that I could say were '*Ya Allah*.' Those words led me to the road of recovery."

Imran's eyes opened and he looked up, silently thanking Allah for Syakirah's candor. Somehow, despite the pain he heard in her voice and tears and felt in his heart, he was relieved that he was not the only one with a past. "Tragedies in life bring us closer to Allah Ta'ala." He quoted a verse in the Quran:

No calamity befalls, but with the Leave [i.e. decision and Qadar (Divine Preordainments)] of Allah, and whosoever believes

in Allah, He guides his heart [to the true Faith with certainty, i.e.
what has befallen him was already written for him by Allah from
the Qadar (Divine Preordainments)],and Allah is the All-Knower
of everything. (Qur'an 64:11)

"Alhamdulillah, I met some good Muslim sisters at my university who helped me pick up the pieces… until I became strong
again…with Allah Ta'ala's love, His mercy and help. Months later
I realized in accordance with Islamic teachings that it was wrong
of me to be in love with a man I was not married to, or certain to
marry. Manaf remains my brother in faith, and I tell myself that
he wanted me to be happy, but I've rejected the idea of marriage
until I met your mother." Syakirah sighed. "So, you see why it
was hard for me when you ask about trust."

Imran was touched. "Thank you for trusting in me, Syira…
and for sharing this with me."

Syakirah responded, "Thank you too for helping me see that
I am capable of trust to some extent. It'll take some time to live
with it again. Let's hope, as friends, we can build this trust in
each other…whatever your decision, insha Allah."

"Insha Allah." Imran had almost forgotten. He did not want
to discuss their marriage over the phone, especially not now that
Syakirah's feelings were exposed and tender. She was right in
saying that they were building the trust through their friendship.
They needed to have trust if they wanted to make their marriage
work insha Allah.

CHAPTER 29

Syakirah and Yasmin were again the advisors for the Language Camp, which was held at Bagan Nakhoda Omar beach this semester. It was a secluded beach in Sabak Bernam district, accessible by a tarred road that ran through several traditional villages. It was an idyllic combination of sun, sand, and sea.

Syakirah and Yasmin were pleased with students' participation in the language games on the first night. Hidayat enjoyed collecting information for his article.

Later, Yasmin studied her friend who was chatting with students. Syakirah had told her that her love for Imran would not let her give up on her marriage. She would be patient and accept Imran's decision as Allah Ta'ala's command.

As she sat preoccupied, Yasmin failed to notice Imran approaching, who greeted her with "Assalamu'alaikum, Mrs. Yasmin!"

Turning her head to the familiar voice, she looked at a smiling Imran with mild surprise and pleasure that Syakirah's husband had shown up at an event that was so important to his wife and brother. "Wa'alaikumussalam…Imran…what a surprise…" Yasmin invited him to sit but Imran was busy scanning the canteen.

Imran spotted Syakirah, who was absorbed in a discussion with the students. Upon discovering her, he looked at Yasmin, distracted, and about to beg a favor.

"It must be really important if you've come here looking for her," Yasmin quipped.

"Something that should be done now or never. I've taken too much time already. It's time I do things right once and for all, insha Allah."

Could he have used a more ambiguous statement? Yasmin thought wryly. She hoped for a happy ending for Imran and Syakirah, but she would have to wait until Imran was ready to spill it.

"I'm lost here but whatever it is, it must have to do with my friend's future?" Yasmin teased.

Imran smiled and nodded. "I need to talk to Syira alone for… maybe an hour tomorrow morning. I was hoping you could cover for her. Maybe after the start of the first activity, insha Allah?"

"No problem, insha Allah. But why don't you talk to her tonight?"

"Tomorrow, insha Allah. Just trust me on this one, okay?" Imran grinned and Yasmin nodded and smiled, recognizing the answer to the unspoken question.

No sooner had Imran and Yasmin set up the plan for the morning, but Syakirah approached their table. Imran stood and they all exchanged salams. Syakirah took her seat.

"How are you Imran?" Syakirah gave him a friendly smile. She was happy to see him. *He looked much happier than the last time they talked*, she thought. He must have come for Hidayat.

"Alhamdulillah. You?" He thought Syakirah looked as happy as he with the unplanned meeting.

"Alhamdulillah…as you can see for yourself. Are you checking on your little brother tonight?" Syakirah sounded calm and cheerful.

"Yes, and my wife too. I just missed tonight's campfire I guess," Imran said to Syakirah and glanced at Yasmin.

"Yeah, you just did. We're closing up the canteen in an hour. So, it's nice meeting you again in a language camp," Syakirah laughed, remembering their last language camp.

"Same here!" Imran grinned.

Yasmin observed the couple's small talk. *What a change a semester makes,* she thought, smiling and thanking Allah. *That's love.*

"Look who's coming now!" Yasmin informed and they all turned to look at Hidayat.

The brothers shook hands with salams and Hidayat filled Imran in on his research and story. A few minutes later, Syakirah cued Yasmin to help clean up the canteen and let the men talk. Seeing this, the brothers insisted on helping, vowing to continue their conversation later in the tent.

A shattering glass interrupted the canteen clean-up. Syakirah dropped a glass and she and Imran instinctively stooped to pick up the glass. Without thinking, Imran reached for Syakirah's hand when he saw that she had been cut.

"Let me look," Imran demanded, holding her hand.

"I'm fine..." Syakirah answered pulling her hand away gently while their eyes locked. "That was clumsy of me."

"Oh, it's... just glass. They shouldn't be using glass cups on a camping trip," Imran commented. They both stood up.

Yasmin called for Hidayat to bring a broom and commented, "We should have brought enough plastic cups. Did you cut your hand, Syira?"

"I'm fine," Syakirah sucked on her finger, embarrassed from all the attention. "Let's get this done."

"Are you sure?" Imran asked again looking at Syakirah with concern.

"Yes," she assured him.

Hidayat came with a broom and swept the pieces. Yasmin, Syakirah and Imran continued clearing, washing, and wiping until the canteen was clean. When they finished, they said good night and went to their tents.

"What exactly happened just now?" Yasmin asked Syakirah curiously as they walked to their tent.

"What? You saw it."

"Well, you looked uncomfortable in the canteen."

"One of the glasses had a chip in it and I dropped it. Cut my finger. That's it," Syakirah answered shortly.

"Then why are you so tense?" Yasmin couldn't see Syakirah's expression in the dark. But she could tell her friend was trying to hide something.

"He held my hand to see if I was hurt."

Yasmin was smiling in the dark. "And?"

"Well, I felt strange for a second... I'm not sure how I'm supposed to act around him. I hope Hidayat didn't get suspicious."

The night hid Yasmin's grin.

CHAPTER 30

And among His signs is that He created for you mates among yourselves that ye may dwell in tranquility with them and He has put love and Mercy between your (hearts); verily in that are signs for those who reflect. (Qur'an 30:21)

"Assalamu'alaikum, ladies!" Imran greeted with a big smile. He looked rugged and handsome in a dark blue t-shirt, black track pants, and dark gray sports shoes.

Syakirah and Yasmin, also dressed for outdoors, returned his salam. "Slept well last night?" Yasmin asked.

"He must have because he's sure in a good mood this morning," Syakirah teased, giving him a quick glance. They all laughed.

"Well, that depends on what Mrs. Yasmin has to say. So, about our deal yesterday?" Imran asked mischievously. Syakirah raised an eyebrow.

With a smile, Yasmin replied. "All set, she's yours until the Scrabble contest at eleven. She's one of the judges."

"Alhamdulillah! Thank you so much Mrs. Yasmin. Insha Allah, we'll be back by then," he assured her. He took a quick glance at Syakirah.

"Anytime, Brother. Assalamu'alaikum," Yasmin smiled.

"You two, what's cooking here? Why all the suspense? Will someone please tell me what's going on here?" Syakirah raised the other eyebrow with impatience.

"Ask Imran! I'm busy! Got to go! Assalamu'alaikum!"

"Wa'alaikumussalam," Syakirah answered, confused. She looked at Imran as he guided her to his car. "So?"

Imran smiled. "This way, Mrs. Syakirah!"

Syakirah stopped short and chuckled at her title.

Imran, working against the clock, urged her, "You are Mrs. Syakirah the last time I checked, right? Just follow me to the beach, please, Madame."

Syakirah followed him. She was surprised at the sudden change in Imran's character. She suddenly felt childishly excited. *What are you up to, Imran?* she asked herself.

They drove out of the camping area silently. Syakirah glanced at Imran once and he seemed composed. Their destination was only a few minutes from the camp. It was a secluded and especially beautiful part of the beach. From the passenger seat, Syakirah admired the scene. Tall coconut trees decorated white sandy fields, their long leaves swaying gently in rhythm with the morning breeze like graceful hands summoning the couple. A few birds dotted the blue morning sky. As the car moved towards Imran's destination, Syakirah's eyes rested on the mesmerizing and lonely sea beyond the coconut pillars.

Imran parked his car under one of the trees. The soft morning breeze greeted them as they got out of the car. Imran led the way as they walked toward the water's edge.

"Here we are!" Imran exclaimed as they stood about two meters from the water.

"Yes, and now what?" Syakirah asked, laughing. She turned to take in more of the gorgeous view. The water melted into the sky in the distant horizon.

Imran sat on the white sand and invited Syakirah to join him. She sat next to him while he stared out at the magnificent sea. The sun proudly sent its neon rays to brighten the new day. The couple was awed and humbled as they witnessed Allah's (swt) creation, one of His countless signs.

Surrendering to the glory of the Creator, Imran whispered. "Subhanallah." Then, without looking at her, he asked her, "Very beautiful and peaceful, right?"

"Yes, subhanallah."

"Beaches are special to my family, Syira. They capture many of our family moments and today I hope it will capture another moment." Imran paused and looked at her.

Syakirah searched his eyes for meaning. Slowly and soberly, she realized the reason he'd brought her here. Imran had finally come to a decision.

"I guess I'd better do this now. I have approximately one hour, twenty minutes." He smiled, glancing dramatically at his watch.

"You're making me nervous, Imran." Her excitement was mixed with anxiety. Her heart began to beat faster, and she was afraid that it would stop as it did on the night of Manaf's last phone call. Immediately she pushed the thought aside and remembered Allah Ta'ala. She prayed that He would protect her and give her strength to face whatever was to come. Imran's face turned serious. Syakirah could not predict what he'd say.

"Hasbi Allah wa ni'mal wakil," she said, calming herself down.

Observing her nervousness, Imran started, "Syira, first of all, I would like to apologize for taking your time and bringing you here. It's the best way I could think of. I could have waited until you returned to KL, but I didn't want to wait and waste any more time. I've wasted enough already."

Syakirah nodded her understanding, if not her agreement.

"I know you agreed with me to wait, but I'm sorry for pressuring you," he continued.

Syakirah interrupted him. "No, please don't apologize, Imran. There was a blessing in it, alhamdulillah. I had been afraid that waiting might lead to a repetition of my experience with Manaf, but this waiting period has been beneficial for both of us. We didn't know each other well enough to build a strong relationship, or even a friendship." Syakirah paused and smiled before continuing. "Allah guided us and we abided by His decision. We've had the opportunity to learn about each other, and since the wedding, I've learned who you are, Imran Hakim." She chuckled, "And if people knew how I felt the first time I met you, they would not believe how civilly I treat you now."

They both smiled as they recalled the incidents at Hillview, Dr. Norman's house and the earlier language camp. Imran nodded in agreement.

"And I learned that you are not Manaf, alhamdulillah," she concluded, disposing of the notion that she could mistrust Imran in the future, whatever it may hold.

Pleased, and taking a deep breath, Imran looked at Syakirah and began to tell her what was in his heart.

"*Indeed in the Messenger of Allah (swt), you have a good example to follow*," he said. "That's verse 21 in *Al-Ahzab* and I've kept it since the first time Uncle Zaid recited it to me many years ago. I was at the lowest point in my life…young and naïve. He wanted to wake me up from my long sleep…my depression after Kaira's death. When *Rasulullah (saw)*'s wife, Khadijah (ra) died, he was very sad and he missed her. His uncle's death and the treatment of the disbelievers, especially in Ta'if, culminated and that era was called the year of depression. But Allah Ta'ala helped him move on with his life. He married Sa'udah (ra). Later Allah Ta'ala cheered him up with a dream that led him to his marriage to A'isha (ra)."

They both looked at the vast space in front of them.

"I haven't brought you down here to give you a lesson about the life of our beloved Prophet (saw), Syira," Imran turned to her and continued. "My point here is I was far from being strong like Rasulullah (saw), but with the help of Allah Ta'ala I woke up from my long sleep. My parents tried almost everything possible to help me, but Allah the Most Gracious sent His help through Uncle Zaid. He helped me build my inner strength and make me closer to the Muslim man I should be. I went through a transformation. I was a man who thought the loss of his wife rendered the world meaningless, and with Allah's help I became a man who, though he still missed his wife, began to see the true meaning of love, life and death…and how all these are parts and parcels of a Muslim's life whose main purpose of living is to serve the only One, the Most Loving and the Most Merciful, Allah Ta'ala. Subhanallah!"

Syakirah was touched by Imran's story. How unexpectedly like her own, she thought. Allah (swt) replaced the loss of someone's presence in his life and in hers with a much better presence—His love and the love for Him!

"Love is a gift from Allah Ta'ala, Syira. Even one of His names is the Most Loving. Islam also recognizes the love a man has for women, children, wealth and others. It's *fitrah*, but these are all temporary possessions. They are all the pleasures of this present world's life."

"And He has reserved Paradise as the excellent return. It's in *Al-Imran*," Syakirah added with a smile.

Imran nodded and returned her smile. "When Allah Ta'ala blesses you with love for someone it becomes 'amanah', a trust that you must guard in the ways shown in His Book and by His Messenger (saw). Your love is only for Allah's sake, not for lust or any other selfish reason. Then He blesses you again when the love blossoms through marriage for His sake. Again you have another 'amanah' to guard. The boat of a new life sets sail. The journey is yet to be seen, but the best of destination is Jannah. So, the journey requires a captain with a solid grasp of Islamic guidelines. A lot of tests, challenges have to be faced and overcome. Some are predictable depending on your actions, but some you'd never expect…like an accidental death. To a Muslim with a solid grasp of Islamic teachings, death is a temporary separation. But, when faith, iman, is not solid, you may fail the test. Suddenly you forget that all these time when you were given love and life, neither were ever truly yours. They have always been Allah Ta'ala's properties. That's why love and life are 'amanah', trusts, to be guarded. When the time expires, Allah Ta'ala will take them back and you are free from the 'amanah.' Every time I reflect on my actions after Kaira died, I am struck by how weak my faith was." Imran paused.

"Kaira was a good Muslim woman, Syira. She inspired me to learn more about Islam when we were in the UK, but I didn't learn enough to understand that marriage was a trust, not a possession. I thought I knew it, but when Allah Ta'ala tested me with her death, I failed. I was suffering in my own boat. Luckily, alhamdulillah, the boat never sank, it just sailed aimlessly on a vast ocean. Whichever direction the wind pushed it, the boat just followed blindly."

Syakirah wondered what Imran meant by that. He did not seem like such a weak man. Then she remembered he was much younger then.

As if reading her mind, he continued. "I didn't drink or take drugs, if that's what you're wondering." He smiled at her. "But I let myself indulge in so much sadness that it consumed me to the point I lost interest in life. I was a sailor who lost his compass. With Kaira's death, I thought I had not only lost the love she had for me, but also the life we shared together. But she was never mine; she belonged to Allah Ta'ala forever, so how could I lose someone that I never owned? She only returned to her Owner. See, that's why when people you love die, you miss them…you miss their presence, the things you did together, time you spent with each other, and so on. Now, when you ponder on the memories, you in fact still have your loved ones. As long as Allah Ta'ala blesses you with good memory, they stay with you until you die. So, reminisce on these moments with faith, not with so much emotion that it would make you blind from seeing the reality of life. You are freed from the amanah; so, you should learn to move on with your life. Hard to do it at first, but not impossible with Allah Ta'ala's help. Just keep seeking for His guidance. That's what Allah, the Most Merciful taught me through Uncle Zaid. Alhamdulillah, he never gave up on me. I was so blinded by emotion and not thinking straight, not thinking rationally. Both Uncle Zaid and Aunt Ani helped me a lot during those days. Alhamdulillah!"

Syakirah commented, "They are good people. I've only known them for a small amount of time, but I believe them to be two caring people with genuine love…love for the sake of Allah. The kind of love and care that make you better people…better Muslims, subhanallah!"

"Yes, they helped my family too. Uncle Zaid and my father were friends, but never really close until Kaira's passing. It was a big turning point for my whole family, I would say. Uncle Zaid and Aunt Ani were our neighbors years ago when we first moved to JB. They were religious people. We, on the other hand, were just like any others who were born Muslims. We observed the Islamic obligatory duties as if they were passed down to us by our ancestors, rather than prescribed by Allah Ta'ala and shown by His Messenger. Later, my family moved to another neighborhood. When Mom and Dad called Uncle Zaid to our house to help me, that was the beginning of the bond between our families, the kind that will last forever, insha Allah."

Syakirah commented, "I've always believed that pain and disappointment suffered through personal tragedies in life only bring us closer to Allah Ta'ala. We need Him to release us from the pain and the disappointment. When we are close to Him, He will reveal the true meaning of happiness. It's like one of Allah Ta'ala's miracles is shown to us right before our very own eyes."

Imran nodded. "True. I was introduced to beautiful characteristics of a Muslim woman through Kaira. She was not perfect, but through her Allah Ta'ala showed me a role model of a Muslim woman. In my line of work, I deal with mostly business people, men and women. Most are very successful and ambitious, career-wise, but I don't see their faith, and don't really spend time to get to know them outside the business world."

"Are you saying you've never met a virtuous woman, close to having the Muslim characteristics you saw in Kaira?"

"You see...there is a fine line between being virtuous and righteous. If you see them through your Muslim heart, that is, with faith, you will see the difference. The presence of these two qualities in someone's actions, given whatever situations life offers, has always been the yardstick for me in looking for a true friend, especially in the world of business. You have to really know who your friends are. The same goes in finding someone to share my life with. I don't hope to meet the perfect woman." Imran paused and smiled at Syakirah.

"There's no such a thing, after all. I only hope to meet a virtuous woman with the righteousness of a true Muslim. These are not qualities one is born with, but once they exist in us, even a little, through proper care of iman, continuous learning for Allah Ta'ala's sake, and with guidance, insha Allah, we can be good Muslims... and companions for each other in the journey of this short life."

"That's true, Imran."

"And that was the end of the story of my past. I tried to tell you once but never got the chance to finish until just now."

"Thank you for sharing it with me." She felt love for Imran as she studied his calm face. For the first time, she would not hide her feelings toward her husband by looking away. She loved him and she hoped he knew it.

"But I haven't brought you here today just to tell a story about my past, Mrs. Syakirah." Again he made her smile with that name. Imran paused.

"Alhamdulillah, the day my mother arranged a meeting with a particular woman, a new story began. Wonderfully imperfect, her detestation of matchmaking and me could not completely mask her piety and Islamic morality. I was intrigued and had to find out more."

He smiled as he teased her.

"You were not easy to deal with either, Mr. Imran," she shot back with a grin.

"I agree. And we both know now what the other really is like, alhamdulillah... though I have to admit we took a winding road to get to here."

"Do you think you've found what you're looking for, Imran?" Syakirah asked, turning serious.

Imran became sober. "Rasulullah said one who turns from his *sunnah*, his ways, will have no relation to him...and marriage is one of his sunnah. We don't want to be denied our relation to him, do we, Syira?"

"No, we don't." Syakirah looked at two noisy birds flying overhead.

Imran watched Syakirah. He knew she needed to be convinced of this. But he wanted her to bring it up first.

"I've told you what I'm afraid of, Imran. Honestly, though I was at peace with my decision to marry you, I never actually trusted you... until recently."

Imran raised his eyebrows at the disclosure. "So, you doubted me since we got engaged? The whole time?"

"Pretty much, yes," Syakirah replied matter-of-factly. She recalled telling Imran about her relationship with Manaf.

"And now?" Imran looked intently at her.

"I trust you now," Syakirah answered and chose her next words carefully. "Believing that you are Allah Ta'ala's choice for me has helped. If one really loves Allah Ta'ala, whatever comes from Him must be welcomed with redha and be accepted with complete willingness. We have to be pleased with His decision, since we cannot perceive the wisdom of His purpose in every event. Sometimes what is good for us is hidden in bad happenings. In *Al-Baqarah* we are reminded of this."

Imran nodded. "Muslims must submit to Allah Ta'ala fully. They can't be displeased with His actions and decisions. In the Quran, we are forbidden from being suspicious of others. Islam teaches us to have good opinions of everybody, how much worse it would be if we were suspicious of Allah the Most Gracious and His acts! Each thing He creates is either good in itself or on account of its results. So, we must be optimistic always, insha Allah!"

Syakirah smiled. "Now that we are being honest with each other, I want you to know that, I like you now after looking at your kindness, your *akhlaq*, and your faith in Allah Ta'ala...your devotion to Him. You are not perfect either, Imran Hakim, but with those qualities I've seen in you, I brave myself to place my trust in you."

"Syira," Imran said emotionally.

"Yes?"

"I'm offering you my complete trust in Allah Ta'ala. I know people don't build trust in one day. It takes time to build it and honesty is one of its foundations. I've nothing to hide from you and I've no reason to not be honest with you, Syira." Imran's eyes looked into hers, searching for a sign that said she trusted him.

Syakirah's eyes glistened with tears as she studied his face. She was touched; his sincerity made it difficult not to cry.

"Syira, will you share a life with me? And share my dream, a dream once wished by Prophet Ibrahim...to have pious and righteous children...a blessed Muslim family to serve Allah Ta'ala?"

Syakirah looked up smiling with tears on her face. Imran wiped the tears away and waited for her answer.

Syakirah closed her eyes as she took a deep breath. She loved him completely. On top of everything, she felt the closeness of the Almighty Allah. Only with His ceaseless love for her she was able to have all these, she thought. She was humbled as she acknowledged this gift from Him. Allah Ta'ala gave her back her ability to trust. Tears of happiness and gratitude flowed down her cheeks.

"Yes, Imran, yes, I'd love to share a life and that dream with you, insha Allah... it has been my dream, too, for as long as I can remember."

Imran took her right hand and with his other, wiped the tears from her face. Then he held both of her hands in his and kissed them.

"I love you, Mrs. Syakirah."

Syakirah studied Imran's face. She was overwhelmed by feelings of gratitude and happiness as she listened to Imran's declaration of love. "Alhamdulillah." She whispered to herself before saying to Imran, "I love you too, Mr. Imran Hakim."

The couple hugged each other, breaking apart only after the noisy birds returned from their morning tasks.

"The beach has just captured another happy moment. Alhamdulillah!" Imran shook himself and glanced at his watch. "I have about thirty minutes left before I must return you."

Syakirah laughed at his remarks. "And you'd better be punctual. 'Insha Allah' is a strong promise a Muslim makes."

"Indeed!" Imran grinned at her.

They both stood up and began the walk to Imran's car. Twenty meters from the car, Syakirah stopped walking. Imran turned to her.

"I've a confession to make." She smiled at him.

"A confession?" Imran asked, arching his thick eyebrows.

She nodded. They stood facing each other.

"Since the first time I met you, I had a feeling that our lives would somehow be entwined forever. That scared me, so I kept fighting it. The more I got to know you, the harder I fought because I didn't want to fall for you...because I was sure you would only marry me to please your mother...and I could not trust you completely...and I would be alone again in the end... that was what I kept telling myself."

"I'm sorry," Imran whispered. The concern in his voice was so genuine. He studied Syakirah's face as he took in the truth about her feelings for him for the first time. Indeed Allah (swt) created women with more emotions than men, he thought. Their sensitivity was not to be taken lightly. "I'm sorry it took me so long."

"Don't apologize, Imran." Syakirah paused. "Remember when you gave me that gift from your mother? ... All your family members were there?"

"You mean when I gave you that ring?"

She nodded. "You said it was a gift from her for our wedding. You thanked me for the time I spent with her. Do you know that ... I thought that night you were going to tell me that you wanted to make the marriage work. And the whole time we were apart I always wondered how it would be different if you did. But Allah Ta'ala knew better. You weren't ready then and neither was I. But I'm ready now...we both are...alhamdulillah."

"Alhamdulillah." Imran was touched by her confession. He admired her patience and faith in the Almighty Allah, that He would see to their happiness.

"Now, will you promise me something?" She waited for his answer.

Imran took her hands and held them in his. He smiled lovingly at her. "Insha Allah."

"Promise me that you will guide me, Imran...lead me to my dream...to be a good solehah wife...the wife who obeys her husband so that she would serve Allah Ta'ala in doing so...so that she would earn Allah's pleasure in this life and the next."

"Insha Allah, I promise."

Syakirah studied his face. She could see a tiny drop of tear at the corner of his left eye. "Thank you, Mr. Imran Hakim."

"You're welcome, Mrs. Syakirah."

Smiling and holding hands, they headed for the car.

∽

They look so happy, alhamdulillah Rabb al-Alamin, Yasmin thought as the couple got out of the car. She smiled at them, believing that the couple had finally set everything straight between them. Not wanting to interrupt them, she left them alone after informing them that the Scrabble contest would begin in ten minutes.

"I wished I could stay, but I've to take care of some important things in KL," Imran excused himself.

"Do you really have to go now?"

"I'm afraid so. I came here with a mission and it's accomplished. I have other arrangements to make before I see you again tonight...hopefully earlier, insha Allah. You are leaving this place this evening, right?"

"Yes."

"So, I'll see you at your house, insha Allah."

"Insha Allah."

After Imran left, Syakirah joined Yasmin at the Scrabble match. When the game finished, Yasmin excitedly confirmed her suspicions. Syakirah briefly told her what happened.

"Alhamdulillah, Syira, I'm so happy for you!"

"Alhamdulillah. Me too, Min. I'm so happy that I can't describe the feeling...I can only say alhamdulillah...Finally, something so right is happening, alhamdulillah!"

~

It was almost five-thirty when Syakirah reached home. As she relaxed after the long day, the telephone rang. It was Imran. He told her that he was coming to pick her up at seven and that he had a surprise for her!

Imran and Syakirah reached the hotel a little after seven. When they arrived at their room, it was almost Maghrib. Imran made a quick call while Syakirah prepared for prayer. She waited for him to enter the room to pray the Maghrib prayer together.

After the prayer, she kissed his hands.

Looking at Syakirah lovingly, Imran told her. "I've a surprise for you! Be ready but stay in here. Come out only when I knock! I'll be right back, insha Allah." Imran left Syakirah still in her praying clothes in their bedroom. She anxiously prepared herself for the surprise. *I love surprises,* she thought contentedly.

At about eight, Imran knocked on the bedroom door. Syakirah came out, wearing her light blue long dress. Imran was captivated by the sight of his wife without her hijab for the first time. Syakirah was smiling and was at loss for words when she saw what was laid out in front of them. The room was filled with flowers and there was a special dinner waiting for them!

CHAPTER 31

The last few months had been blissful for Imran and Syakirah. Though their careers temporarily kept them apart, they kept in touch at least once a day on the phone, and visited each other as often as they could. Syakirah voiced her thoughts about moving to JB for good but Imran asked her to consider it thoroughly because he knew she loved teaching at the college.

"Imran, I feel like we're a couple of school kids in love…on the phone all the time…it feels funny to go through this again."

"Oh, who was that first guy?"

Ah, Syakirah thought happily, *he wants to play.* "Honey…do I detect some jealousy here?"

"Well… the thought of you and another man…you know… in love…" Imran teased her.

Syakirah laughed. "Someone from high school… I had a big crush on him. It obviously didn't work out, as evidenced by our own marriage. Nothing to worry about, my love."

Satisfied, Imran changed the subject. "Are you still coming to JB for the seminar next week?"

"Well, yes. I wouldn't want to miss it. I've been looking forward to that seminar at UTM for months. As soon as I'm done with marking the final papers…"

"Really? I thought it was because you miss me and want to see your husband… but if the seminar is more important, then… fine with me…" Imran said, pretending to be hurt.

Syakirah teased her husband lovingly, "Oh, honey…I'm sorry…but it's the seminar of the century!"

"I know…and I miss you too," he said laughing.

After the call, Imran sat in the study room and the thought visited him again. Living apart meant a lot of commutes from KL to JB. This worried him. Lately, Kaira's accident had been on his mind more than usual.

"I place my trust in You, ya Allah." Imran calmed himself.

~

A week later, Syakirah and two other English lecturers left for the seminar in JB. She called Imran that morning, Imran suggesting that she take the flight but she insisted on taking the college's transport. He was worried for her safety because it had been raining. He had to stop himself many times from thinking about Kaira. He kept telling himself that it would not happen again.

Imran bought his wife a cell phone the week before so that she could call him on the road. He insisted that she call him on the road.

The first time she checked in with him, Syakirah called from their lunch stop. Imran was anxiously waiting for the call.

"Assalamu'alaikum honey, it's me."

"Wa'alaikumussalam! Alhamdulillah you called. Ten more seconds then I would be the one calling you. Where are you guys now?"

"We're in Seremban taking a short break for lunch. We can't go that fast because it's still raining. I'm glad we have a good and very careful driver. Insha Allah, we will get there before five."

"Insha Allah, I'll be in my office until six. Call me once you get here."

"I will…. and honey, try not to worry. Everything will be fine, insha Allah. I can't wait to see you."

"Me too but I cannot *not* worry. Just be careful, okay? Tell that to the driver. He's driving my wife."

Syakirah laughed and kept reassuring Imran not to worry. After the call, Imran tried to work but he could not concentrate. He called Umar to ask him to drop by his office and Umar said he would be there. He kept himself busy throughout most of the afternoon by halfheartedly investigating new manufacturing techniques, sales projections, and last year's profit & loss statement.

It was almost four when the office phone rang. A wave of dread washed over Imran. *Allah protect me from my thoughts!* Imran thought as he shook himself. *Silly man!* He picked up the phone and his heart stopped when his secretary said it was a call from the JB police.

"Hello."

"Hello, is this Mr. Imran Hakim Kamal?" A male voice on the other end of the line asked.

"Yes."

"Mr. Imran, I'm sorry. I'm afraid we have bad news for you. There has been an accident. We need you to come to the hospital…"

"Subhanallah," he said disbelievingly. He mechanically put down the phone and called in his secretary, telling her to make the appropriate phone calls, and left the office.

He got in his car, but before he left, he closed his eyes and whispered, *"Ya Allah…Inna lillahi wa inna ilaihiraji'uun…To Allah we belong and to him we return"* (Qur'an 2:156). He was in his own world, alone with his Creator. He needed Him, the only One to offer him solace in this time of crisis.

Then Umar tapped on the window, and Imran had his best friend with him, confirming his faith.

"Imran, remember Allah Ta'ala. He will see to it. Let me go with you to the hospital. Everything is going to be fine, insha Allah. Just pray to the Almighty Allah, pal."

∼

Fifteen minutes later they entered the emergency room and saw two police officers there.

"I'm Imran Hakim...you called me about an accident... Syakirah Sulaiman? Where is she? Is she..." his voice trailed off.

The officers let Imran catch his breath before telling him, "She's in the trauma-one room. The doctors are working on her. It seems that she had some cuts on her arms and legs, and she suffered a head injury."

"How....when did this happen?"

"From what we've learned, it took place around three, about fifteen kilometers from JB. It was raining hard. A lorry skidded and went out of control. It collided with their Pajero. Luckily we found your business card in her purse. One of the passengers told us that you're her husband." Imran closed his eyes and ran his hand through his hair. The police officer said something about confirmation and asked for his signature.

When the police left, Imran and Umar went to sit on the chairs outside Syakirah's room. Umar sat close to Imran who was bending forward in his chair, his elbows on his knees and his head in his hands. His eyes were glistening with tears. All he could hear was the officer's words *"she suffered a head injury"* and he recalled Kaira's accident. The painful memory came rushing back. He felt numb. He didn't hear Umar talking to him. He snapped to attention, however, when the door to trauma-one opened. He approached the doctor.

"Doctor, is she going to make it?"

"And you are...?"

"Imran Hakim... her husband." It sounded almost strange to him.

"We really cannot say much yet. We've done what we could but she needs an operation. She had a concussion and an internal bleeding. We will do the operation as soon as we get your consent."

"Yes, I'll sign the paperwork..."

"We'll do our best, Mr. Imran. The rest is in Allah Ta'ala's hands."

"Can I see her?"

"Just for a few minutes. We've to get her ready for the operation."

Imran followed the doctor into trauma-one. "Be quick, sir," a nurse told Imran as he approached Syakirah's bed.

Holding her right hand, Imran whispered to his wife. "Sweetheart, you have to be strong and fight this. I love you, Syira...I love you."

A nurse came a few minutes later and told him that it was time to take her for pre-operation procedures. Imran reluctantly left the room.

While he was at the nurse's station filling out the paperwork, he saw the orderlies wheeling Syakirah into the operating room. He stood motionless until Umar told him that they had to wait in another room.

Imran sat with his head in his hands in the post-op waiting room. Umar met Iskandar and Marina as they got off the elevator, summoning them with hand motions, then explaining the injury and procedure to them. Iskandar and Marina sat on both sides of Imran.

"Imran, how're you holding up? Iskandar asked his brother. Marina looked on tearfully.

"The best I can, insha Allah."

"I'm sorry, Abang Imran." Marina said. "The operation will take some time. Why don't you go get some air? Iskandar and I will be here while you're gone." Iskandar agreed with his wife. Imran got up and weakly walked to the elevator with Umar. They stopped at the mosque nearby the hospital. Due to the chaotic event, his Asr prayer was delayed and he felt guilty. After the obligatory prayer, he stayed in the mosque praying to Allah (swt) to save his wife. They left after Maghrib prayer and returned to the hospital.

The operation continued. Imran sat with Iskandar and Marina. Iskandar told him that Syakirah's parents were on their way and that their siblings were taking the night flight. Ani would be there soon, too, insha Allah. Imran listened to his brother talk, nodding at the appropriate times. Then as if remembering something, he interrupted, "You guys heard anything about her two friends and the driver?"

Iskandar answered. "Yeah, while you were gone I asked the nurse. She said the teachers only had minor injuries. They are in the outpatient room. The driver broke a couple bones, but alhamdulillah, is doing well."

Two hours later the light above the operating room turned off. Imran's heart stopped as he stood up and walked toward the OR doors. Iskandar, Marina, and Umar followed him. The doctor came out.

"How is she?"

"Alhamdulillah, we managed to stop the internal bleeding. She's stabilizing now. But she's not out of the woods yet. The next twenty four hours are the most critical." Imran stared at the doctor as he listened to this. Then Syakirah was wheeled out of the OR. The doctor said she would be moved to ICU and they would monitor her closely. Imran asked if he could stay with her. The doctor told him to wait for a couple of hours. After the doctor left, he sat on the couch and closed his eyes.

"Abang Imran, she is going to be okay, insha Allah. Allah Ta'ala will take care of her." Marina softly said to her brother-in-law. Imran looked at her dazedly and in shock. Iskandar softly squeezed Imran's shoulder. He agreed with what his wife said and suggested that Imran go home to freshen up. His brother was right. He looked and felt worn out. He said he would go but would be back in an hour.

"Thanks, Umar. I really appreciate this. Alhamdulillah. You should go home too. I'll be fine, insha Allah. I'll drive back to the hospital myself. Just need to take a shower." Imran tried to smile. Umar understood that his friend needed to be alone for a while.

"Okay, call me if you need anything, insha Allah."

Imran nodded.

Mak Jah asked if he wanted to have dinner but Imran shook his head lightly. Tears welled up in the old lady's eyes as she watched Imran so exhausted, worried and sad. She told him Hidayat called a few minutes ago. His youngest brother could not get a flight that night. Yasmin and Hidayat would take the first flight in the morning. After taking a shower, he prayed the night prayer followed by a prayer in which he sought Almighty Allah's help.

"Ya Allah...the Most Gracious, the Most Merciful, I bestow my prayer upon you as a weak creature of Yours. I know whatever

You decide I will have to abide. Please, Allah save her...save my wife. Give me the strength to face the final decision of Yours. Keep my faith strong with me. If her time to meet You is here, if another one I love is leaving me to return to You...let her die in faith...*husnul khatimah*...and give me strength to face it again. Amen."

After drinking some coffee, he called Iskandar only to find out that there was no news yet. Before leaving for the hospital, he told Mak Jah he would stay there for the night.

CHAPTER 32

Imran stepped out of the elevator to the ICU. Iskandar was alone as Marina had gone home to check on the twins. Iskandar informed his brother that Ani was in Syakirah's room and that he himself needed to get out for a while for some air. Imran sat outside Syakirah's room.

Imran was lost in thought when Ani approached. He looked up and tried to force a smile. Ani sat next to him.

"I'm sorry Imran. I know how you must have been feeling since they brought her in here...I called your Uncle and he sent his salam. He promised to pray for Syira."

"Wa'alaikumussalam...I appreciate that. That's the best thing we could all do now...pray to Allah Ta'ala...And, thank you for being here, Aunt Ani." The presence of this woman, who was so like his mother, was just too much for him. His eyes glistened with tears.

"This is just another test from Him, Imran. We must accept it with redha, as always for everything that happens in our lives. Only He (swt) knows best. And remember, Imran, when a good Muslim experiences hardship, he faces it with patience and perseverance because he knows that is good for him."

Imran agreed with her.

A few minutes later, Imran accompanied the nurse into Syakirah's room. He examined Syakirah's pale face. Her dark hair, which was partly bound by a bandage, contrasted sharply with her face. Despite everything she went through tonight, she looked beautiful, he thought.

"I've missed you." He couldn't take his eyes off her. He moved the chair closer to the bed so he could hold her hand without letting go. He held her cold hand to his cheek and then brought it to his lips and kissed it.

He sat watching her until the nurse shooed him out of the room. In the bright light of the waiting room, he watched Iskandar talking with Ani and told the two that he needed to go out for a while. He asked his brother to call on his cell phone if Syakirah woke up. Imran went to his car and sat there. It all came back to him.

～

"Kaira…?" Imran had asked for Kaira as soon as he was conscious. The nurse called Umar, who had been waiting for hours outside Imran's room.

Imran saw Umar quietly enter his room. "Umar?"

Umar was silent as he took stock of his friend's condition. Imran's head, right arm and left leg were bandaged. There were bruises on his face and on the other arm. Umar was relieved that his friend survived the accident and looked pretty good, considering.

"Umar, Kaira…?" Imran groaned. He searched for an answer from his friend's face.

"You're going to be okay, Imran."

"Where am I?"

"You're at the hospital. You remember you were in an accident?"

Imran nodded slightly. "Where's Kaira?"

"You need to get better, Imran. I'll see what I can find out about Kaira."

Imran fell asleep after that. When he awoke, Ita and Izwan were sitting beside his bed. Ita was crying.

"Kaira…?" Imran asked Izwan.

"They tried their best Imran…"

"No…no … not Kaira…" Imran began crying.

"I'm so sorry, Imran. They tried but…." Before Ita could finish, Imran was screaming Kaira's name hysterically. A doctor came in and administered a sedative.

The next day Umar and Izwan came to flesh out Imran's vague recollection. Imran was the only one who survived the accident. Tamrin died on the spot and Farah died on the way to the hospital. Kaira died in the ICU. As he listened to the news he sobbed, "I'm sorry, I'm so sorry Kaira…"

The memory, long hidden, brought fresh tears to the mature Imran, who now understood his obligation in the face of catastrophe. He took a deep breath. "*La haula wala quwwata illabillah…* There is neither might nor any power, except with Allah… I was so young then, Allah, when she left me to meet You. Forgive me for not being strong, then, to face Your test. Right now, I need your Mercy more than anything…for Syakirah and for myself. I know she would leave me too eventually…but, if You have decided for it to happen now, please give me enough faith to accept everything with much redha and be pleased with Your final decision. I place my whole trust in You, oh Allah!"

～

An hour later he stepped out of the elevator. He saw Iskandar talking to Syakirah's father whose face was drawn and troubled.

He approached his father-in-law and asked when he had arrived.

"About half an hour ago, Son. How're you holding up?"

"I'm okay. Have you seen her, Dad?"

"Yes, I went in for a while. Your mother's with her right now. Only one person at a time. She looked…" Syakirah's father choked up and could not continue. Imran grasped his arm and nodded, as he understood the old man's feelings. Syakirah's stepmother came out of the ICU. She cried softly as she sat with her husband.

"Mom," Imran called softly.

"Imran, she looked so pale and weak. I…I can't bear seeing her like that." Syakirah's stepmother buried her face on her husband's shoulder.

"Imran, you go ahead and see her," his father-in-law directed as he consoled his wife.

Imran nodded. "Iskandar, why don't you take them home. It's past midnight. You two must be tired. You could use some rest yourself, Iskandar."

After they said their salams and left, Imran quietly entered his wife's room. "Assalamu'alaikum, honey. It's me again," Imran told his unconscious wife. He sat and held her hand again until the nurse shooed him out again.

"I'm going to check on her. Would you…" The nurse said.

Reluctantly Imran let himself out of the room. Ani watched Imran come out from Syakirah's room. He sat next to her without speaking. With his head down, he stared at the floor until he heard a new set of footsteps. Looking up, he saw Hanim, who rushed to her brother and they held each other.

"I'm so sorry, Abang Imran. I couldn't believe it when I heard. I came as quickly as I could."

"Thank you for coming, alhamdulillah. I could use your company right now, Sis. Hidayat will be here tomorrow, insha Allah. He's taking a flight with Yasmin."

"Hidayat must be worried sick. Iskandar told me Hidayat was taking a test when he called Kak Yasmin."

"Yes," Imran answered hollowly.

"She'll be fine, insha Allah. She'll pull through this, insha Allah…"

"I'm praying for that, Hanim. We all are…"

"I know, Abang Imran," she answered sympathetically, seeing the pain in her brother's eyes.

The nurse came out and Imran motioned for Hanim to go in and see Syakirah. Hanim walked into the room.

"Kak Syira, you have to fight this. We all love you and hope that you won't leave us so soon, insha Allah. Abang Imran may keep all the pain inside, but I know he's hurting so much right now. If only you knew. You must wake up and see him. You can't leave him yet, insha Allah." Hanim wiped the tears from her face. She could not imagine how her brother would cope with losing another wife. *She* could not bear to witness him go through it again. She held Syakirah's hand. "This is a big test from Allah Ta'ala for my brother…I really hope you can hear me, Sis." Hanim prayed in the room for Allah (swt) to save her sister-in-law. She decided to stay with Imran a while before heading home to get some rest and meet Syakirah's parents. Ani left with Hanim after asking Imran to call her if there was a change.

After Hanim left, Imran went into Syakirah's room to stay the night while he held her hand. He woke up at four in the morning when the attending nurse rushed into the room. Syakirah's vital signs had flattened for several seconds, triggering the nurse's call, but apparently she was fine now. Imran sat with Syakirah until almost Fajr prayer time. He heard someone at the door. The nurse was coming in for her morning routine. Imran left for Fajr prayer at the mosque nearby.

Imran reached home as Syakirah's parents were about to leave for the hospital with Hanim. Imran took a shower, ate, and fielded several calls from well-wishers before heading back to the hospital. Hanim was sitting alone in the waiting room. She told him Syakirah's parents went to the canteen and Syakirah's condition hadn't changed.

Imran was worried. It had been thirteen hours since the operation, and Syakirah should be responding by now, according to the surgeon.

As the siblings talked, Yasmin and Hidayat arrived. Hanim smiled sadly to Yasmin as their eyes met. Yasmin went into Syakirah's room as Hanim talked to her younger brother.

Yasmin was in tears when she approached Syakirah. She stood very close and watched Syakirah's face. She pushed aside a few strands of hair on her friend's forehead. Then she sat down and held Syakirah's hand.

"Hey, best friend. Assalamu'alaikum. You have to wake up, okay? We still haven't finished the English workbook we're writing. Don't disappoint me, Syira. I mean it…no joke about that…" Yasmin was choked up with tears. "You're the best friend I've ever had," she grinned through the tears, "… well, other than my Nik. And I don't want to lose you yet. To whom will I complain about those students?" Yasmin squeezed Syakirah's hand. "Syira, your parents, brothers and sisters need you. Imran needs you. I'm sure he is sick worrying. Please, wake up. Oh Allah… make her wake up…" Yasmin said a prayer for Syakirah. Then, she wiped her tears and got up to leave. She placed a scarf she found near the bed on Syakirah's head to cover her hair. She went out to see Hanim and Hidayat. Hidayat got up and Yasmin nodded, telling him to go in to see Syakirah.

Hidayat entered Syakirah's room and stopped short when he saw her lying on the bed. He did not quite know what to do. However, he slowly approached his sister-in-law. Then, before he realized, words just came out of his mouth.

"Assalamu'alaikum, Sis. You don't mind me calling you that, right? We're not at the college right now. But if you don't want me to call you that, you'd better wake up to stop me yourself." Hidayat smiled, with sadness in his eyes. "You know what, we've all missed you. And I bet you know who misses you the most. He's the guy I respect the most in my life. And he's waiting for you to wake up." He sat beside Syakirah for a while and said a prayer for her before leaving.

Yasmin and Hidayat went to visit the other two lecturers and the driver. Imran left to make a call. As Hanim was about to leave to for the cafeteria, two nurses rushed into Syakirah's room.

"What...what's happening?" Hanim asked.

"We're not sure." That was all Hanim received for an answer. She started pacing nervously. A few minutes later a doctor came and entered Syakirah's room.

"Ya Allah, please don't let anything happen to her. What am I going to tell her parents and Abang Imran. Please..." She whispered to herself. Just about then Yasmin came back. She stopped pacing.

"What's going on, Hanim?" Yasmin asked. Hanim sat down, her head dizzy.

"I don't know. I was here when suddenly the nurses ran into her room. Kak Yasmin...they are working on her. What if..." Hanim stopped as she saw Hidayat, who could tell that something was wrong from her face.

"Hidayat, why don't you go and find Abang Imran. I'll get her parents." Hanim told her brother.

"I'll wait here." Yasmin said. Hanim ran to the canteen and Hidayat went to the elevator. A few minutes later the nurses and the doctor came out of Syakirah's room.

"Is she going to be okay?" Yasmin immediately asked the doctor.

"She's stabilizing now, alhamdulillah. Just pray for her."

The doctor left and Yasmin went into Syakirah's room. She looked the same. Yasmin pulled the chair close to Syakirah's bed and sat down. Yasmin held Syakirah's hand. "Syira, please fight. Don't give up yet. We need you, Syira." Yasmin heard the door opened. She turned and saw Syakirah's parents. Yasmin went out to let them be with Syakirah.

"How is she?" Imran asked Yasmin nervously as he waited to see Syakirah.

"The doctor said she's stabilizing, alhamdulillah."

CHAPTER 33

"*And put thy trust in Allah and enough is Allah as a Disposer of affairs*" (Qur'an 23:3).

Imran entered Syakirah's room. He stood beside Syakirah and watched her, wishing there was something he could do to wake her up. He couldn't take his eyes off of her as he held her hand. He kissed it and then he placed it down. He rubbed her hand slowly. Then as he touched the side of her face, Syakirah's eyes slowly opened. Imran took her hand again and held it in both hands.

"Hi," Imran said in a jubilant whisper, trying to smile. His eyes glistened with tears.

"Im…Imran?" Syakirah softly spoke, her mouth and throat parched.

"Yes, it's me, honey. Assalamu'alaikum."

Syakirah looked at Imran. "Wa…'alaikum…salam…"

"I thought I'd never look into your eyes again." A tiny tear escaped his eye, which he wiped quickly. "How're you feeling now, honey?"

"Tired. What happened?" Syakirah looked around the room.

"You had an accident. Remember you and your friends were on your way to the seminar? Well, it was raining hard and the

Pajero crashed into a lorry. They took you to this hospital. They operated on you yesterday, and you've been unconscious since." Imran briefly explained to Syakirah about the driver and her two friends.

Syakirah closed her eyes and slightly nodded. "Honey, I'm sorry I worried you." A tear rolled down her face. "But mostly," she whispered seriously, "I'm sorry I missed the seminar of the century."

Alhamdulillah! he thought as he laughed out loud, eyes glistened with happy tears. *I married the right woman.*

Syakirah squeezed Imran's hand. She realized how the accident must have reminded Imran of his last day with Kaira. She smiled at Imran, but her pain was a torment for him to watch. "I'd better get the nurse and tell them you're awake."

Syakirah shook her head, saying, "Don't go." She wanted to assure him that she was alive and would not leave him, insha Allah. Life and death were parts of Allah's (swt) miracles. He was the All-Wise and All-Knower of everything that He created and made happen. As His servants, she and Imran had to be pleased with Allah's (swt) decree in all matters in their lives, thought Syakirah. Imran stayed and held on to Syakirah's weak and outstretched hand until the attending nurse rushed in.

As Imran left the room, he passed the doctor who'd been summoned when the change in Syakirah's vitals was observed in the nurses' station. Imran told Syakirah's parents in the waiting room the good news, and waited with them until the doctor and nurse gave her parents the OK to see her. Imran went outside to call all the people he loved to let them know that Syakirah was conscious and would recover insha Allah. Yasmin, Hanim, and Hidayat all made short visits to Syakirah's room, grateful to the Almighty Allah that the nightmare was over.

"She's sleeping now." Hanim told everyone when she and Hidayat closed the door to Syakirah's room. Hanim took Yasmin and Hidayat home. Imran stayed with Syakirah's parents for a while before telling them that he had to go somewhere.

∽

The cemetery was peaceful and quiet. Imran found his mother's grave, which was next to his father's. The rays of sunlight, breaking through the shady leaves, were rays of happiness brushing clean the last gloomy hours of Imran's life. The late morning breeze, rustling through the branches, caressed his cheeks softly. He felt loved. He sat between his parents' graves and recited a prayer for the dead. Then he touched Saleha's stone and took a deep breath.

"Mom, thanks for your advice," Imran whispered, referring to Saleha'a words of encouragement when he was at his lowest.

"I almost went through it again, Mom. I'm so grateful to Allah Ta'ala for giving me the chance that I did not get with Kaira. And Mom, alhamdulillah…through you I met Syakirah. I promise you that I will love and take care of her, insha Allah. I know it made you happy that we are now together. May you rest in peace, amen. Alhamdulillah …your wish was fulfilled."

∽

Almost a week had passed since the accident. Imran was grateful to Allah (swt) more than ever. He survived another test from the Almighty, and had become stronger for it, accepting Allah Ta'ala's will with redha, accepting it as His decree. *As always and ever, there was a blessing in every event that happened in someone's life,* Imran told himself. *Strong faith will always be the power to pull one through any of life's ordeals!*

Yasmin and Hidayat left the day after Syakirah regained consciousness. Hanim, however, stayed for a week and her husband would be joining her later to visit the family.

Imran and Hanim drove Syakirah's parents to the airport. He told his in-laws that he would drive Syakirah back to the college when she was released from the hospital. Then the siblings went to the hospital.

"Assalamu'alaikum, Kak Syira." Hanim called out as they entered her room. She was up reading a book. She smiled, delighted to see them.

"How're you today, honey?" Imran said as he and Hanim sat on either side of her bed.

" Alhamdulillah, I'm bored silly! The doctor said I could leave in two days. I can't stand being here any longer. I just want to go home. And back to work." Imran and Hanim smiled at each other, recognizing Syakirah's fussiness as a symptom of recovery, insha Allah.

"Well, two days are not that long, Kak Syira. Besides we'll come everyday to check on you, insha Allah."

"Unless she gets bored with us…" Imran grinned and Hanim laughed.

Syakirah grinned at her husband. "Nothing could be more boring than what I do when you aren't here. All I do is eat, sleep, and read. Sometimes I sneak out of here to visit the children in the next wing, but the nurse has caught me twice now, and she scolds me!"

Imran and Hanim laughed at the admission. "Just hang in there, Kak Syira. When you get out of here we'll have lunch before you go back to KL, insha Allah," Hanim said. "Abang Imran can drive this time, right?" Hanim looked at her brother, teasing.

"Insha Allah. Anything for you, my ladies…" The two women laughed at his remark and his deep, dramatic bow.

~

Imran drove Syakirah back to KL. He stayed a day then returned for an important meeting at KS Holdings. Syakirah made up her mind to move to JB for good. This semester would be her last at Pine College. She told Imran before he left for JB.

"Are you sure you won't regret this? I mean leaving the college and being even farther from your parents…your home?" Imran asked her with concern.

"Honey, my home is where you and I build it, insha Allah."

"Insha Allah."

They smiled lovingly at each other.

EPILOGUE

Syakirah watched the peaceful night from the balcony facing the beach. The sky was beautiful with the brightest stars complementing the full moon. Indeed, Allah (swt) made them, as said in the Quran, to decorate the heavens. She prayed to Him to share many more nights like this for the rest of her life with Imran.

"Finally, we're alone and I have you to myself, Mrs. Syakirah. No more relatives hanging around." Imran stood next to her, joining her to admire the night sky.

They had a thanksgiving dinner after she had moved into Imran's home. That would be their home for the rest of their lives, Imran had told her.

"You have me for the rest of our lives, Mr. Imran Hakim, insha Allah." She glanced at him with a smile.

"I will hold on to your words. I want to have you for the rest of our lives, insha Allah."

Syakirah turned and faced Imran. They looked into each other's eyes and smiled. "I've always liked the little boy in you. I guess I was attracted to it the first time I saw you."

Imran grinned. "I remember we almost had an argument that day."

"I said the little boy…" Syakirah repeated with a small laugh.

"Yeah? What about the grown up in me?" Imran asked playfully.

She answered him seriously, "That too…but that part was so good at hiding your true feelings, at shielding your pain and your scars. You looked tough on the outside but beneath that tough exterior was the vulnerable little boy waiting for me."

"And now you're here… to hold and to love me."

"Really." Syakirah smiled playfully at her husband.

"How come you're so good at this? Did you study me like you studied each of your students?" Imran teased her.

"I'm good at what I do, aren't I?" she answered, winking. She whispered, "And your mother wanted me to take good care of you too."

"She did?" Imran smiled, flashing his dimples.

"She didn't have to ask. I knew it the first time I saw the two of you. But you were too much to handle then."

"Am I still?"

With a flirtatious smile Syakirah answered. "Sometimes…"

Imran took Syakirah's right hand and kissed it. Then, he whispered to her. "I love you, Mrs. Syakirah."

"I love you too, Mr. Imran Hakim."

Happiness was written on their faces.

"Alhamdulillah. Thank you for making her dream come true."

"Alhamdulillah. Of course, my love. It is Allah Ta'ala's play and I'm the actor… we all are… I really miss her."

"Me too. She gave me one of the best gifts in my life…you." Imran remembered the card in the wedding present Saleha had left for them. It said:

"I leave you to Syakirah. I'm grateful to Allah (*swt*) knowing that I can be at peace. Be happy my son. May Allah Ta'ala bless you both forever. Amen! Love, Your Mother

And Allah give them a reward in this world and an excellent reward in the hereafter. For Allah loveth those who do good (Qur'an 3:148).

Glossary

A

Abang – brother (older male sibling)

Akhlaq – Islamic disposition / manners (based on the Islamic
  teachings)

Al-Ahzab – a chapter of the holy Quran

Al-An'am – a chapter of the holy Quran

Al-Anfal – a chapter of the holy Quran

Al-'Araf – a chapter of the holy Quran

Al-Baqarah – a chapter of the Holy Quran

Alhamdulillah – All praise be to Allah

Al-Hujurat – a chapter of the holy Quran

Āli-Imran – a chapter of the holy Quran

Al-Isra' – a chapter of the holy Quran

Al-Kahf – a chapter of the holy Quran

Allah – God

Allah Ta'ala – Allah the Most High

Al-Talaq – a chapter of the holy Quran

Amanah – trust

Aameen – O' Allah, respond to our du'a (supplication)

An-Nur – a chapter of the Holy Quran

'Aqad – the solemnization of a marriage in Islam

'Aqiqah – the sacrificing of one or two sheep on the occasion of the
  birth of a child, as a token of gratitude to Allah Ta'ala . It is a
  deed, which pleases the Almighty just as the prayer at an instance
  of joy pleases Him

Ar-Rum – a chapter of the Holy Quran

Asr prayer – an obligatory prayer offered in the afternoon

Assalamualaikum – Islamic greeting (Peace be upon you)

Astaghfirullah – a word uttered to ask forgiveness from Allah (I ask
  Allah's forgiveness / Pardon me o' Allah)

At-Taghabun – a chapter of the holy Quran

B

Baju kurung – Malay traditional long dress for women
Bismillah – with the name of Allah s.w.t

D

Dato' – A title awarded by the King/Sultan
Dhuhur prayer – an obligatory prayer offered at midday

E

Eid – Islamic Festival

F

Fajr (prayer) – an obligatory prayer offered at dawn
Fitrah –a pure innate or natural disposition

H

Hadith – the statements made by the Prophet (s.a.w.), e.g. his sayings
Hajj – a pilgrimage to visit the sacred house of Allah Ta'ala in Makkah
during the days of Hajj (8th –12th of Dhulhijjah)
Halal – lawful and permissible by the Islamic law
Hijab – a head covering prescribed by Islam to be worn by a Muslim
woman
Husnul Khatimah – felicitous/blessed end (to die with one's faith in
Allah)

I

Imam – The person who leads others in a salat (prayer); also refers to
the Muslim Caliph (or ruler)
Iman – faith, belief
Insha Allah – If Allah Ta'ala wills (God willing)
Isha' (prayer) - the fifth obligatory salat (prayer) of the day offered
late evening
Istikharah – a voluntary salat (prayer) offered to seek guidance from
Allah Ta'ala in making a decision, regarding a certain deed / situ-
ation which one is facing.

J

Jannah – Paradise
JB – Johor Bahru (the southern state in peninsular Malaysia)

K

Ka'bah – the Holy House of Allah located in Makkah
Kak – Sis (sister)
KL – Kuala Lumpur (capital city of Malaysia)
KB – Kota Bharu (the north eastern state in peninsular Malaysia)

L

Luqman – a chapter of the holy Quran

M

Maghrib (prayer) - an obligatory salat (prayer) offered after sunset
    (evening salat)
Maryam – a chapter of the holy Quran
Masha Allah – Whatever that Allah Ta'ala wishes (to give, He gives)
Masjidil Nabawi – The Prophet's (pbuh) mosque located in Medina
Mawaddah – the tender love Allah Ta'ala grants a man for his wife (or
    vice versa)

Q

Qadar – Divine preordainment of Allah s.w.t

R

r.a. (radhi Allahu anhu)– May Allah be pleased with him/her
Rahmah – compassion / mercy (also refers to a man's gentle care and
    treatment of his wife so that she would live in comfort with him)
Rasulullah (pbuh) – the Prophet of Allah (may peace and blessing of
    Allah be upon him)
Redha – be pleased with what (the decree) has been ordained by
    Allah (s.w.t)

S

Salaam(s) – Islamic greeting, i.e. Assalamualaikum – peace be upon you

s.a.w (sallallahu 'alaihi wasallam) – p.b.u.h. (may peace and blessing of Allah be upon him)

Solehah – pious (woman)

Songkok – a Muslim man's headgear

SubhanAllah – Glory be to Allah / How perfect Allah Ta'ala is

Sunnah – the actions of the Prophet (s.a.w) including his sayings, deeds and approvals

Surau – a place to offer prayer (smaller than a mosque)

s.w.t (subhanahu wa ta'ala) – Allah is pure of having partners and the exalted (most high)

T

Ta'ala – The exalted (the Most High)

Tahajjud (prayer) – a voluntary prayer offered after waking up from a sleep (after past midnight and before dawn)

Tahlil – reciting 'La ilaha illa Allah' (There is no god except Allah). It also refers to a traditional get-together (practiced in some countries in South East Asia) to say prayers for the dead and ended with serving them a lot of food (lasted for 3 to 7 nights)

Taqwa – Fear of displeasing Allah when one is close to Him

U

UiTM – University of Technology Mara

UK – United Kingdom

UTM – University of Technology Malaysia

W

Waalaikumussalam – And upon you is peace

Wallahu'alam – And Allah knows best

Y

Ya Allah – O' Allah (O' Lord)

About the Author

Zaipah Ibrahim, a Muslim born and raised in Terengganu, Malaysia, is an English teacher. She was a graduate of Southern Illinois University at Carbondale. She was an English lecturer (1990 – 2001) at Kolej Agama Sultan Zainal Abidin (KUSZA), presently known as University Darul Iman Malaysia (UDM). She devotes her time writing Islamic books for young and adults, teaching English as well as training teachers at Islamic kindergartens.

The author has previously published two books, *Islamic Word Games Book 1* and *Book 2*. The books are suitable for children above seven years old as well as adults. Readers have fun solving the word games while learning some basic Islamic knowledge. Contact the author if you would like to know more about these fun books and/or obtain copies:
emaani1@yahoo.com

The Gift II, the second book in Zaipah's series is also an Islamic romance novel which will be published in Malaysia by *Telaga Biru* publishing. To read more about this exciting, new, and soon to be published novel go to: http://polariswriter.blogspot.com/

ISLAMIC FICTION BOOKS

Muslim Writers Publishing is proud to have published *The Gift*, a quality Islamic Fiction book for teens and adults. You can learn more about the availability of Islamic fiction books and Muslim authors by visiting: www.IslamicFictionBooks.com.

Islamic Fiction Books: This refers to creative, non-preachy, and imaginative fiction books written by Muslims and marketed primarily to Muslims. Islamic Fiction may be marketed to secular markets, too. The content of these books incorporates some religious content and themes, and may include non-fictionalized historical or factual Islamic content with or without direct reference to the Qur'an or the Sunnah of the Prophet (pbuh). The stories may also include modern, real life situations and moral dilemmas. Islamic Fiction may be written in many languages.

Islamic Fiction books do not include any of the following Harmful Content:

- vulgar language
- sexually explicit content
- unIslamic practices that are not identified as unIslamic
- content that portrays Islam in a negative way

Linda D. Delgado, Publisher
Muslim Writers Publishing

Muslim Writers Publishing (MWP)

Print Books Available at www.MuslimWritersPublishing.com

Non-Fiction Titles

The Beautiful Names by Saaleha E. Bhamjee

Power Poetry For Wide Awake Youth by Habibullah Saleem

Star Writers by Amatullah Al-Marwani

A Muslim's Guide to Publishing and Marketing
  by Linda D. Delgado

Halal Food, Fun and Laughter by Linda D. Delgado

Islamic Fiction Titles

The Runaway Scarf by Corey Habbas

Sophia's Journal: Time Warp 1857 by Najiyah Diana Helwani

The Size of a Mustard Seed by Umm Juwayriyah
  (Forthcoming - Summer 2009)

The Gift by Zaipah Ibrahim

Muslim Teens in Pitfalls and Pranks by Maryam Mahmoodian

Grandma & Hijab-Ez Family Activity Book
  by Linda D. Delgado and Shirley A. Gavin

Islamic Rose Books series 1: *The Visitors* by Linda D. Delgado

Islamic Rose Books series 2: *Hijab-Ez Friends*
  by Linda D. Delgado

Islamic Rose Books series 3: *Stories* by Linda D. Delgado

Islamic Rose Books series 4: *Saying Goodbye*
  by Linda D. Delgado